COLLARS & CURSES

Sharon Skinner

Brick Cave Media
brickcavebooks.com
2017

Brick Cave Media
brickcavebooks.com
2017

To my parents.
We didn't always see eye to eye, but there
was always love in our hearts.

Also by Sharon Skinner
Available from brickcavebooks.com

POETRY, SHORT STORIES AND ESSAYS
In Case You Didn't Hear Me the First Time

FANTASY, PARANORMAL & SCIENCE FICTION
The Healer's Legacy (Book 1: The Healer's Trilogy)
The Matriarch's Devise (Book 2: The Healer's Trilogy)
The Nelig Stones
Mirabella and the Faded Phantom
Sacrilege (Futurewords: A Brick Cave Anthology)

The Exile's Gift (Book 3: The Healer's Trilogy)*

* Forthcoming

COLLARS & CURSES

Sharon Skinner

Brick Cave Media
brickcavebooks.com
2017

CHAPTER ONE

When I walk into the Coffee & Cues with Joey Marsh on a Monday afternoon in April, it seems like my life has finally taken a turn toward normal. Just two teens stopping for mochas. No big, right? Yet, the sun shines brighter, the coffee smells richer, and our rinky-dink hometown is suddenly less claustrophobic. It feels big enough to finally let me breathe—if I can just calm my pounding heart enough to catch my breath.

Joey grips my hand in his, refusing to let go even as he digs out his wallet and I can't stop the smile that spreads across my face.

Two weeks and three days. That's how long it's been. I'm still dizzy at the newness. I'd pinch myself, but I don't want anything to spoil this moment. For most of the year in tenth grade, I'm this girl no one has ever noticed. Till one day I trip over my big size elevens and dump my books in front of this guy in a leather jacket, and the next thing I know, I'm dating the best-looking boy in school.

I glance over. Joey's dark hair that's just a little too long, hangs down in blue eyes the color of a summer sky. He sees me looking and smiles, that amazing dimple destroying every girl within range.

Including me.

Okay. So, he isn't perfect. His grades aren't the best and I know my parents don't like him because he's been in trouble. He's even spent time in the Youth Detention Center. But he's stayed out of trouble since then, and he's been really sweet to me. Anyway, there's something exciting about a guy who rides a motorcycle, and yeah, maybe I'm attracted to bad boys. Which makes sense if you know my genetic history. Plus, he smells great. Leather and motorcycle oil with an overlay of chocolate.

"Let's grab a couch." Joey leads the way into the store-front-turned-game-room that's connected to the coffee shop. Mochas in hand, we skirt the pool table, snake our way around the kids playing video games, and head for the alcove where secondhand furniture surrounds a low table with a chessboard painted onto the top.

We just reach the couch when I hear a shout. "Hey, Merissa! I've been lookin' for you." Kandi Johnson, the biggest, meanest girl in school, stands in the doorway, hands on her hips, and glares.

"What's up with her?" Joey asks.

I shrug, trying not to look concerned, but adrenaline crashes through my veins in a fight-or-flight frenzy. "I don't know." I step toward the couch, only to freeze when Kandi yells again.

"Hey! I'm talkin' to *you*." She points at me. "What'sa matter? You too stupid to know your own name?"

My hackles rise as I swing around and watch her march toward me. Crud. Kandi Johnson is a bully—a great big Amazonian-sized bully—and she is headed right for me. Things go quiet. The crowd vibrates with anticipation.

Kandi crosses the room in three steps, stopping in front of me, scowling like she's just eaten something nasty. Or is about to.

She's taller than me, and I have to look up to meet her stare. It feels like there's a heavy rope wrapped around my chest and the longer we stand there, the tighter it gets.

I force myself to breathe.

"What's going on?" Joey asks, but I can hardly hear his words over the rushing sound in my ears.

Kandi's voice is right inside my skull when she growls, "Stay out of it. This is between me and her." She jabs a finger in my direction.

When Joey shrugs and sits down on the arm of the couch, something inside me withers.

"What is it you want?" I ask, trying not to look as betrayed as I feel. My teeth are clenched. My voice sounds thin through the storm in my brain.

"I heard you called me a bitch." She steps closer, flexing her thick arms.

"Wh—what?" I take a step back and bump into the coffee table. First off, there isn't anyone I know well enough to talk to like that. Second, it's a compliment I'd never bestow on her. But I sure as hell can't tell her that.

"I heard you called me a bitch!" Her hands squeeze into tight fists, knuckles cracking loud in the quiet room.

Is she making it up, or . . .? I look around, wondering if the jerk who put me in this situation is in the room. A dozen faces stare back like feral animals waiting for blood, but no one moves. "I don't know where you heard that, but it isn't true."

"Well, that's what I heard. And now you're gonna be sorry." She spreads her feet and raises her fists.

"I don't want to fight you." My voice sounds throaty, the roaring in my ears louder.

"Too bad," she snarls. "'Cause you don't get a choice. But I'll tell you what, I'll let you take the first shot."

"Excuse me?"

"Go ahead. Hit me." She opens her arms.

My mom is going to kill me if I can't talk my way out of this, but all I can think to say is, "I'm not going to fight you."

"Yeah, you are. Hit me." She feints toward me.

I shake my head, digging my nails into the palms of my hands to keep from swinging on her.

"Hit me!" Kandi yells, smacking her chest with a balled hand.

"Listen, Kandi—"

Her left fist comes up quick, lands hard on my right cheek. My hand goes up to my stinging face and I spin around. Everything goes red, then black. There's a buzzing noise; a screaming wind; a cyclone tearing through me. Until, slowly, a gray mist fades from my eyes like I'm coming out of a fogbank.

I'm sitting on Kandi's chest, my hands wrapped around her neck. My teeth are bared and an angry growl tears from my throat. Her eyes are wide and a look of fear-coated surprise has replaced her former sneer.

Panic rises and I stare at my hands. It takes me a moment to realize they're still human. Then relief flutters over me like flapping crows' wings. "I said, I won't fight you," I tell her through gritted teeth. "Understand?"

She tries to nod her head and I loosen my grip. I draw in a raspy breath and stand, trembling with the adrenaline rocketing in my blood. I step back to give her room. She crab-crawls backward to the pool table, hits her head with a loud thunk, then leaps to her feet and runs. I watch through the big storefront window as she streaks past outside.

The room is quiet. Not one video game bleeps and every kid in the place seems to have stopped breathing. They're all watching me, staring at me like I've grown fangs. Or ears and a tail.

Not this time.

I purse my lips and give them a shrug, trying to be nonchalant, but my body feels rubbery from

5

bouncing between anger, fear and relief. With the show over, everyone breathes normally, including me, and the plink and blip of video games slowly resumes.

When I turn back to the couch, Joey is gone.

For a second, I think I might actually cry. But then I get angry, again. He could have tried to help. He could have made some kind of effort instead of backing down like a useless jerk, just because Kandi told him to. Not that I needed his help, obviously. But he couldn't have known that, could he? I mean, I'm not model-thin and helpless-looking, but it's not like my body is covered in muscles, either. And, anyway, what kind of boyfriend just sits and watches when the girl he's dating is attacked by the school bully?

So much for *bad boys*.

I plop down onto the worn sofa and stare at the coagulating mochas. Across the room, kids are totally absorbed in their games. Not surprising. It wasn't much of a fight, after all. But if my mom hears about this, I'll be grounded till I'm forty-seven. Why did Kandi have to pick a fight with me? And why today, just four days before the full moon?

I always knew something was wrong with me. I mean, *different*. That's what Mom calls it. "It's not wrong to be different, Merissa," she says in her completely logical (meaning totally out-of-touch-with-reality) way.

Shows how much she knows.

Even as a little kid, I hated being indoors. I wanted—no, I *needed* to be outside, touching the fertile ground, inhaling the fierce air, the sun's warmth and light soaking into skin and bones. I could hear sounds the other kids couldn't, and I could smell in color.

Weird. But true.

Back in preschool, when the other kids would settle down for naps, I could never sleep. My ears followed the sounds of insects crawling along the walls, bees buzzing in the bushes outside the windows. And heartbeats. All of them thump-thumping in a chaotic rhythm that slowed down as the other kids nodded off to sleep. In the quiet, my ears would begin to pick up the rustlings of small animals—squirrels in nearby trees, rodents in the grass—and then my stomach would begin to rumble.

Only, I wasn't hungry for graham crackers and milk.

I slump forward. The mochas have turned a cold and sludgy charcoal gray. I pick mine up and stare into the gooey layer of melted whipped cream that floats on the surface like scum on an abandoned fishpond. My nose wrinkles before I can even get the cup to my mouth and I want to sneeze. I set the cup back on the table in a rush so I don't spill it all over myself.

Needless to say, I've never had anyone I could tell my secret to. That's why it was such a total high when Joey started paying attention to me. I guess I wanted to believe that the old saying is true. You know, the one about love being blind. Not that I thought he was actually in love with me. I just hoped he might like me enough to be a little near-sighted. Obviously, he's got his eyes wide open now. Seeing me lose it that way was probably like laser eye surgery. Who wants to date a girl who can out-bully the school bully?

I sink back into the sagging couch. Across the room, a group of kids huddles around a video game, one of those big retro game consoles with the old original games on it, stuff like my parents used to play.

One of the kids at the console is watching me. I haven't figured out which one, yet, but I can feel her eyes on me—I know it's a girl—boys feel different when they look, the way they stare, measuring, questing, imagining. This is different. It's like she's trying to decide if I'll bite.

I might, I want to tell her, *but probably not, today.* I look past the group of kids, out through the big window, at the street outside, the cars rumbling past. I pretend to be interested in a bright yellow Prius that stops right out in front. Even with my human ears, I can hear it purring quietly, its electromechanical hum like the buzzing of a giant bee.

Of course, I couldn't care less about the car; it's just something to focus on while I figure out which girl is watching me. Slowly, I inhale through my nose, sensing the air in the room, tasting it on the back of my tongue. Letting it settle into my brain.

At first, I can't separate the overabundance of smells. All the colors in the room are woven together. I generally try to ignore the too-many

8

rushes of scent and color that mingle inside my brain. But now, I slow my breathing and concentrate. Then, bit by bit, I begin to unravel them and each one takes on its own special tint. Finally, I isolate her scent, her particular hue.

She's pale vanilla mixed with dead leaves, or some kind of green wood covered with dusty flowers, mossy greens and pale lavender. Hard to pin down exactly, but unique. My nostrils flare. My nose twitches. I exhale and lean over the mochas to try and get her out of my brain. But, like every new scent the first time I catch it, she's stuck there.

An indelible imprint.

One thing I know for certain, she's different. Not different like me, exactly, but not like the other kids. Not one of the Norms.

Finally, I raise my eyes.

She's standing at the far edge of the group, acting like she's watching the girl working the game's controls. But her lilac-colored eyes are focused beyond her. Focused on me. Like they recognize me. Even though I know I've never seen her before. She tilts her head just a bit, her hair falling to one side like a dark curtain, and her lips quirk up in a secretive smile. It feels like a dare. I want to get closer, find out who she is, what she is, but before I can get to my feet, she's across the room and out the door.

I'm sitting up straight, the hairs on the back of my neck sticking out like quills on a porcupine, but the other kids are just as casual as before, totally engrossed in their stupid game of Space Invaders, or Pong, or whatever it is. They didn't even notice when she left. Not one of them showed any sign of even seeing her. Like maybe they hadn't known she was there to begin with, so didn't recognize the vacant space she suddenly left in the room.

But I noticed. And now I'm worried.

She definitely isn't like me, and she's not a Norm. So, what is she?

Mom's always saying there aren't any Others like me in this part of the country, because this region belongs to Papaw. He lives high up the Sierras and only comes to visit in the summers when the roads to his cabin aren't blocked with snow and ice. Papaw says if it weren't for me, he'd have moved up to Alaska or someplace even farther away like Iceland or something.

Our "condition" sometimes skips a generation, or two, like it did with my dad. Papaw told me there was even a time, way back a couple hundred years ago, it skipped so many generations, the family thought they'd lost the ability all together. But they didn't. And I sure didn't get skipped.

Lucky me.

What matters is that the girl with the wisteria-colored eyes and the earthy smell doesn't belong here. At least, I don't think she does. I don't know what it means that she's here, but I'm sure as hell not going to ask my mom. Who knows what she'll do? She might even contact Papaw and get him down here to investigate. And as much as I miss him, for some odd reason, that's the last thing I want.

I lean back, away from the murky sweetness of the mochas and breathe in the last of her scent. Odd. It's already nearly gone. All I can find is a pale green mossy-ness with a hint of spider web.

* * *

Dinner is over and I'm rinsing the last of the plates before sticking them in the dishwasher. It's been a good night. I haven't broken a single thing. *So far,* I think, as the plate I'm holding starts to slip out of my grasp. I manage to juggle-catch it and set it down in the sink with a glassy clink. Then I breathe again. If I break any more of Mom's dishes, she'll make me buy her a whole new set.

I don't know why I'm such a klutz, but ever since I hit puberty, I've been clumsy, awkward, like the skin I wear is an oversized sweater.

Carefully, I pick up the plate and slide it into the dishwasher, add the soap, and close the door. I push the button and listen to the rush of water streaming in as I clean and rinse the sink. My mom doesn't understand how I can be such a butterfingers with normal stuff like doing the dishes when I can play video games and zap monsters for hours without losing a single life. I tried to explain the difference to her, but she just doesn't get it.

Or me, for that matter.

Out in the living room, Mom is watching one of those annoying reality shows. I don't understand the attraction. I get more than enough reality every day. If she really wants to see a bunch of drama, she ought to come to my high school. Not that I get involved in any of it, as long as I can help it. Other than my recent run-in with Kandi, no one really notices me. At least they didn't, before Joey. They also barely talked to me. Not like they'll start now. Not after everyone hears what happened at the coffee shop. And everyone will, probably before first period tomorrow. Although, I can't figure out if that's a good thing or bad. I mean, the other side of me grins every time I think about it, but the human side . . . Well, since I can't really sink through the floor and disappear, what difference does it matter what that side of me thinks?

Except it does.

Because, while I never really fit in before, now I never will. What boy is going to want to date a girl who can practically tear someone's throat out in ten seconds or less? If I were a Norm, it would sure creep me out. Although, for some reason, I'd really expected more from Joey. Thinking about him just sitting there on that couch rakes a claw across my heart and makes a part of me want to cry. Except the other part of me, yeah that part, just wants to bite him.

I let out a slow breath and rinse the sink, letting the spray of water wash the stainless steel clean. I'm not sighing over a stupid boy, I tell myself. Honest. I'm just breathing, like Papaw taught me. *Yeah, right.* I dry my hands on a dishtowel and head out into the living room.

Mom lifts the remote and pauses her program. "You done with your part of the kitchen?"

"Yes."

"Homework?" She gets up to go wipe the kitchen table and sweep the floor.

"Not much," I tell her. "Just a small section on human anatomy. I did everything else in class."

She gives me that Mom look.

"I'll be in my room finishing my homework." I clomp down the hallway, wishing I walked like other girls, smooth with a swish or a little bit of a hip swing. But I'm not graceful like that. Especially, not now.

My body wants to stretch, reform, run outside. The waxing of the moon drags at my insides, tugging me toward the change. Only, I know better. I'm not a little kid anymore. I have to maintain control. I'm only allowed to change when the moon is so full I can't resist, and even then I'm not allowed out on my own. Mom drives me to the nearby wooded preserve and I have to stay "within earshot." On top of that, I have to wear the collar. Sometimes, the lure of a scent, or the rustle of a rabbit pulls me away and before I know it: *ZAP!* It's only a mild shock, but enough to remind me of who and where I am.

I settle in with my biology text, memorizing the names of the bones in the body. Wouldn't Mr. Rajanni be freaked if he knew that my bones, so unlike those of an ordinary human's, can actually transform into a wolf's?

CHAPTER TWO

If the bell doesn't ring soon, I'm going to lose it. It's always like this the last few days before the full moon. I used to have to stay home this time of the month, because I had no control. Most of the time, I can usually just breathe through it, calm myself down the way Papaw taught me up on the mountain. But not today.

I caught that strange girl's wild scent in the hall outside the admin office. And for some reason, it's made it harder to control my body, to stay human. Barely a trace of her green-earth undertones lingered, but I know she was there. Like I said, once I catch a scent, I have it forever, logged into my brain like a permanently locked file on a computer hard drive. Anyway, for some reason it's making me crazy that I can't get away and track her, figure out who . . . what . . . she is.

Maybe she's still on the school campus. If I could find her, get close enough . . . But I'm stuck in English class. Can't get a pass because we're supposed to be writing an in-class essay.

English is the one subject I'm usually good at, but right now I'm struggling just to stay in my seat. I really hate how I feel this close to the full moon. It's like being schizophrenic. No. More like major mood swings.

Every five seconds.

I stare at the smart board in frustration, wishing I could erase the teacher's fat cursive essay assignment: "If you could be any animal you wanted, what animal would you be, and why?"

I've been staring at a blank sheet for twenty minutes, wanting to shred the paper into tiny bits. I can't write what I really want to write, can't tell her that I'd rather not be an animal at all, that I'd rather be a Norm, but there's no way I can ever be like everybody else. And I sure can't tell her I want to be a wolf, which is the only animal I really know well enough to write about. Even if the teacher believed it was creative writing, my mom would have a cow.

Great. Now, I'm hungry.

I try to think about being something else, something other than what I am. If I could choose to change into something other than a wolf, what would it be? But, even though I can't stand being who I am, there's nothing else I really want to be.

Except normal.

What would I write, if I were a Norm? What kind of animal would a perfectly regular human want to be? A bird maybe? People are always talking about how they wish they could fly. Yeah, I guess it could be pretty okay to be a bird. But it would have to be a big bird, one that wouldn't be easy prey. An eagle or a hawk. A hunter. Diving down on rabbits with lightning speed. My mouth starts to water and my blood begins to pound.

Breathe in. Breathe out. Focus on becoming blank.

That's it.

I begin to write, scribbling across the page. *If I could be any animal I wanted to be, I would be human because humans are not driven purely by instinct and they have the ability to manipulate their environment, to use tools, to find solutions to complex problems.* I keep writing until the bell rings. If the teacher tries to take away credit from me because I didn't choose an animal, I'll just tell her that according to my biology book people are included as part of the animal kingdom. And she did say we could choose to be any animal we wanted.

Who am I kidding? I'll probably get accused of being a smart-ass, but better that than not finishing the assignment. And there's no way I can stay focused on being some kind of an animal if I keep getting a hunting urge while I'm trying to write. Besides, she's supposed to be grading on format and grammar. Right?

I think most people imagine that being a shifter would be cool. There are all these books and movies that romanticize shape-shifting and make it seem so great to be other than normal. But it's not like that. It's really a huge pain, if you ask me. I mean, who wants to worry about their canines showing whenever it gets close to a full moon?

Or how about catching the scent of a squirrel when you're walking down the street and trying to act like there's absolutely nothing wrong with you, when all you really want to do is chase it up the nearest tree?

I know you're thinking it would be great to be faster and stronger than most everyone around you. You'd think it would make sports so easy. And it would. If I weren't such a klutz. And if my parents hadn't driven it into my brain for years that I can't do anything that might bring attention to myself or my so-called abilities. Not to mention that if I'm not really careful, I could hurt someone just blocking a basketball pass or kicking a soccer ball. Which pretty much sucks the fun right out of most sports. That's why I stick to track. It's easier not to hurt someone if you're not making contact. Plus, fear of tripping over my own feet keeps me from winning all the time and standing out. Besides, what would be the point of outrunning a bunch of Norms I could chase circles around any day of the week if I didn't have the gracefulness of a hippo with a peg-leg?

There's other stuff, too. Like, how much I want to stick my head out the window when I'm riding in a car. Seriously. What is up with that?

Okay. There are some positives. Like, for the most part, I keep to myself and most people leave me alone. Or did until recently. Although, now the whole Kandi scene has probably been seared into everyone's brain and there's no telling the fallout that will come from that. Of course, my mom will slaughter me if she ever finds out I got into a fight. That's why I usually try to keep my head down and stay out of trouble.

On the other hand, the whole running the woods at night? Pretty sweet. Or would be if Mom ever let me really go. It's easy to get caught up in the scents and the feel of the rushing wind, muscles pumping and the ground blurring beneath your paws. Of course, it's not like I get to do it very often, even though we live so close to a nature preserve.

The biggest suck is that I can't tell anyone my secret. I'm not really sure when my dad told my mom about what he is. Or, rather, about his bloodline. She doesn't talk about it. Gets real quiet when I ask. So, I don't anymore. I guess everyone has stuff they don't want to talk about. I just wish she'd tell me more. She always says that I know all I need to for now and when the time comes that I need to know more, I will.

Whatever that's supposed to mean.

I drop my paper into the "First Drafts" basket on the teacher's desk and head out into the hallway, letting myself get carried along in the crush of kids moving between rooms. My ears are ringing with the sounds of trampling feet and hundreds of talking, mumbling, calling, chatting voices. I reach for my ear buds, ready to shove them in my ears and turn up the volume, when the scent hits me again, dusty and brown, with an earthy-green undertone. My vision narrows and the noise suddenly diminishes to a whisper.

I look around and see her staring at me, violet eyes so intense I feel the need to look away. But I don't. There's something about her that teases my brain, pulling me in. I don't want to lose sight of her. I try to change direction, head toward her. But the crush of bodies is like trying to fight a heavy ocean undertow and I get swept past her. By the time I manage to pull myself free, she's gone.

Again.

I'm still standing there, trying to track her when the warning buzzer sounds. Biology is in the next building over. I have to run or I'll be late.

I'm panting when I slip through the door just as the bell rings. I jog up front to an open spot and nearly trip over the stool legs as I take my seat.

Biology would be so much better if the classroom didn't always smell like formaldehyde and sweaty sneakers, all metallic colors swirled with eraser pink. And if we didn't have to partner with a classmate on every single project. Mr. Rajanni says partnering builds teamwork skills we'll need to be successful later in life.

He's a great teacher and I like his class well enough, but he obviously has no idea that I will never actually fit into society and that, later in life, I'll be living alone in a cabin out in the boonies, like

Papaw. Besides, I hate getting paired up with someone who doesn't do their share of the work.

Mr. Rajanni stands at the front of the room, waiting for everyone to stop shuffling through backpacks and sliding into lab seats. It doesn't take long. Everyone knows Mr. Rajanni doesn't put up with anyone messing around during class. He would have made a great policeman, the way he hands out infraction slips.

He's in the middle of taking attendance when the door opens and a waft of earth-scented air washes across the room, all loamy browns and deep forest jade. I turn and there she is, standing in the open door. She's wearing a long blue skirt and a black t-shirt with silver stars airbrushed across the front. Her midnight hair is held back from her face by a braided headband. In her hand is a half-sheet of blue paper.

She scans the room, catches me staring. I drop my gaze, my neck growing warm.

"May I help you?" Mr. Rajanni finally asks.

She walks to the front of the room and hands him the paper. "I'm new," she says. "I just transferred here and I've been assigned to this class."

Mr. Rajanni examines the girl's schedule and frowns. "I see." His face is tight in the way that shows he's unhappy. He likes having an even number of students to pair up for labs, hates it when the admin office messes up his count, hates it when he has to triple up on a team. But he forces a smile and introduces her. "Class, we have a new student with us. Her name is Breanna Massey."

"Bree," she corrects him.

"We are just beginning a new section, Miss Massey." He hands the paper back to her. "You may take a seat in one of the extra chairs at the back of the room until we assign lab partners for this project."

I watch as she slips to the back of the room, her blue skirt swishing, flat baby-doll shoes barely making a sound on the tile floor. A shudder runs through me. *What is she?*

Mr. Rajanni's voice pulls me back to the front of the room, but my head is so filled with Bree's unusual scent that I barely hear him describing the new assignment, until he says, "We will continue our section on vertebrates by dissecting rats."

A wave of groans and murmured complaints ripples around the room, but Mr. Rajanni keeps talking. "Anyone who is vegetarian or vegan, or who has a formal excuse on file, will work on an alternative assignment." He stops for a moment and shakes his head at someone whispering at the back of the room. "And, no, you will not be dissecting a vegetable. Students will, as usual, work in teams of two. So, as I call your names, you will please move to your lab stations."

Mr. Rajanni calls out pairs of names and students begin moving, taking new seats as he assigns partners. Suddenly, I realize that my best chance to find out more about this new girl is to get assigned as her partner, but before I can get my hand up, I hear Mimi Rubo's fake-sweet voice.

"Mr. Rajanni," she says. "You really ought to pair me with Merissa this time. We haven't worked together at all this semester."

What? Damn! I've waited too long. Most everyone else has already been assigned a partner and the few people left are probably just as freaked out about touching dead things as Mimi.

A quick surveillance of the room shows that Mimi's BFF, Jorja, who she usually manages to manipulate into being her lab partner, is absent. Mimi isn't trying to partner with me out of friendship. In fact, the only nice thing she's ever said to me is how much she likes the red and silver highlights in my otherwise brown hair, and that's only because she was trying to find out who does my hair. She actually accused me of lying when I told her it was natural. The only reason she wants to partner with me is because she expects me to do all the dirty work.

I hold my breath as Mr. Rajanni checks the roster. Maybe I'll get lucky and he'll assign her to work with one of her other cliquish friends.

But my hopes fall when he nods and makes a mark in the roster. "That will be fine," he says. "Just be certain you do your share of the work."

"Oh, I will," Mimi smiles sweetly at him as she glides across the room and parks her trendy, popular-girl butt in the seat next to mine. As soon as Mr. Rajanni moves on, Mimi gives me a smirk. "I need an A on this assignment," she says in a low voice. "And I'm not touching anything gross."

I glare at her. Does she really think I'm going to

do all the work and let her take credit for it? No way. Especially not after she went and ruined my opportunity to partner with Bree and figure out what she is and why she's here. And an A? Who is she kidding? "I'm not the science geek you're looking for," I say, but I resist waving my hand in her face. A quick glance tells me the class is still uneven. Someone else must be absent. I can't help but look toward the back of the room to see who Bree will get paired up with.

Mr. Rajanni is speaking quietly with her.

He waves her over to the lab table in the corner at the front of the room. The one where he does his teaching demonstrations. Is she going to be working with the teacher? He's done that before. I guess it does keep everything evened out.

I watch as she sets out the equipment she'll need, laying everything out on a clean mat. Mimi jabs me with an elbow and hisses in my ear. "What are you gaping at? Don't you think you'd better set things up?"

"Your arms aren't broken," I tell her.

"I'm not about to ruin these." She wiggles her fancy manicured fingers in my face. "Besides, I told you—"

"Right. You're not touching anything gross."

"Exactly," she says in her squeaky voice, "and all of this stuff looks gross to me."

I roll my eyes, but it's probably just as well. At least if she doesn't touch anything, she can't screw it up. The only thing worse than doing all the work is losing points because your lab partner doesn't know a milliliter from a dram. Not that I'm a great whiz at biology myself. In fact, the teachers all think I'm ADD, and in a way they're right. Dealing with my kind of split personality, reining in my animal side all the time is utterly distracting and makes it hard to concentrate on stuff like reading and lectures. The last thing I need is a prissy diva weighing me down like a dead albatross.

I begin setting up, pulling out the dissecting tools. Even though I usually have to work at it, I like science. It's just so pure. Either something is or it isn't. A substance reacts or doesn't. The answers end up being certain. Unlike the weirdness that is my life. I mean, I started out basically as normal as the next kid, or so I thought, but then all of a sudden, it turns out I'm not. Just don't get me started on how everything they teach in biology and anatomy are basically only true if you're completely human.

From the outside, our family looks uber-normal. My parents are still together and they both work. Mom at the local pharmacy and Dad driving a truck, long hauls, which keeps him on the road a lot. We live in a small but decent house. We recycle. All the surface stuff is there. But underneath we're totally not normal.

Especially me.

"Earth to Mersa," Mimi says.

I glare. It's an old joke and a bad one.

"Oh, sorry. Muh-Riss-Uh," she intones each syllable, eyes wide in mock innocence. "You need to go up and get our, ugh, rat-davor." Her upper lip curls with distaste.

A half-dozen students are lined up at the front of the room, waiting to take the stainless-steel trays Mr. Rajanni is handing out.

I walk up to the front of the room and get in line for a specimen, watching the parade of metal trays being carried back to lab tables. The new girl, Bree, has set out all of her instruments in meticulous order. I bet *she* knows a scalpel from a retractor. If I had her as a partner, I'd not only get to know more about her, I could easily get an A on this section.

I step up to the front of the line. Mr. Rajanni reaches into a big tub with a large pair of tongs and lifts out a sopping wet pink and white body, sliding it onto a metal tray. He nods at me and I pick up the tray and carry it over to my lab station. Mimi peers into the tray as I come near and wrinkles her nose. "I'm not touching—"

"Anything gross," I finish for her. "I got it." My own nose twitches at the deep scarlet smell of death mixed with chemicals, which fill my head with metallic shine. Then, just as I begin to set down the tray, the rat's whiskers twitch. I jump and the tray slips out of my hand, crashing onto the lab table and splashing liquid onto Mimi's frilly pink blouse.

She shrieks and stumbles backward, arms flailing, and sweeps the next lab station clean. Tray, instruments and deceased rodent crash to the floor in a thunderous clatter and a wet splat.

"Ew, that reeks," Mimi squeals, sniffing at her sleeve. Her face is screwed up in disgust.

"It is only formaldehyde," Mr. Rajanni assures

her. "It will not harm you."

"But it's got dead rat in it!"

Raucous laughter gurgles from the back of the room. From the front station, over and around the other voices, Bree's laughter rises like music. Not in a fairy tinkling kind of way, but a deeper melodious way, like a hushed symphony. It makes me think of heavy rain falling on a forest canopy. But there's also a mysterious undercurrent that seems to creep in underneath the warm notes. A whisper of cool secrecy that teases my brain that I can't quite hold onto.

Mimi's face flares. She turns her steely glare on the class. "It's not funny!"

"Students," Mr. Rajanni raises his voice to be heard. "In this classroom, we do not laugh at the misfortunes of others."

"Look at my blouse!" Mimi shouts. "It's ruined."

"Many fabrics contain formaldehyde to reduce the possibility of mildew growth," Mr. Rajanni says.

He really does believe every moment is a teaching moment.

Mimi's face contorts. "This isn't fabric, it's haute couture! From New York!!" Her protest is so high-pitched it hurts my ears.

"Please, calm yourself, Miss Rubo."

"I can't do this," Mimi wails, waving her hands in the air like they've been contaminated. "It's just too gross." She grabs her designer book bag and rushes out of the classroom, yelling, "I quit." The door swings shut behind her.

There's a stunned silence in the room and then a

low snicker bubbles up. Bree appears to be biting her lips to keep the laughter from bursting out of her.

"Merissa, please clean up your station." Mr. Rajanni says in his calm-before-the-storm voice. He glowers at the class and the laughter dies. The partners at the lab station next to mine are already gathering up the instruments Mimi has knocked to the floor.

"I expect everyone to be set up and working when I return." Mr. Rajanni strides after Mimi, but stops at the door. "Merissa, you and Miss Massey will become partners for this project." Then he's gone.

I glance at the new girl. She's already put away all of the instruments she had laid out on the table, as if she knew the teacher would reassign her. With a shrug, she picks up her book bag and saunters over to my station.

"I'm Bree," she says.

I stand there, not sure what to say. I thought she was avoiding me, that I had to chase her down, like some wily prey, that I might never catch her. Now, here she is and I have no idea what to say.

"That was hysterical," she says. "Though, I didn't think it would cause quite this much of a mess." With a smirk, she stoops to pick up the lab stool that's still lying where Mimi left it, sets it right and slides it up to the lab station. In a heartbeat, she's straightened out all of the instruments, her agile hands dancing over the table. When she's finished, she sits down on the stool, ready to work. "Where shall we start?" she asks, her lilac eyes smiling along with her lips.

Before I can answer, Mr. Rajanni returns and all side conversations stop. Long minutes later, we've cut through the skin on the rat's stomach and pulled it back to expose its insides. I'm ignoring Bree's scent, the electricity that seems to pour off her. I'm trying to focus on the diagram in my biology text, follow it so we don't miss anything.

"Go ahead and ask me," she murmurs, busily making tiny labels and attaching them to the pins we'll use to mark the different organs.

"What?" My heart is thudding away so hard she can probably hear it.

She tilts her head and looks up at me. "I said, go ahead and ask. I know you're dying to know."

"To know what?" I keep my head down, eyes locked on the rat.

"If I can tell about you, the way you can tell about me."

I give a noncommittal shrug. "I'm not following you."

"Don't be obtuse," she says, wrapping a tiny post-it note around a pin so it sticks out like a little flag.

Suddenly, I feel like this is all wrong. That my mom is right about everything. That I need to keep my secret to myself. "Not only do I not know what you're talking about," I tell her, "but I don't really want to know." I turn back to the rat, scalpel poised above it, but my hand is shaking and I've forgotten where I'm supposed to cut next.

"I've actually been wanting to meet you, probably just as much as you wanted to meet me." Bree puts down the pin and glances around the room surreptitiously. "We have something in common and you know it." She sighs. "We could be friends. You can be yourself around me. Unlike the lame Normals in this backwater town. I know you're not one of them."

My hands shake so much I can't make the next incision. I don't know what to say. Mr. Rajanni, who has been circulating around the room, stopping at each station to check progress and ask and answer questions, pauses at the lab table behind us. I hear him compliment the students on their neatness, correct the placement of a label.

Then, it's our turn.

"You need to focus on what you are doing." Mr. Rajanni makes a few corrections to our work, then moves to the front of the room and parks himself, leaning back to sit on the edge of his desk and survey the room.

He's within hearing distance, so we don't dare talk about anything but the task at hand. Personally, I'm relieved. Now that I have the chance to expose my secret, I decide I don't I want to. Maybe it's all the years my parents have spent pounding caution into my brain, but there's something unsettling about the idea of sharing information with this girl. There's something about her that bothers me. Being so close to her sends my nerves into overdrive. But the way she talks about the Norms, voicing my worst thoughts, making me feel so much more an outsider, is disquieting.

I don't know why it should make me so uncomfortable. I mean, none of them are really my friends, but most of them aren't horrible. They may not be lining up to invite me to their parties, but for the most part, they leave me alone, which is pretty much all for the best.

I continue to work. It's really sad the number of rats they kill just for science. Think of all the science classes in all the high schools in all the towns and cities across the country. How many rats a year is that? Half a million? A million? More? Not that I'm a huge rat fan, but millions of rats dying in the name of science? What is that about? Some sort of plague vendetta or something? Maybe next time I'll partner with the vegans and cut up a carrot.

As long as I don't have to eat lunch with them.

Bree starts to say something and I glance up at Mr. Rajanni, who is watching us work. She hands me a pin. "This one goes there, I think." She points to the rat's heart. The label on the pin has Kandi Johnson's name printed in block letters.

I shake my head and tear the label off the pin, ripping it into tiny pieces before tossing it in the trash. "I think you better check the reference."

"I'm sure I had it right," she says, but she makes a new label and hands it to me. This time it's correct and I slip the pin into the specimen's organ.

Bree leans close and hisses in my ear. "Meet me by the back gate after school. We need to talk."

CHAPTER THREE

After school, I decide to go straight home, but Bree catches me at the corner, grabs my hand. My fingers tingle at the touch of her cool skin and I try not to blush as I quickly slip my hand out of hers, afraid someone might see us; two girls holding hands. Her amethyst eyes practically sear me and I feel warm all over. She's looking at me in an appraising way and smiles as if she likes what she sees.

Whoa. What does that mean?

My neck and face grow hot and a small shiver runs across my skin. What the hell is wrong with me? I like boys, Joey Marsh in particular. Although, after his cowardly retreat in the Coffee & Cues, maybe not as much as I did.

I let out a small sigh.

Bree's eyebrow lifts. "Heart troubles?" She asks it like she can read my mind and I flinch.

"No," I say. "Not really." I fiddle with the strap of my book bag so I don't have to look at her

"Just as well," she says. "None of these losers are good enough. Especially not for someone with your special talent."

Startled, I look up at her. What is she saying? She can't really know what I am, can she? Or maybe she can. It's been clear to me all along that there's something Other about her, even though I'm not sure exactly what, yet. And what about all those things she said in biology? It's obvious she knows something, and there's something about her that I find really intriguing. But I'm not about to spill my guts to someone I hardly know. "I told you before, I don't know what you mean."

She gives me a crooked smile. "Right. And you're not the least bit curious about me. So, I guess we don't actually have anything to discuss." She folds her arms, watching me and waiting, like she's expecting some big reaction.

I shrug, trying not to look as interested as I am. Although, it's practically killing me to know what she is, how much she knows about me. Maybe, like I can tell with her, she can sense that I'm not a Norm. Maybe that's all she can tell. Or maybe she doesn't actually know anything and is only guessing.

"It's possible I noticed you around town before you came into biology class and wondered who you were," I say.

Her smile widens. "That's because you have special senses."

I catch myself toying with the zipper on my bag. "Not really," I say. "This town isn't all that big, and neither is our high school. It's not like we get new students all the time. I just happened to see you in the hall." Not exactly a lie. Of course, I'm not about to tell her I smelled her before I saw her.

"Come on. I'll show you my grandmother's weed garden." Her smile is full of secrets. I know my parents will have a fit if they find out I'm talking to an outsider about family issues, but it's clear Bree's not a Norm. Not really an outsider, right? So, what can it hurt?

Her grandmother's place is crouched in the back of a cul-de-sac that rests up against an old apple orchard. The house is small, with a narrow porch that wraps around two sides. With its peeling paint, it looks like some sort of shedding beast. Wildflowers and strange plants fill the yard; creepers and bushes and odd succulents that twist and coil like knots of writhing snakes. Potted plants line the porch and perch on every windowsill—a greenhouse on steroids.

As I follow her up the steps and onto the porch, a gray cat leaps up onto the rickety railing and meows, sniffing the air and raising a paw in my direction. It startles me because cats don't usually like me. At all.

"This's Vesta," Bree says, reaching for the animal.

The little creature crouches, meows again, then waltzes away from Bree, tiptoeing along the railing until she's even with me, then nudges my arm with her head.

"I think she likes you," Bree tells me. "You'd better pet her before she changes her mind."

I raise my hand tentatively, and slowly stroke Vesta's head. She pushes against my fingers until I have a handful of soft furry ears and head. "She feels like velvet, only warm."

"Yep," Bree says. "She likes you. The little traitor." There's a hint of humor in her voice, even though she's frowning.

"I can't believe it," I gasp. "I've never been able to get this close to a cat before. Not even when I was little." I can't keep the awe from my voice.

Bree cocks her head to the side. She laughs and it sounds like children's voices echoing in a wood, warm and velvety like Vesta's fur.

"She's a witch's familiar. Believe me, she's seen stranger things than you."

This time I can't keep the surprise off my face. "Your cat is a witch's . . . familiar?"

"Of course," she says. "What did you expect, a duckbilled platypus?"

I knew she was Other, but a witch? And I just can't believe she said it so matter-of-factly. *Wait. Stranger things than me?*

I stop petting Vesta and drop my hand. The cat meows in annoyance, then leaps down off the porch railing and saunters across the lawn into the orchard.

Bree watches the cat leave and laughs. "As annoying as they can be, cats are pretty standard. Oh, there are plenty of other animals we could attach to, but cats are easy to care for and don't draw as much attention as say a bear or a falcon would. Especially these days. Unless you're a rock star or something."

I've never met a witch before. Papaw didn't tell me much about them. He just said there was more to witches than most people knew. When I asked him if he'd ever met one he just grunted and changed topics.

Suddenly, Bree's eyes go wide and she slaps her forehead with her hand. "You can tell I'm different, but you couldn't identify me. You've led a really sheltered life here. And we have a lot to talk about."

I stare at her. "I don't know what you mean."

"Uh-huh," she says, unconvinced. "Well, it's nice to know you can keep a secret, but I'm getting tired of this. So, I guess I'll get to the point." She glances around, like she's making sure no one is nearby. Then she leans forward and whispers, "Neither of us fits into this town, because neither of us is normal. We have special powers that ordinary humans do not have."

I can't keep the surprise from my face. Or the worry.

"Just getting it out in the open," she says. "I know you can tell about me. We can always recognize one another."

My brain tells me to leave. Go home. Now. But for some reason, I'm still standing here on the porch.

She watches me intently, waiting, but I keep my mouth shut. Between Papaw and my mom, I've learned not to say anything. Not to anyone. Not ever. But, if Bree really is a witch, and she can tell that I'm not a Norm, what else does she know?

I know I should probably be on my guard, but there's something fascinating about her, and I'm curious to know more. Like, is her grandmother a witch, too? And why did they move here? Papaw's territory stretches so far, I guess I just thought that the turf thing included all Others and non-Norms. But apparently, I was wrong. I guess it only applies to shifters.

"Come on," she says, leading the way toward the front door. "There are fresh cookies in the kitchen."

I sniff the air, but even with my wolf's abilities I don't smell anything except the pungent plants surrounding the house. "How do you know that?"

"Because I'm psychic," she says.

"Really?" I hesitate.

"Just messing." She opens the door and spicy sweetness spills out. "Today is Tuesday. Grams always bakes on Tuesdays."

Inside, the house is dark and quiet, almost too quiet. Thick drapes and heavy wall hangings absorb the sound and make you feel like you should be whispering. It kind of creeps me out, but it's not like what I expected. Although, now that I think about it, I'm not sure what I expected. It's clean and smells of fresh-baked cookies and there's no boiling cauldron hanging in the fireplace. The floors are made of a dark polished wood covered with thick area rugs. Most of the furniture is wood and looks kind of old, like it's probably all antiques.

I follow Bree into the kitchen. There's a modern stove and refrigerator and a perfectly normal sink. The table is covered with a bright green tablecloth with white flowers embroidered along the edges. A rack hangs from the ceiling, filled with dried plants and flowers.

"I hope you like cinnamon." Bree sets a plate of cookies on the kitchen table and takes two tall glasses off a shelf. "And almond milk." She pours us each a cup. "Grams is lactose intolerant."

I've never had almond milk before. I take a small sip and decide I like the creamy nutty flavor of it. It goes really good with the cookies, which are still a little warm and stuffed with oatmeal and chopped walnuts.

I glance around the kitchen and Bree smiles. "Grammy is probably out digging up mandrake root or collecting devil's claws."

My eyes widen and I nearly choke on a mouthful of cookie.

Bree laughs. "JK," she says. "Besides, those are really just ordinary plants. She doesn't have a magic broom, either. In case you're wondering. Although, she swears her new vacuum cleaner works like a charm." She laughs at her own silly joke and I can't help joining in.

We both reach for another cookie at the same time and our hands collide. Bree wraps her fingers around mine and gives them a squeeze before offering me the last cookie. I feel a blush rising up my neck, creeping toward my face, and I try to pretend I'm not flustered, not embarrassed at all.

I leave the cookie on the plate and drink the last of my milk. "So, how did you know about me?" I ask her, fingers still tingling from her touch.

She leans forward. "Maybe it was magic," she says in a conspiratorial voice. "Or I might have followed your scent, right?"

I go tense, breath held, senses on alert.

Bree holds up her hands, palms out, and sinks back into her chair. "Okay. I checked you out. You know. Just to be sure."

I give her a blank look.

She rolls her eyes. "Anyway, I've really been wanting to meet you." She gives me a quick confident smile.

I don't believe what I'm hearing. Every time I caught a glimpse or a whiff of her scent, she seemed to be heading away from me.

"Sure. Ever since I saw what you did to that girl in the coffee shop. Nice moves, by the way."

Part of me wants to revel in the praise, but what happened with Kandi shouldn't have. I was out of control and I know better. I shake my head. "I should have talked my way out of it, found a way to back down." I look down and see that I've shredded my napkin into tiny pieces.

"She totally had it coming," Bree says, in a hushed voice. "None too bright to pick on someone like you, eh?" She wriggles her eyebrows and I feel a small smile turning up the edges of my lips.

After Bree rinses the cookie plate and glasses

and sets them in the sink, she guides me through the house to her room. It also looks pretty normal, except that she has scarves draped over her lampshades. Also, the pencil holder on her desk beside her computer monitor has things sticking out of it that look a lot like the wands in the Harry Potter movies. That, and the top of her bookshelf has some odd-looking stuff on it. I move closer. There's a brass bowl filled with dark glittering sand and some fragrant-smelling ash. Several candles, all in different kinds of holders, line the sides of the shelf. There's a glass dish full of what looks like rock salt, along with a bunch of feathers and a whole jar full of rocks. "Are all these things used for magic and spells?" I ask, pointing to the shelf.

"Some." She shrugs and flops down onto the bed. "Some are just things I like and picked up, like those seashells right there." She nods in the direction of the bedside table.

I look around, trying to decide which things are magical and which aren't. A silver picture frame lies face-down on her dresser. I pick it up. A young Bree stares out, smiling between an intense-looking woman and a pale man with dark, curly hair. Before I can ask if the people in the photo are her parents, she snatches the picture from my hand and shoves it into a drawer and slams it shut.

I stand there stunned.

"Sorry," she says suddenly. "Bad mojo." Her voice is strained, mouth pulled down in a severe frown. "Put the past in the past, as Grams always says." The words slide out of her like a sigh. "Of course, it's easy to say when you seem to forget so conveniently."

The last is said under her breath and I don't think she's really talking to me.

I sit on the bed and glance around the room. The window curtain flutters and Vesta leaps from the open window onto my lap, surprising me. Tentatively, I scratch between her ears and she pushes her head against my hand. Her loud purring soothes the tension from the room.

"Bree," I say, suddenly curious, "are witches born?"

"Of course we are," she laughs. "We're basically human, after all."

My face grows hot with embarrassment. How many times has my mom told me I'm "basically" human? And how many times have I said I don't think basically means what she thinks it does. "I don't mean that," I say. "I mean, does it run in families? Is it genetic, like with me?"

She stops laughing and looks serious. "I guess it depends."

"On what?"

"On what type of witch you're talking about."

"Types?"

"Sure." She plops back down onto the bed and scratches Vesta on her rump. The cat hunches her back and begins kneading my leg with her front paws.

"How many types are there?" I wonder if she can tell me all the stuff Papaw left out of his five-minute witch lesson.

Bree bites the inside of her cheek and thinks about it before answering. Then she holds out her fist, opening her fingers one at a time as she counts them out loud. "The main categories are white, black, green, kitchen, solitary." She pauses for a breath and holds up her other hand, counting off again. "And then there's coven, eclectic, elemental and ancestral."

"Really? What do all those things mean?"

"It's mostly about where they draw their power from and what kinds of tools they use." Bree leans against the pillows stacked up at the head of her bed. "White witches use light energy to make spells. Black witches are into the dark arts like demonology. Green witches are really earth witches, people who use plants and natural connections, like my grandmother. Kitchen witches cook their spells. Solitary witches practice alone, unlike coveners who raise power as a group. Eclectic witches are kind of like borrowers. They find and use whatever works best for them in a given situation and don't restrict themselves to a single style or a particular set of tools." She pinches a leaf off one of the potted plants on her bed stand and rolls it between her palms, releasing a pungent minty smell that hangs in the air around us and fills my head with white fire.

"So the tools of an elemental witch would be fire, earth, air or water?" I ask.

Bree drops the crushed bit of plant into the wastebasket next to her bed and sits up. "Those, and also metal, stone and wood." She raises a hand as if to stop me. "Don't ask," she says. "I wouldn't have included them as elements if it were up to me. And neither would any scientist. Especially not wood or stone. But magic isn't science and, like my grandmother always says, no one asked me." There's a bitter edge behind her words.

I'm not sure whether or not I should ask, but I really want to know. "So, what kind of witch are you?"

"Undetermined." She laughs, throaty and deep. Her shoulders sag and she grows quiet, then glances at me from under her thick lashes.

"What kind of shifter are you?"

There's something unnerving about the way she says it and the look in her eyes. She leans forward and suddenly she's kissing me and I feel a tingle of warmth all over my skin. It's a lot like kissing a boy, but also different. Softer. Sweeter.

With a start, I realize I'm kissing a girl.

And liking it.

I jump up from the bed and back toward the door, breathless. For a moment, I don't know what to say. "I'm dating someone," I blurt, a part of me still hoping it's true, even though Joey hasn't called since the coffee shop. Then I rush out of the room, lips still buzzing from connecting with hers.

CHAPTER FOUR

It's hard to avoid someone in a school as small as mine, yet I manage to steer clear of Bree most of the morning. But there's no way I can get out of biology. We have a quiz and unless I'm on my deathbed, my mom will have a fit if I miss any kind of test. The amazing thing is that somehow Joey has managed to avoid me at the same time that I've been avoiding Bree. I guess I was lying after all when I told her I was dating someone.

Thinking about Bree reminds me of what happened in her room and, for about the billionth time, I find myself comparing it with kissing Joey. It freaks me out that I'm not sure which I liked better, and I can't get the mental loop to stop playing in my brain.

For the most part, I'm being ignored by the rest of the student body again. Just like before Joey took notice of me. And BK—Before Kandi.

It almost feels like Joey and I never even happened. Only, it did, and so did the coffee shop. A couple of kids have eyed me with that freaked-out gaze. The one that says they heard all about the Coffee & Cues debacle. Luckily, most of the rest of them are too busy gossiping about each other to care about me. Either that, or they haven't all heard about it, yet, which is more likely. It's really not the upper echelon of kids hanging out at the C&C. However, there are some, probably the ones who were there, who are looking at me like I'm some kind of alien.

When the lunch bell rings, I grab my sack lunch out of my locker. A piece of folded paper flutters to the ground as I start to close the beige metal door. It's a note. From Bree. She wants me to meet her at lunch. Apparently, to apologize. I can feel my face redden. I slip the note into my jeans pocket and gently click the door to my locker closed, hoping no one is looking at me, that I have once again become invisible.

I don't really want to talk to Bree, I have no idea how I'm supposed to feel about what happened, or what to say to her, and besides, I've got a report to do. It's make-up work for English. Ms. Linde says the essay I wrote was only worth partial credit since I didn't actually follow the directions. I wasn't going to argue. Partial credit plus no parental involvement plus the opportunity for make-up credit equals win.

Anyway, I have to find an animal I can relate to and write a report on how its habits and behaviors are different from a human's. Not rocket science. I know I can pull something together, if I can just focus. I won't need to do a ton of research, and I could probably wait till tonight and get the information off the Internet, but I like the smell and feel of actual books. Not to mention, I'm still in Bree-avoidance mode. So, I slip out of the hallway and fast-walk across campus.

The library is a riot of smells, paper and glue, leather and wood, history and computers. The bright colors swirl around the room, hovering over a foundation of deep browns and woody earth-tones, and edged with the silver and ice blue of electronics. The library has been housed in the same building practically since the town was founded. It sits right next to the High School campus and serves as both the school and public library. The only thing that's really changed in decades is the addition of electricity and modern equipment, like the copiers and computers.

I like the old parts of the library the best, the way the tall wooden shelves hold the books close, like they're protecting them. I know they're inanimate objects, but I don't like to think of them that way. Some of the characters in my favorite books just seem so real and alive to me. Rows of books, side-by-side, nestle together like they're sharing their stories with one another. I guess I like to think of them as being safe and happy, resting between their covers when I'm not with them living in their worlds.

I set my book bag down on one of the polished tables. Unlike the school cafeteria, where the tables are made of some kind of cheesy plastic, the furniture here is real wood, sturdy and solid. Old, too. Yet, under the varnish and wax, beneath the years of civilization they've accumulated, I can still smell the wildness of the trees they once were. It's comforting to be here, to settle in with the friendliness of wood and words.

I grab a couple of random encyclopedias and set them on the table. I figure it'll be easier to find an animal to write about by playing page lottery than by drilling through the index. Holding one of the books balanced on its spine, I close my eyes and gently let it fall into my waiting hands, allowing it to open to a random selection.

But before I open my eyes, I know she's there. Not only do I smell her, I can sense her staring at me from across the room. I blink open my eyes and there she is, just as I knew she would be. She's dressed in a brown skirt and a purple top that accents her eyes, her hair pulled back into a braid. She has an expectant smile on her face, like she's been waiting for me to notice her.

Part of me suddenly wants to run across the room and grab hold of her, so she can't leave again. I need to talk to her, need to know more. But another part of me wants to sneak out the back door, keep avoiding her. Before I can do either, she swishes across the room, her full skirt billowing around her legs, sandals slap-slapping against the floor.

She sits down across the table from me and leans her elbows on the table, chin on her fists, smiles and says, "Hi." Just like nothing ever happened.

There's a new scent overlaid across her normal dusty earth smell. A brown sandalwood and pale yellowy jasmine smokiness that drifts off her clothes and hair, like she's been burning incense. She watches me and I realize she's waiting for me to speak, but there's something about her total ease that makes me even more uneasy, and all I can do is stare.

She tilts her head to one side, regarding me. "You could say hello," she says. This knack she has for knowing where my thoughts go is unnerving, not to mention a little creepy. "I really am sorry," she says. "I thought you liked me. Or that you at least found me attractive." She raises her eyebrows.

"I have a *boy*friend." My voice sounds husky and uncertain, even to me.

She shrugs like it's no big deal. Only, there's something in her eyes that makes me want to take it back. But I don't. "How did you know I was here?"

She leans forward and tilts back her head to look up at me, and I realize I'm still standing there, the encyclopedia open in my hands. I glance down at the page and see a picture of a wolf. I shut the book too hard, slamming the pages together with a loud smack.

The librarian looks over his glasses at me,

eyebrows raised, and I quickly sit, sliding into the chair as silently as possible.

Across the table from me, Bree is biting her cheeks. Eyes filled with laughter, she shakes her head in tiny jerks.

"I can't believe you're laughing at me." I glare at her. If looks could bore a hole through someone's forehead, she'd be shy her entire frontal lobe right now.

"Hold on," she says, putting up her hands in a defensive gesture. "I wasn't laughing at you; I was laughing at the situation."

"How is that different?" I hiss.

"Come on. Don't be like that. I'm the one who got rejected here. And for a boy, at that. Can't we still be friends?" She fake pouts and I can't help noticing how her eyes sparkle and smile, even when the rest of her face is making that sad little look. It drains me of my anger.

I shake my head and let out an over-the-top exasperated sigh.

"Let's go get a cup of coffee or something." She jerks her head toward the librarian's desk and raises her eyebrows. "Somewhere we can talk. There's so much you don't know, and I think I can help." She gives me a knowing look.

I hesitate, emotions roiling, curiosity warring with confusion and uncertainty. "Lunch hour is half over," I whisper. "We'll never get back in time for next period."

"You have study hall next period," she says. "No one is going to miss you."

"You know my schedule?"

"I told you, I checked you out." She smirks. "I'm your very own stalker."

I just sit there, not knowing if I should be flattered or appalled.

"Oh, come on," she says. "I'm not the one who bites." She laughs and it's that musical laugh from before. A warm secretive laughter. No anger, and nothing suggestive, just a laugh.

My mom will kill me if she finds out I skipped class, even if it is only study hall, but Bree's comment is dead on target, and I just have to know what else she knows. I need to know, well, everything. All the stuff about shapeshifters, witches and Others that no one else will tell me, all the secrets I'm dying to know, no matter the consequences.

I stand up, grab the encyclopedias off the table and dump them onto the sorting cart and follow her toward the exit. But before we get to the door, with a sudden swirl of skirts, she veers to the left and flits between two tall bookshelves.

I trail behind her, wondering where she's going. The exits are at the front and side of the main room, the restrooms near the front door. There's nothing back this way, except more books. Waving her hands in the air in front of her, she slips past the rows of books lining the old wooden shelves.

She turns a corner and I hurry to catch up to her. She zigs across an aisle and into a different row of shelves and I increase my speed, nearly slamming into her as I round the end of a tall bookshelf.

She's standing in front of a row of old, faded books, the writing on their spines rubbed to invisibility. Her hands are outstretched, palms forward, like a blind person trying to find the way. Except, her eyes are open. Only when I look closer, I can see she isn't actually seeing anything. Or, rather, what she sees is something far off.

Her fingers flutter then suddenly light on the spine of an especially dusty book. A sigh floats out of her as her she slides the book out, a shush of air being released that matches the soft shirring sound of the book leaving its place on the shelf. Her hands slide over the cover, caressing its moldering surface. In the shadows thrown by the bookshelves, it glistens with an oily sheen and a shiver tickles its way up my spine.

"What's that?" I ask.

Bree starts in surprise, spinning around like she doesn't expect to find me there, and nearly drops the book. Her eyes are wide, pupils dilated, and I sense something behind them, something dark and angry, something eerily not-Bree. "Just a book." Her voice is cool, controlled, but there's a deeper timbre to it, like there's something stuck in her throat.

"Yeah. A book. I know. We're in a library." I try to say it lightly, flash her a smile, but there's something about the change in her, a subtle shift in her scent to something layered in ozone, that sends a shiver that makes me want to walk away. Instead, I say, "I meant, what's it about?"

"Just stuff." She slips the book into her bag and when she looks back up at me her eyes appear normal.

"You can't just take that," I tell her. "You need to check it out."

"I don't have my library card with me," she says, sounding more like herself. "Besides, did you see the dust on it? This old thing hasn't been checked out in eons."

I shake my head, begin to protest, but she stops me before I can say anything.

"I think this book may have some answers . . . for both of us," she says in a conspiratorial whisper.

"So, just check it out," I say. "Or let me do it for you." I reach for the book, but she jerks her bag away with a cat-like hiss. I take a step back and eye her warily, hackles rising.

Her smile is suddenly back. "The thing is," she says in a placating way, "I may need to keep it longer than the usual three weeks. It's really no different than using a card. Look, it's not like I'm stealing it. I'll just be borrowing it on the honor system, which is really the basis of the library lending process anyway. I mean, how many people never even return books when they check them out on their cards? And it's not like I'm planning to keep it. *Forever.*" She shakes her head dramatically.

She sounds sincere and everything she says makes a sort of sense, but there's a resonance of panic beneath her reasonable arguments that make me uncomfortable. I know she can see the disbelief in my face.

"Loosen up," she says. "Let go just a little. You know you want to. It won't kill you to ignore a stupid rule once in a while."

Maybe not, I think, but following the rules is my mom's number one rule. She's made it clear that not following them could give away who I am. What I am.

"What are you going to do?" Bree asks in a thick voice. Her face is strained, ashen against the shadows. "Are you going to follow me nonchalantly out the door? Or are you going to rat me out to the librarian?"

I can hear my mother now, her I know-what's-best voice scratching inside my head: *Following the rules keeps us safe.*

The skin on my scalp feels tight, like I'm wearing pigtails that are too snug, but I shrug it off. "Whatever," I say. "It's your karma."

Bree grins, then turns and casually strides across the main room.

I give her a good, long head start, expecting the book alarm to go off as she passes between the magnetic sensors. But nothing happens. Maybe the book is so old it isn't tagged?

She even gives the librarian a cute little wave as she leaves, and I nearly swallow my tongue when the librarian glances up, hesitates, then smiles and waves back. My heart feels like it's chewing its way out of my ribcage as I follow her out the door.

CHAPTER FIVE

Bree orders a triple iced mocha with whip and chocolate syrup. The idea of coffee and chocolate is tempting, but I haven't wanted a fancy coffee drink since Joey walked out and left me sitting alone with two lukewarm mochas. What's wrong with me? Why can't I just forget about him? In all reality, he didn't walk out, he ran. Like a scared rabbit. The more I think about it, the easier it is to picture him high-tailing it out the back door with his head down. If he'd had a tail, it would have been tucked between his legs. Before I realize it, I've barked out a little laugh.

"What's so funny?" Bree asks.

"Nothing," I say. "I was just thinking how good a tall hot mocha would taste."

"Go ahead," she says. "It's on me."

We take our drinks and sit outside the Coffee & Cues at one of those plastic and metal tables. A strong breeze flutters the edges of the colorful umbrella sticking up out of the center of the table.

I watch as Bree uses her straw to feed herself small dollops of whipped cream from her drink with a feline grace. She looks up to see me watching her and tilts her head to the side. Her plum-colored eyes practically glitter.

I blush and look away, embarrassed that she caught me looking.

She frowns. "They've really got you wrapped up tight, don't they?"

"What do you mean?" I toy with my cup.

She stirs her mocha with her straw, swirling the whipped cream into her drink. The ice makes a swishing noise as it spins around inside the plastic cup. The white cream swirls into the chocolate, a mesmerizing counterclockwise whirlpool of colors that marble together moving deeper and deeper and a calm gray haze sends tendrils whispering inside my head.

The hair on the back of my neck rises and I pull myself up and away from the soft darkness. The silence that had begun to envelop me falls away and I push back from the table, my hands gripping the edge, a growl fizzing at the back of my throat. "What the—"

"Well played," she says with what is clearly respect gleaming in her eyes. She's no longer toying with her drink and her focus is fully on me.

I feel my lips curl into a snarl and it's all I can do not to lunge across the table aimed for her throat, sink claws into the throbbing pulse of life at the base of her neck. A low sound reaches my ears and I know it's me, a deep angry growl, the kind that's nearly inaudible, but clear warning for any animal stupid enough to stand in my way. "What was that?" My voice is a throaty hiss.

Her eyes go round, the pupils dilating in automatic fear. "I was only testing." She's whispering, but her voice rings with the high-pitched notes of panic. "I wouldn't have . . . not really . . ."

I unwrap my fingers from around the table's edge where my fingernails have carved half-moons into the plastic surface, force the animal back down inside.

"You tried to spell me!" I'm watching her now, every breath, and I know my lips have thinned to that ugly straight line that says I don't like what I see. If I were in form, I'd be baring my canines, letting her know I'm ready to bite.

"I'm sorry." She says it like she means it. "I didn't mean to. I mean, I didn't think it would work at all. It shouldn't have. You're just so . . . unique."

I can smell the truth mingled with her fear. But I don't trust her, don't believe what she's saying. She's too changeable, too unpredictable, too schizoid. Even her scent won't stay set.

"I may not know exactly what you are, Witch." I grind the words out between clenched teeth. "But I know I don't want anything more to do with you." I stand up to walk away and she reaches for my hand, sending an electric jolt of energy up my arm. I jerk away from her, confused and angry.

"Please, don't go." Her voice is pleading, now. "I really didn't mean it. I'm so sorry."

I know she means what she says, I can smell it, sense it. She smells like forest again, but with a silky overcast of sorrow, fear and guilt. Only, there's something older underneath. It's weird the way her scent keeps changing. Not just in the usual ways, where emotions color the odor, but like there are more layers that I haven't yet detected.

Part of me wants to relent, to sit back down and start over. But the animal inside me is repelled. Self-preservation gnaws at me.

Only, instead of leaving, instead of turning my back, I find myself folding slowly back into the chair, curiosity compelling me to discover the truth about this girl who smells like earth and spiders. This girl whose feelings are so powerful they are nearly visible to me. This person who makes me forget what I am beneath the rush of human feelings that wash over me.

This girl who kissed me.

Relief floods over her as I settle back into my seat. "I can explain," she tells me. Her smug self-assurance has slipped away.

"No more games." I fold my hands on the table.

"I wasn't playing games."

I start to stand and she swallows hard.

"Okay," she says, her eyes downcast. "No games. Honestly. I really am an undetermined witch, and

I . . . I didn't think that spell would work on you."
She looks at the ground and whispers. "It shouldn't
have."

"Oh, gee, that makes it okay then. Not." I sip at
my mocha, make a face. Maybe I should switch to
chai.

"Can you change into anything else?" Bree asks
suddenly, breaking the silence.

Startled, I shake my head. "I have only two
forms. This one, and my . . . Other self."

She nods slowly, like she's taking a moment for
the information to settle in.

"I thought you were all-knowing about everything
Other," I accuse.

She sighs. "I don't know everything. That's part of
the problem. And why I need you."

She sounds sincere and it's my turn to sigh. "It's
obvious you know a lot more than I do. You were
right about me. I've been short-leashed all my life
and only know what I've been taught. I knew you
were Other, but not what you were beyond that, but
I can't imagine how I could possibly help you."

She reaches for her drink, but when I start to
growl, she slides her hand back into her lap. "We
need each other," she says quietly.

"Oh, really? And why is that?" My tone is
condescending now, but I don't care. I'm tired of
being messed with and she deserves it.

She opens her mouth, hesitates.

"What happened to no more riddles?" I say. "No
more games?" I'm practically shouting now. "I give
up." I grab my stuff.

She springs out of her chair. The table wobbles and her drink spills, ice and liquid splattering across the surface and onto the ground as she grabs my arm.

I yank my arm out of her grip. "I was doing just fine before you came to town. I don't need you." It sounds cold, but I'm flustered and tired and being here with her is just so confusing.

"It's not like anyone else around here is worth hanging out with. They're all so . . ."

"Normal?" I can see where she's going, relate to the loneliness I sense in her.

"Exactly." Bree leans closer to me and lowers her voice. "They, the Norms, they don't understand us. Can't . . ." There's sadness in the way she says it. Like she's speaking from experience. And not the good kind.

I feel my defenses drop. "So, you're saying you need a friend?"

Her face crumples, then her eyes flash. "Don't be dense," she huffs. "I don't *need* anyone."

What the hell? What is wrong with her? "That's it. I'm done being called stupid and I'm completely done with being played," I shout. A man on the corner waiting for the light to change, turns and stares.

"Lower your voice," Bree shushes me. "You're drawing attention."

"Who cares?"

"I do. Your folks obviously do, and if you had any sense at all, you would, too." She reaches for my hand again, but I yank it away.

She looks hurt, then shrugs and settles back into the iron patio chair.

I glare down at her. She's shading her eyes with one hand, staring into my face and for just an instant I can see something there. Something dark and hungry. Something that gives me the creeps.

"Will you help me or not?" she says, her voice soft. The odd thing I thought I saw is gone, now I'm not sure I didn't just imagine it.

"Help you what?" I shake my head. She's just so . . . "No. Never mind. Not interested."

"Not even if I can answer all your questions? Tell you everything you ever wanted to know about Others like us? Help you learn about yourself?" Now, she sounds desperate. As if she'd give me the world if she could, just to get me to stick around.

I'm wary, but curious, despite this likely being another ploy on her part. What if she really does have knowledge I don't about Others? Not much of a stretch considering how in the dark I've been kept. What if she can tell me the things my mother can't, or won't? The parts that Papaw clearly left out? Wouldn't that be worth at least listening to her?

I can feel myself wavering. I know my mom will be pissed. Bad enough to discover that I've met a witch and haven't told her. Not to mention that if I do find out what she and Papaw have been keeping from me—whatever it is they don't want me to know—she's going to have a royal fit.

I sit back down.

CHAPTER SIX

"So far," I say, with a fake yawn. "You haven't told me much I didn't already know." My cup is empty, and the iced mocha we didn't manage to sop up with a huge stack of napkins is a gray sticky mess. "I already know being what I am is genetic, runs in families, skips generations, yada-yada-yada."

She opens her mouth to speak, but I cut her off. "And what you've told me about witches is fascinating, but where's the deep, dark info that is supposed to make cutting class and risking an all-star grounding worth it?" I sound like I mean business, but there's such a sense of relief in being able to finally talk about all of these things with someone other than my parents, that the rest of it has dwindled to low-level importance.

The sun has moved across the sky. School must be out by now. Traffic motors past. For the first time in my life, I have cut school, and not just one class, but an epically huge entire afternoon. I shiver at the thought of my mom finding out, but push away the guilt and worry. My parents don't actually socialize all that much, so I might get away with it. I hope.

Bree notices me watching the cars go by. "All Norms, all the time." Behind the sneer, she sounds almost wistful, which surprises me since she seems to think Norms are so beneath her. But maybe she doesn't like being Other any more than I do.

"Don't you like being, you know, different?" I ask.

"Do you?" she shoots back.

"It's not the same," I say.

"Oh, really?" Her voice is more quizzical than angry, but she's obviously bothered by my statement.

"It's not like nature has turned you into some kind of freak the way it has me."

She smirks. "So, now we're playing who's the bigger weirdo?" She pushes up the sleeve of her shirt, uncovering the inside of her arm up to her elbow. A pattern stands out stark against her pale skin, a green swirling line as fine as thread. There's something familiar about it, but as I stare the line twists and bends, weaving into something new.

She pushes her sleeve back down.

I wait, expecting her to say something, explain what that is on her arm.

After another minute, she grins at me. "You should see the one on my butt."

"Really?"

She lets out a peal of warm laughter that slides against my skin like sunlight. I can't help but laugh along, the sense of unease from earlier replaced by a familiar comfort.

"That's a heck of an ice breaker," I say, and we both start laughing again.

Then, just like that, she's all serious again. "We're not freaks. We're special." She says it kind of mocking, like it's something an adult has told her, probably hundreds of times.

"Yeah, right," I say. "Only we don't get our own bus."

That makes us both laugh, again. Only not so hard as before.

"All right." I pick up my empty cup and toss it into a nearby trash can. "We're both *special*. But you don't have to deal with this." I raise the leg of my jeans and show her my shin, covered in fine dark hair. "Do you know how often I have to shave? I hardly ever bother to wear dresses anymore. It's just not worth it."

"That must really suck." She shakes her head. "But at least it *can* be shaved off." She points to her arm. "This doesn't come off. Ever."

"But you were wearing a tank top the first time I saw you," I say.

"Cover up spell." She shrugs. "Doesn't last long, and so far, the only one I've really perfected smells so horrible, I can barely cover that up, even with pure essence oils."

I wonder if that's the reason her scent changes all the time, the spells and magic affecting her and the oils she wears to cover them up. "Why can't you just do another spell to cover up the smell?"

"It doesn't work that way," she tells me. "Mixing spells is not only difficult, it's dangerous. They don't just layer. A lot of the time, they combine and become something altogether different from what you intended. You have to be really careful."

"I didn't know that."

"Why would you? No real need to know unless you're a witch." She frowns. "Or a sorcerer, I suppose."

"True. But then why is it you know anything about shifters?"

"Mostly from books."

"There are books about shapeshifters? Actual, factual ones?" Now, she has my undivided attention and I wonder what might be in that old book she 'borrowed' from the library.

"Sure," she says. "There are books about pretty much everything Other. They just don't tend to keep them in your local library." Her hand drifts toward the bag on the table. Her fingers twitch lightly against the strap, and her face takes on an odd faraway look.

"Where do you get them, then?" I ask, alert and ready for . . . I don't exactly know. I just feel the need to be poised for a defensive move.

She pulls her hand back and examines her fingernails before answering, and the tenseness leaks out of my muscles. "Personal collections mainly. There are a few covens with their own libraries, but you generally have to be a member— or really close to one—to see them. Used to be magic journals and grimoires and such were kept hidden and only passed down from generation to generation. But nowadays there's a lot you can find by connecting to the right people on the Internet. You just have to make sure you're communicating with the real deal." She makes a face. "There're a lot of scammers out there, trying to make money off people who just wish they were witches."

I realize with a start that Bree and I have more in common than I first thought. More than just being Other. We both have a problem with the way people romanticize what we are. And the worst part is, I had fallen into that trap. I thought that being a witch must be so much better than what I am, that no matter what, I have it tougher than anyone else. But maybe there are worse things. And, as much as it pains me to admit it, there are a few good things about being a shifter. Like the way it feels to run in the night, sensing everything amplified ten times. At least when I'm allowed to really run, which is practically never since the last time we visited Papaw. My fingers drift to my throat as I consider Bree with fresh eyes.

But, if she doesn't like being different, then why does she seem to despise Norms so much? How can you think you're better than everyone else when you don't really like who you are? "You mean like those people who idolize the idea of being actual

Werewolves or Vampires?"

"Worse than that," she says. "I mean there are legitimate witches and covens and people with some minor magic, or those with just enough magic to do basic things. But there are also Norms out there who think they can just read a book or start a coven and wield powerful magic. People who think that's all it takes. People who delude themselves into thinking they're raising power when they don't have an ounce of real magic or the first idea of how to connect to the source. People who have no idea of the existence of Other, or what it's really like, but who dream it into some kind of uber-paradise." She rubs at her fingers with a napkin, like there's something sticky on them that won't come off. Then she tosses the napkin down onto the table. "Idiots and morons who wouldn't know real power if it snuck up and burned the flesh from their bones."

Her voice has filled with so much anger and disgust it's as if she's suddenly become someone else. Someone I don't like. Again.

I decide to change the subject. "So, how do I get my hands on some of those books about shifters?"

She looks at me, forehead wrinkled in confusion, then shakes her head and shrugs. "How should I know?" She narrows her eyes at me, reaches over and yanks her bag closer.

I can see my hopes doing a swirly and flushing away. This is not the time for someone to be messing with my emotions. Not when I've got more than just hormones yanking my strings. "What's with the Jekyll-Hyde act?"

She doesn't answer, just glares at me, like I've committed some heinous offense, and I've had enough. The last thing I need right now is to get jerked around by some obnoxious witch whose emotions are on the roller coaster ride from hell. The stupid moon does that to me enough. So much for finding out any big dark secrets, or even whether or not being what I am affects my taste in ice cream.

"Thanks for the coffee." I tell her. I've got more important things to do than play games with a psycho, witch or otherwise. "See you in class."

I swing my messenger bag over my shoulder and walk away, a part of me wishing she'll place a cool hand on my wrist and stop me, again. But all she does is slide her bag into her lap and hug it close.

CHAPTER SEVEN

The next couple of days are tense in biology class. I try to stay focused, but I literally have to work to keep from biting off Bree's head when she starts handing me pins with stupid things written on the labels. Things like, *Eye of New Moon,* and *Wolf's Bane.* She smirks every time I peel one off and rip it up. I guess she's decided that having a friend isn't all that important, after all. She sure hasn't bothered to try and make up, much less make nice. So, neither do I.

By the end of the period, my teeth are gritted so hard, I'm surprised my jaw doesn't snap. One more day, I keep telling myself. I just need to keep it together for one more day. The full moon will peak early tomorrow evening. Then I can run and, afterward, the moon will begin to wane. I'll have a reprieve—both from my beast and from dealing with Bree—at least until Monday.

When the bell rings, Bree takes her time gathering up her things, while I place our dissection tray on the metal storage cart. She seems to be waiting for something, but I really don't care, as long as she doesn't bother talking to me. It's lunchtime and I'm famished. So, I pick up my books and jam them into my bag. I'm heading for the door when I see him waiting in the hallway outside the classroom.

Joey Marsh. Dark bangs drape across his gorgeous eyes. My heart drops out through the bottoms of my feet and I feel the smile start to spread across my face. Maybe he wants to apologize for running out on me the other day at the coffee shop.

But when he looks past me like I'm not even there, my brain freezes.

His eyes lock onto something and he grins, showing his amazing teeth and deep dimples. I can't bear to turn around, can't bear to know, but my body betrays me, curiosity winning out. The only student left in the room other than me is Bree. And when I see that's who he's looking at, even though he's a total jerk, my heart cracks open like a fragile bird's egg and spills itself out into my ribcage.

Bree brushes past me, tulip skirt swishing around her long legs, her purse and book bag draped over one shoulder. "Hey there, handsome," she purrs, slipping her arm through his, linking herself to him like they're a couple. I'm frozen in place, too stunned to do anything but blink. She turns and gives me a wink, then saunters away with Joey in tow.

The room goes gray, then hot white, and I spill onto my knees. The beast wants blood, rips at my insides in a raging attempt to be free of my humanity. I wrap my arms around myself, fists curled into my armpits, nails digging into my palms.

There's someone at my side, a voice in my ears, but I can't make sense of the sounds. The room is metallic grays. I'm dimly aware that my eyes have already made the change. My skin is too tight and wants to come unzipped. I'm being consumed, choking back a throat-searing howl, when something touches my shoulder.

I jerk away. Swing around. Bare my teeth.

"Merissa?"

A part of my brain knows that voice, recognizes my name.

"Merissa!"

I muzzle my growl. Breathe deep. Exhale a slow stream of air. Breathe again.

My eyes begin to focus and color seeps back into the room. It's Mr. Rajanni and his face is filled with worry. "Are you all right?"

I can't make myself speak, so I just nod. Still breathing, deep and slow.

In. Out. In. Out.

"I am going to call the nurse," he says, rising

from the floor where he's been kneeling beside me.

"No, please." I finally manage in a hoarse whisper. "I'm fine. I'll be okay." I'm clutching my stomach, but I force my fists to unclench.

"You certainly do not appear to be fine," he argues.

"No, really. It's just so embarrassing," I tell him, using the standard excuse. "It's just, you know, that time of the month."

His eyes go wide in surprise and his face colors. He has no idea what I really mean, but it's not a lie, and is usually enough to stop the questions, especially from male teachers. "Can you stand?" He offers me his hand.

I unwrap my arms and push myself up. Rise. The beast is barely under control, and I don't dare take his hand. I don't want him to see the gouges in my palms, the fine red lines where I pierced the skin with my nails when they tried to become claws. I reach inside my bag and grab a handful of tissues, pretending to wipe my eyes and nose as I carefully sop up the drops of blood from my hands.

Mr. Rajanni is still eyeing me like he needs further convincing. I sniffle into the tissues. "Please, Mr. Rajanni." I plead. "Don't tell anyone. I just couldn't bear for anyone to know."

He blinks at me, then his face fills with empathy. "Are you certain you do not wish to see the nurse?"

"It's usually not so bad. It's just sometimes, you know, they hit me so hard. Stupid cramps!"

Despite his being a biology teacher, the word hits its mark and his face flushes darker. "Yes. Yes, of

70

course," he mumbles. "As long as you are certain you will be all right." He leans forward and makes a show of brushing the dust from his pants.

"I'll be fine," I assure him, hitching my bag over my shoulder.

"Well, then," he says brightly. "I hope you feel better on Monday."

"I'm sure I will," I lie, pasting a big fat smile on my face.

I'm sure that after the weekend I'll have less of an urge to tear out someone's throat, but that doesn't mean I'll feel any better.

CHAPTER EIGHT

The full moon shines down through leaves and branches and sweet night scents fill my brain with a wash of color that tints the shades of gray I see through my wolf eyes. The cool ground cradles my paws as I pad between the reaching oaks. This is what I've been waiting for, the freedom to let go and run off the persistent animal energy that makes it so hard to focus.

A rustle in the brush causes my ears to prick. A rabbit sprints for its warren and my legs tremble. I long to give chase, but the buzz collar chafes my neck, reminding me that I am not all fur and instinct. I am a shifter. Still able to reason within my animal form. Still able to think. Still able to exercise control.

Control. I'm beginning to hate the word. It's like I can never relax. Not in one form or the other. I'm always on guard, always protecting my secret.

I snarl, my animal side urging me to let go, to be fully wolf. But Papaw's lessons echo in my head. Lifesaving rules of survival that go beyond survival of the fittest. Rules that keep us all safe. Keep us alive.

A whine slips out as I focus on breathing. *In. Out. Pause. In. Out.* It's harder in this form. Every breath fills my head with the odors of forest and earth, trees and animals, plants and prey. If I had a choice, I'd run away. Run up to the mountains. Live apart, like my Papaw. But I don't. I didn't get to choose who I am. I didn't get to choose to be born. Everything in my life was chosen for me. All I get to do is follow the rules, do what I'm told.

Suddenly, I'm running. Racing through the brush, headed into deeper woods. The cool night air rushes through my fur. My paws barely touch the ground. A million scents converge, whipping past as I sail between the trees. A howl wells up from somewhere deeper than I can fathom and lets loose as I soar through the blurring landscape.

Zap!

I screech to a halt and flop on the ground, choke back a whine of frustration. Talk about a buzz kill! I want to gnaw the controller out of my mother's hands. Crunch teeth into plastic. Grind it down. Destroy the connection. Instead, I lie on the ground, panting.

And how the hell does she always know when I

let loose? There's something almost unnatural about the way she seems to know exactly when to rein me in. I said something to Papaw about it once and the tips of his ears got all red like they do when he's super angry about something and ready to blow. Then he stalked off and I didn't see him again until the next day.

I'm still lying on the bare earth, head on paws, wondering about it when the impatient dog whistle calls me in.

CHAPTER NINE

After my run, things are basically back to normal. At least, as normal as they get for me. Except that every time I think about having to go back to school on Monday, I have a horrible urge to eat grass and throw up.

I keep telling myself that Joey is just a stupid boy, and that Bree is a completely screwed up person, who totally messes with other people's emotions. Neither of them is worth my time or trouble. But knowing Joey—the only boy I have ever kissed—is dating Bree—the only *girl* I've ever kissed, and who it turns out is a real witch—in more ways than one—makes my canines hurt.

For the zillionth time, I wonder what it would be like to be just one thing. Girl or wolf. Right now, even being one hundred percent wolf would be preferable to feeling like I do. Of course, being anything or anyone other than me would be preferable.

Trying to sleep on Sunday night is a waste of time, so I slip out of bed and log onto my computer. I surf the net and, before long, I find myself googling witches and witchcraft. There are so many hits—more than forty-seven million for the first topic and almost thirty million for the second—that I don't even know where to start. Not that I'll probably find anything useful. Based on what I've found about shifters on the Internet, we non-Norms keep our secrets extremely well.

My eyes begin to blur as I wade through multiple pages of the same dreary information. Like a lot of things, the subject of witches tends to send people off on rants, either for or against, with no real in-between. There are places to buy spells and books and all sorts of witchy tools, but I can see what Bree was saying about all the Norms who are wannabes. There can't be that many true witches in the world, can there? I can also see that I'm wasting my time.

If only I knew how to get my hands on some of those books she told me about. If they actually exist. I picture her smiling face, the way she smirked at me as she strolled out and took Joey's arm, and my heart contorts into a twisted gnarl. The sound of cracking plastic yanks me back into the room. I loosen my grip on the computer mouse and roll it across the mouse pad. Luckily, it still works.

I creep back into bed, curl myself around a pillow. Completely tucked beneath the covers, I will myself to dream of mossy trees and rich earth.

CHAPTER TEN

Monday morning sucks. In algebra, I scrunch low in my desk, trying not to look like I'm avoiding the teacher's gaze—even though that's exactly what I'm trying to do—and ignore the spring sounds that filter in through the high bank of windows that stretches along the outer wall.

Francis Loring High, named after some founding father of the town, used to be a factory that my dad says made widgets, whatever those are. The city bought the old buildings, refurbished and turned them into a high school, and made the existing high school into a junior high when the town's teen population exploded sometime way back in the 1980s. Some days, like today, it feels exactly like we're being stored in an old warehouse.

Blowing off my homework and staying up to surf the net last night doesn't seem like such a good idea anymore. Normally, I can catch up during each class period before the homework is actually due, but today has been a nightmare of pop quizzes and essay questions. Luckily, with all the strange things that have been going on in school today, everyone seems to be on edge, so none of the teachers appear to have noticed my extreme lack of enthusiasm for school work. Yet.

During first period, in Digital Arts, the computers started to make strange grinding noises and then one after the other went into total meltdown. There wasn't any smoke, just an eye-stinging stench. Not that bitter smell of melted plastic and electronics, more like the yellow-green of sulfur and wet garbage. The entire classroom had to be evacuated.

US History didn't go much better. We were all just sitting there having one of Mr. Beladi's discussion/debates about class and equality when a crap-ton of insects flew out of the air vent and swarmed overhead. After circling for a few seconds, they dropped down and started dive-bombing every person in the room. Mimi Rubo screamed like a banshee and tore out into the hallway with her entire crew in tow, followed by the ugly swarm and that same sulfur smell. That was second period and Mimi's troop was still locked in the girl's bathroom, last I heard.

By the time we got to third period English, Ms. Linde wasn't taking any chances, so we were told to remain in our seats and read. Things stayed quiet.

Although, Ms. Linde tried really hard not to look up at the air vents, and failed miserably the entire period.

Anyway, I hate math. Especially algebra. On the plus side, since it's the last class of the day, all the bizarro stuff seems to be over with. On the minus side, algebra is already my worst subject, and double negative, I don't have homework done and Mr. Lo is not as flexible about assignments as Ms. Linde.

I'm trying to come up with a good excuse to give him when there's a sudden commotion out in the hall.

Mr. Lo rushes over to the door and looks out. "Wait here and stay in your seats," he tells us. But as soon as he's out of the room, everyone is crowding the door to peer out into the hallway and see what's going on. Water pours out from under the door of the boy's bathroom across the hall and Mr. Lo is trying to figure out a way to get over there without ruining his shoes. At least this time the janitors can't blame the girls for the school's bad plumbing.

CHAPTER ELEVEN

Things stay pretty quiet until Friday. But then the entire kitchen staff lets loose in a humongous food fight, totally trashing the cafeteria. Principal Tyler's face was as red as a splattered tomato when she went rushing into the dining area and skidded across the floor to land in a pile of smashed food and empty ketchup bottles.

The staff was just standing there, all of them with stunned looks, and claimed not to remember what had happened. Of course, in addition to the comedic scene with Tyler—sure to get a lifetime run on mobile devices all over town—the video cameras in the cafeteria showed every hurled vegetable and squirted condiment. And the entire school had access to the footage the second it was anonymously posted to WeView on the Internet.

Teachers are saying someone must have spiked the coffee or some such. It'll be a while before the blood tests come back, so it's hard to say.

Not that I really care why they did it. Early release is early release.

Lot of good it did me, though.

Mom was waiting for me when I got home and she hasn't paused long enough for me to wedge in a word for the last hour.

"I just cannot fathom what got into you," she says for the hundredth time since she started in. "Where is your head at?"

"I told you, it wasn't my fault. *Kandi* jumped *me.*"

"Don't take that tone with me, Merissa." Her face is hard.

"It's not a tone."

Her jaw gets tight. "And you talk back now?"

I glare at her, then realize I'm pushing it and drop my eyes. "If you'd just let me explain—"

"All right," she says, anger still riding the edge of her words. "Go ahead. Explain to me why you can't stick to a few basic rules. Rules, I might add, that are intended to keep our family safe."

The quiet intensity in her voice as she utters that last part causes me to look up. Her face is hard, but—in her eyes—I see what looks like fear.

I've never seen my mother frightened before. Everything I'm about to say slides back inside me. I force myself to swallow my words along with the resentment at being accused of something I didn't cause. "I'm sorry," I tell her, trying to sound sincere. And, while I hate apologizing for something that was totally not my fault, I do sincerely want to chase the fright from her eyes.

She blinks a few times and purses her lips. "Being sorry won't be enough if anyone ever finds out about . . . our secret, Merissa."

The way she says it makes me angry all over again. "Don't you mean *my* secret? Seems like I'm the only one around here having to hide what she is." I spit the words out.

For a moment, she just stands there, apparently stunned into silence. But just when I think I've hit her broadside and I can celebrate the win, she grabs me by the shoulders, locks eyes with me, and says low and quiet, "You have no idea what you're talking about, young lady. The world is a much bigger place than what you know and there are things going on in it you can't begin to understand."

I feel like I'm sinking through the floor and something ominous closes in around me.

Then she lets go and takes a step back, sucking in a deep breath, and suddenly I'm just standing in the kitchen facing off with my mom again.

She wipes her face with her hands. "Go to your room."

"I'm not a five-year-old," I complain, but it's only half-hearted because I'm a little more than freaked out about what just happened.

"Go. To. Your. Room." She stares at the ceiling like she can't stand to look at me anymore.

I know when it's time to beat a hasty retreat, but

I just can't help getting in the last word. "Fine." I grab my books and stomp off down the hallway.

At least I'm not grounded. Not yet, anyway.

CHAPTER TWELVE

The following Monday, Mr. Rajanni stands at the front of the room, eyeing the smart board warily, as if afraid the boogeyman is about to jump out of it. I'd laugh, but at this point the appearance of a boogeyman wouldn't be a surprise. Although, it'd probably be one of the look-a-likes and not the actual boogeyman. At least, according to what my mother told me once when I had a nightmare about him. When most moms were confusing their kids by telling them there's no such thing as the boogeyman, my mother was explaining that he was not only real, but had a horde of underlings pretending to be him. Sort of like department store Santas pretend to be the supposedly real Santa, only in this case the boogeyman and all his proxies are real. Now that I think about it, the truth actually confused me as much as other kids' parents' denial probably confused them.

I suppose people are afraid of a lot of things they know are there, even though they've been told those things don't really exist. And it doesn't help when strange things happen, like all the stuff that's been happening here at school this past week. There's something about all of it that reeks of Other. But why would that be?

Today began about as crummily for me as any school day in the history of school days, with too many smacks of the snooze button, followed by the sudden adrenaline-rush-filled realization of being late, decorated with a large dose of spilled juice and no breakfast.

For most of fourth period, Mr. Rajanni has been standing at the smart board, clicking from one illustration to the next, droning on about the digestive systems of mammals while most of the class, including me, gaze at the front of the room with bleary eyes. But for the last couple of minutes, he's just been standing there, silently staring at the last slide, a picture of a lion tearing at the carcass of a gazelle as if it's the first time he's ever seen it.

When the smart board starts oozing a dark red, I think I'm falling into a bad dream. I rub my eyes and blink hard, but the oozing just gets worse.

Then, the smell hits me.

Blood.

Charcoal shades surround me, turning to black and ringed with the yellow-green of sulfur. At first,

I'm afraid to look around the room. Afraid I'll discover I'm the only one seeing the red dripping from beneath the dark smudginess. But there are muffled gasps from behind me and then Mr. Rajanni stops staring. He reaches out, putting the tips of his fingers to the board. They come back covered in crimson and he tries to back away, slipping in the pool of dark liquid that has formed on the floor, and falling.

His head hits the edge of the desk with a loud thump.

There's a moment of stunned silence, then a fresco of chaos and noise as kids run from the room, some of them screaming for help, others just screaming. I sit stunned, trying not to inhale. The blood is causing my insides to bristle. Then, one of the girls from the volleyball team rushes to the front of the room. She kneels by Mr. Rajanni and touches his neck, then leans in to put her ear near his mouth. Sitting up, she pulls off her team hoodie, rolls it up and tucks it under the teacher's feet, then surveys the nearly empty room. Her brown eyes lock on mine as I stand there, still stuck to the spot. "Help me," she commands. "I think he's in shock. We need more elevation."

Time slows and my brain watches while my body moves, bending to scoop up my messenger bag and hauling it to the front of the room. I hand it to the girl who tucks it under Mr. Rajanni's legs with her hoodie.

The teacher groans.

"Bring me some books," the girl orders, ignoring

the sticky blood that coats her hands.

Keeping my brain turned off, I grab the textbooks off the nearest desks and hand them to her. She stacks them beside the teacher's head and holds out her hand for more. Breathing through my mouth to keep the blood scent at bay, I scavenge four more books, which she piles on the stacks and slides in close on either side of the teacher's head.

Mr. Rajanni's eyes begin to flutter and the girl puts her hands against one of the stacks of books, motioning for me to hold the other side. "We need to immobilize his head, in case of neck injury. Don't push them in, just hold them in place in case he tries to move."

Like some remote-control robot, I do as she tells me.

"Did anyone call 911?" she asks.

I look across the room to the door. A crowd has gathered in the hallway, kids pushing forward to see, but refusing to enter the room. I shrug.

Then, the crowd parts, and two EMTs stride into the room. In a flash, they've taken over, ushering us out of the way. Time seems to speed back up and the next thing I know, they've got Mr. Rajanni strapped to a board and lifted onto a gurney.

"Is anyone else hurt?" one asks.

I stare blankly at him.

"Where did all this blood come from?"

"Would you believe the white board?" Volleyball Girl asks.

He shakes his head. "That's about the worst prank I've ever heard of. Your teacher could have been really hurt."

"How is he?" I ask.

"Thanks to you two, I think he'll be okay," the female EMT says. "Good job, girls." They wheel Mr. Rajanni out of the room.

Volleyball Girl is wiping at her hands with some moistened towels the EMTs gave her and the smell of antiseptic and blood coats the back of my throat, making me want to regurgitate.

I need air.

I reach for my bag, but it's sitting in the pool of animal blood, sticky and congealed. I have to get out of this room, but as I head for the door Volleyball Girl touches my arm, offers me a moist towel. "You okay?" I shake my head, pull away from her and push through the crowd of kids. By the time I reach the outside doors, I'm nearly running. It's all I can do to keep myself from dropping to all fours . . .

I lean forward, hands on knees, and take deep breaths, but the blood smell has followed me, clinging to my clothes and my skin. My scalp tightens. I can almost feel the hair on my arms and legs grow longer. Then I'm on my knees in the grass, tearing up huge handfuls of green, rubbing the blades between my hands. The pungent odor of chlorophyll permeates the space around me, clean and fresh, clearing my head.

A shadow falls over me. Volleyball Girl sets my bag, most of the blood cleaned from it, on the ground in front of me, then squats down beside me and sits cross-legged. "You did good in there," she tells me, pulling up a few blades of grass and twirling them between her fingers. Concern and curiosity swim in her almond-shaped eyes as she looks over at me.

For a moment, we sit in silence. Then she shakes back her dark hair and smiles. "Mr. Rajanni is going to be okay, thanks to you." She's pretty, streamlined and athletic without being too muscular.

"Thanks to you, you mean. I just did what you told me to." I brush the dirt and grass from my hands. "How do you know all that stuff, anyway? I sure had no idea what to do."

She shrugs. "I want to study medicine. I do a lot of volunteer work with the rescue service. You'd be surprised how many people go hiking off-path in our local mountain ranges without the slightest clue on how to survive, even for a day." She laughs. "Anyway, thanks for your help. Everyone else was too freaked out to do anything, except dial 911. I think they got about a hundred calls." She rolls her eyes. "I'm Kat, by the way." She extends her hand.

"Merissa," I tell her as we shake hands. Her skin is cool against my hot palm.

"You feel warm," she says. "Are you sure you're okay?"

"I'm fine. Just . . . the blood. It . . ."

"Yeah," she says. "Some prank, huh? It looked really real, too."

"It was—" I begin, then correct myself, "—some prank, yeah." I know it's not. At least, not a prank that any Norm could pull off. I can't help wondering if Bree is somehow connected, except she wasn't even in the classroom. In fact, she hasn't been around when any of the weirdness has occurred. But all this stuff only started happening after she showed up, which makes her completely suspect in my book.

* * *

The rest of the day goes by like a scratched-up DVD movie that sticks on some scenes and skips over others. By the time I get to final period, I think maybe this day will relinquish its hold without anything worse happening, but who am I to dream of better things?

Just after the bell rings to signal the start of class, and everyone is nearly settled down for Algebra, the fire alarm screeches, followed by a chorus of cheers and the commands of the teacher to "Leave everything here and head out of the door, single file." A few kids linger to grab cell phones, or lipstick, or whatever other stupid thing that would probably cost them their lives in a real fire, but the teacher intervenes and everyone finally gets herded out the door, through the hallway, out the back exit, and onto the track field where half the school is standing, grouped by classes.

The other half of the student body will be standing in the church parking lot across the street from the front of the school. Teachers will be calling out the roll and checking off students. Hopefully, no one is cutting last period or smoking in the bathroom, or we could be out here forever while they track down the MIAs.

Once everyone is accounted for, teachers lighten up and kids start drifting from one group to another, chatting with friends, or hooking up with boyfriends and girlfriends. I've got the toe of my shoe shoved into the grass, trying to dig myself a hole to crawl into when someone touches my elbow.

I look up into violet eyes and take a step back. "Bree." She smells the way she did when I first met her, spider webs and earth. The burnt sulfur reek is nearly gone and the green forest loamy-ness almost completely overwhelms the lingering traces.

"Hey, 'Rissa. Long time, no talk."

I don't know what to say to her, so I say nothing.

"Oh, come on," she says, "I thought we were friends." Her face is pale, red rimming her eyes. I'm ready to walk away, but there's something about her today, something vulnerable. I have the urge to reach out and take her hand. Only, I don't.

Instead, I sniff again, trying to adjust. Usually, even with perfumes and colognes, a person smells pretty much the same way all the time, just more or less of it depending on their mood. But Bree's scent bounces back and forth, from one extreme to the other, like a tennis ball in a professional match. I suppose it could be because of the spells she uses, like the one that covers her strange tattoo.

Bree gives me an odd look and I realize I've been inhaling her scent as if it were the rich aroma of freshly baked bread or cookies fresh from the oven. The memory of sweet cookies baking reminds me of her grandmother's house, the mismatched ceramic planters lining the porch, overgrown with all sorts of strange plants. And the soft, gray cat that let me scratch behind its ears. I let out a sigh. The day we'd spent in that warm little cottage just being exactly who we were, without having to be cautious of what we said, was the one time since finding out who I truly am that I felt comfortable inside my own skin. I think about being in her room and search her face, looking for the girl I saw that day.

"Hey," Bree says. "How are things in Merissa-land?"

"Great," I tell her, but it's clear I don't really mean it. "How about you?"

"To be honest," she says, pulling her long hair out of the tight braid and running her fingers through it, "I'm feeling off. Like I don't fit inside myself anymore."

"Join the club. That's the way it's been for me pretty much my whole life."

"Yeah? Well it sucks."

I let out a snort. "I hear that."

She's fidgeting, her hands moving like they're missing something, as she re-braids her hair.

"You okay?" I ask. "You seem sort of nervous or something."

A scowl crosses her face. "I'm fine," she grumbles. "Just that the stupid drama teacher wouldn't let me bring my bag. It was just sitting there on the front row aisle seat, I could have run out and grabbed it, then gone out the main door, but she made us leave the theater by the stage doors and no one was allowed to go back in." She laughs, a low mirthless sound, and rubs at her shoulder. "It's just weird not having my bag with me. I feel kind of naked without it."

Weird? I want to tell her what's weird is how she's all nice one minute, then an uber-beast the next. I'm not sure what's stopping me. Except that it's kind of nice that she's talking to me like a person and I don't want to do anything to trigger her mean-girl attitude. Deep down I know the nice act is probably just that, an act. But I wish we really could be friends. My skin heats up and I catch myself remembering that kiss, a part of me wanting to reach for her. Instead, I say, "Maybe you should take that old book back to the library and stick it on a far back shelf."

She gives me a confused look. "What book?"

"Come on. You know. The creepy old book you took from the library and have been hauling around with you everywhere ever since."

She stares at me for a moment, then her look of confusion turns into a sneer. "What makes you think that anything I do is any of your business?" Her hands fly to her head and she begins to shake and her eyes go from plum to black and back again. It happens so fast I think I might have imagined it. Then, as if it never happened, she drops her hands and smiles at me. "We should bake cookies, sometime. My grandmother has an awesome recipe for caramel snicker-doodles."

I know I'm staring, that my mouth is open, that I look like an idiot, but I'm so creeped out and stunned, I just can't help myself.

"Are you okay?" She reaches toward me and I step back.

Her face scrunches up in consternation and she drops her hand. Her eyes go wide for a moment, then the angry sneer is back. "You really need to figure out who your friends are." Her words come out in a hiss. "When the time comes, you'll need to pick a side. And you don't want to be on the losing team. Trust me."

She spins around and hurries toward the building before the teachers give the okay to go back inside.

I stand there unmoving, shocked into place as kids stream past, flowing around me like I'm a rock in the middle of a river. Then a dark hand is laid on my shoulder and I look up to see a boy. No. That's wrong. He's not a boy, not a hundred percent boy. In fact, he's one hundred percent Other. I can tell by his scent. Only, there's something off about it. Like it's a mixture of things, part boy, part something like Bree and another part that's completely wild and alien, oak leaves, milkweed and Other with a hint of burnt copper.

He's wearing jeans and a t-shirt, a pair of dark glasses perched on his nose. Gray eyes stab at me over the top of his sunglasses as he pushes a lock of silver-tipped hair off his forehead. Without a word, he walks past me and heads toward the double doors, as if he's just another student, but veers off at the last minute and disappears around the corner of the building, his enticing scent trailing after him.

My fingers reach up to my shoulder where he placed his hand and my scalp tingles. I start to follow him, wanting to find out who—what—he is, but a teacher stops me, herding the last of us back into the cool dark of the building. There's still time to finish out last period and they don't want us to miss a single exciting moment of learning. Or lose any more contact hours than they can help, seeing as the state only pays for butts in chairs. My mom's words, not mine.

With a shudder, I wonder when I started actually quoting my parents.

CHAPTER THIRTEEN

I decide to take the long way home from school, along Main Street, past the Coffee & Cues. I slow down as I pass in front of the big picture window that looks into the game room. The usual crowd of kids is inside, huddled around the video games.

"You interested in a cup of coffee or a latte?" a low voice purrs.

It's the boy from the fire drill. He's leaning against the building at the edge of the picture window, dark hair shining in the sun. He wasn't there a moment before, but now he's slouched against the building as if he's been there for ages.

I narrow my eyes and inhale. Rain-soaked tree bark, milkweed and something else I can't quite place. I know I was distracted when I walked past, but I'm generally not that oblivious to the people around me. In fact, I tend to be what my mom calls hyper-vigilant, always knowing where other people are and where I am in relation to them. So, I know I would have seen him. Or at the least, smelled him, his nighttime rainforest mix of warring scents; pine green and browns ringed by a shimmer of black. Only, I didn't.

My nostrils dilate, as I try to catalog him, attempt to match his here-and-now aroma with the scent at the school, and realize that, like Bree, his scent is elusive and changeable. He's definitely not a Norm.

He smiles at me. It's friendly, but there's something dark behind it and when his lips part I can see his teeth aren't smooth and rounded like a human's. They're pointed.

"You don't go to my school." I say in a low voice. "Who are you? Why are you following me?"

"My name is Jeryd and I need your help recovering something that belongs to me." He tilts his sunglasses up so I can see his eyes. They're dark gray with specks of silver and clearly not human. At least, not any human I've ever seen.

My breath rushes out in a whoosh. I search my memories, all the things that Papaw taught me, the signs and scents, but I can't quite place this Jeryd person. "What are you?" I finally ask.

He looks down at the ground as if the answers to the universe might be written there at his feet, then he raises his head and says, "What I am, is what you would call an Otherworlder. The details aren't really important."

This is impossible. I've lived in this town for all sixteen plus years of my existence and I have never seen the slightest sign of anyone other than me who wasn't a full-fledged, ordinary—nothing more special than a talent for whistling or baseball or tap dancing—Norm. Not that I know all there is to know about it, but seriously, there is no way that all of a sudden, out of the vast external world into mine, could there just coincidentally step two Otherworld beings with no connection to one another whatsoever.

"Are you related to Breanna?" I ask, thinking he must be a cousin Bree neglected to mention, a witch or a warlock, or whatever the male version of Bree would be. Although, that's not exactly what his scent says.

His smile dissolves. "Not that I'm aware of," he says in a harsh tone. "Although, as my mother never ceases to remind me, my parentage, at least on my father's side, is extremely questionable."

As paranoid as ever about being outed, I look around to see if there is anyone nearby who might overhear this odd conversation and report back to my mom about it. "Then what are you, and where did you come from?" I demand, once I'm certain the coast is clear.

He shifts his weight, and pushes off from the building. Standing up straight, he's taller than I am, which most boys my age aren't.

"A bit of this and a little of that," he tells me, shrugging as if it isn't important to him, but I can tell it is. He stares at me hard, like he's looking for something. "Fancy that," his eyes light up suddenly. "You and I have something in common."

"What are you talking about?" I ask, thinking that if he's not related to Bree, he may be another kind of shifter. Or something I don't even know about. Yet.

"We're both half-breeds," he says.

"Half-breeds?"

"Sure," he says, taking a step in my direction. He holds his hand up, palm facing toward me. "I'm half Sidhe, on my mother's side, and half my father's son, which makes me a whole lot of nothing." An odd look washes over his face and he lowers his hand. "You're—"

"Half-she? What's that supposed to mean?" I catch a glimpse of a pointed ear peeking from beneath his shaggy hair.

He wrinkles his forehead and gives me a funny look. "Fay. I'm half Fay."

Fay! I gasp.

"Now that I think on it, perhaps we don't have so much in common, after all." He lets out a small sour laugh, as if he's just told a joke that is somehow offensive.

I quickly sift through everything Papaw taught me about the Fay. It's not a very long list, but one thing has stuck, mainly because he jack-hammered on it like it was life or death. Never trust anything that comes straight out of Other. Not ever.

Jeryd is still smiling. I narrow my eyes at him, wondering what I missed. Every hair on my body stands up, and I'm zinging with nervous energy.

And what the hell does he mean by half Sidhe? According to everything Papaw has shared with me, which admittedly wasn't much, and the little bit of info Bree managed to offer up before going Ms. Hyde on me the other day, the term can refer to just about everything that comes out of Other. Which means he could be half just about anything Other on both sides, which would make him completely Fay and therefore one hundred percent dangerous.

I glance through the picture window, expecting an audience of faces to be pressed up against the glass staring at us, or rather at him actually. Oddly, absolutely no one is paying any attention to us. Somehow this calms me.

"Never mind that, it's not important." He eyes me as he inches closer, moving slowly, the way I would if I were stalking a wild animal. "If you're not in the mood for coffee, how about a short walk? We need to talk, and there are too many curious humans around here for my taste." He nods in the direction of the bus stop and I see the woman on the bench with the book open in her hands has tilted her head to try and listen to what we're saying. Fact really is stranger than fiction, I want to tell her, but I don't. Instead, I glance back at Jeryd and give him a quick nod.

He steps up beside me and I feel that zinging again, but this time it isn't nerves. I take a step back.

"How about we take the short trail through the Hollows?" he asks.

"The Hollows? That's not a place I know." My mouth is dry. I rummage in my bag as nonchalantly as possible for my water bottle and take a sip, but I keep my eyes glued on Jeryd.

"Sorry, sometimes I forget that in this world names and places change over time." He gives me a quick sad smile and juts his chin toward Fielder Park, an area that stretches from the other side of the main highway out to the edge of town. "I meant your town's outdoor recreation area."

"Fielder Park? Okay," I say. The park isn't usually crowded this early on weekdays, but it never seems to be completely empty. I could probably attract attention, call for help, if I really need to. But for some odd reason, I don't think I will. I'm not actually afraid of Jeryd. I don't feel like he's planning to try anything. It's more like there's something resigned about him, like he's accepted the way things are, given up the fight. Although, I have no idea what fight. Maybe Papaw was right, maybe I shouldn't trust him, but there's suddenly a whole lot more going on in my boring little town than I ever thought possible, and I am dying to know what the hell it's all about.

We cross the road and walk into Fielder Park, following the jogging trail that winds along one end of the green field before zigzagging across the open area where the town's annual Easter egg hunts and other such events are held. There are a few people out playing Frisbee golf and walking dogs. So, it's not like we're alone out in the forest or something, but we are far enough away from people that they can't hear us.

I turn my head to look at him. His face in profile is a collection of sharp lines, his chin just a bit on the pointy side, but somehow he's even more attractive from this angle. I stare at him, trying to get another glimpse of his ears. Wondering what they might feel like. "What do you want?" I snap, then clamp my teeth together and look away.

A kid rolls up behind us on a mountain bike and Jeryd steps closer to me to let him pass. His arm brushes against mine and a tingle of heat rushes between us.

Dammit! What the hell is wrong with me? It's not enough that I'm already mixed up with a boy and a girl? Now, I'm getting revved up over a Fay? Half Fay, I remind myself, but Papaw would still have a heart attack or, in his words, a conniption fit.

The kid on the bicycle goes by and Jeryd steps away from me. The absence of his closeness leaves me chilled and more alone than I felt before he brushed up against me. "This is ridiculous," I mutter under my breath.

"What's that?" he asks.

"Nothing," I watch the kid on the mountain bike disappear into the trees where the trail winds through the wooded area before slanting down along Crystal Creek. "I was just thinking out loud."

I can feel Jeryd watching me, his gaze lingering on my face, and I wonder what he sees in my profile. Just a plain human girl with a high brow and thin nose, or can he see the real me? I've never really thought about it before. I've always just hidden behind this shape, blended in with the Norms, passed as one of them. But now it turns out there are Others who can see me for what I really am, can tell I'm different. That I'm like them.

Dangerous. The word comes unbidden into my brain and I find I like it, like being the person someone's mother should be warning them about.

Jeryd brushes the hair out of his eyes and I remember he's asked me for something. "Maybe you should tell me what specifically you think I can do for you," I say.

"Your friend, the witch—"

"Breanna is not my friend," I tell him in a rush. "I barely know her." And she's kind of freaking crazy, I think, but don't say.

He gives me a look of disbelief, then nods. "Okay," he says, "this Breanna, who you aren't actually friends with, has something of mine."

"I'd say that's between you and her." I shrug. "So, why tell me?"

"Because," he says slowly, like he's teaching something to someone who is having trouble understanding him, "I need your help to get it back."

"Why don't you just ask her for it?"

"First off, because I can't let it, I mean her, know it was me who hid it in the library. And secondly, she's put a barrier around it that I can't penetrate."

"The library? Are you saying that old book she took is yours?"

He glances around like he's afraid someone is listening. "Yes, for all intents and purposes. I thought it would be safe there. It should have been." His shoulders droop and his face grows severe. "Seems a poor choice now."

"I guess." I shake my head. "Hiding a book in a library, a place where people go to find books does seem to be a little on the not-such-a-good-idea side."

His mouth quirks up in a sardonic smile. "It seemed like a fair idea at the time." He gestures toward town. "And it was well guised. A normal human would never have noticed it. And this town isn't a popular destination for Otherworld visitors."

"So, if this book is really yours, why don't you just go get it back? What do you need me for?"

"I told you," he says, "she's established a barrier spell. I can't get within three lengths of her."

"Lengths?" For some reason I find this really funny. "You mean she's cast some sort of restraining order spell?" I can hardly get the words out, I'm trying so hard not to laugh. That sure would have come in handy against Kandi Johnson the other day.

"I guess you could call it that." He frowns. "Not exactly true, but technically correct as to the outcome." He scuffs a foot against the trail.

I think about this for a minute and can't help but wonder what kind of spell could do that. "So, why doesn't it work against me? I've seen her in school and there's no barrier that keeps me away from her. If you and I have so much in common, why is it that I can get close to her while you can't?"

"Because the restraining order spell as you so

creatively called it, must be selective. I don't suppose it would make much sense for her to cast a spell that would keep you or your kind away. It would probably make school very awkward. That, and she probably doesn't think you're a threat or that you might ever come between them."

"Them?"

"Her and the book."

"She's right," I say. "Not my monkeys, not my circus."

"What?" He looks at me like I'm speaking a foreign language.

"None of my business," I say, turning to leave. "And not my problem."

"It is if you treasure your quiet existence here, and that of everyone else in this town," he says, in an ominous tone.

I turn back. "Are you threatening me?"

He shakes his head and takes off his sunglasses, to look directly into my eyes. "Not I."

"You mean Bree?" I start to laugh, then stop. "What the hell is in that book?"

"Chaos," he looks away from me. "Chaos and slow but certain doom for the Silver Realm, the place you call Other, and likely all of its inhabitants, some of whom I would be sorry to see destroyed. The entity inside that book was imprisoned to keep it from doing great harm. You have no idea what havoc will be wreaked, if it is released."

"Why should I care?"

"How can you not?" He steps closer. There's an

air of menace about him that wasn't there before and hot pin prickles skitter across my scalp. "Both our worlds, and the people in them, are at risk."

I think about my parents and the rules I've already broken. I *cannot* get mixed up in this. "This is not my problem," I say. "Why don't you get your whatever-she-is mom or your deadbeat dad to help you?

He mutters something under his breath.

"What did you say?"

He shoves his hands deep into his pockets and leans forward. His eyes are practically glowing, reflecting the afternoon light in a creepy-evil-creature-about-to-explode way. "I said, you're acting like a stupid wolf."

I choke down the growl that's formed in my throat and turn to go.

"Just like that? You turn your back?" He calls after me, shock and frustration ringing in his voice. "Now, you're just acting like a stupid girl."

"Up yours." I leave him standing in the middle of the jogging trail and speed-walk home. I can still smell him, but his intoxicating aroma is fading and even my odor-cataloguing brain is having trouble recalling the exact scent, though the haze of Other clings to me like metal dust to a magnet. Luckily, I don't need to hide any trace of his scent from my parents. For once, being different from them is a relief. I nearly laugh out loud when I realize this, but a sobering tendril of thought niggles at me. What if the jerk is right? What if there really is something sinister going on? What if the book does contain a cursed entity trying to escape its bounds? And what if in escaping, it could hurt my family?

Get a grip! I tell myself. The creep is just trying to con you.

It's obvious he's after something for himself. What other kind of behavior could you expect from a whatever-kind-of Fay he is. All Papaw's warnings shudder their way through my brain and I shiver at the thought of all that trickery mixed with equal measures of arrogance and selfishness, then heaped with an extra helping of charm. But just because his nature is to be self-serving, doesn't mean there isn't at least a modicum of truth to what he's saying. It would explain all the weirdness that's been going on at school. Dozens of kids are out sick, including the entire drama department. And I can't deny the whole schizoid way Bree's been acting, nice one minute and vicious the next. Not that that's proof of anything other than the girl needs to be medicated.

Although, if there is something sinister exerting its influence on Bree and the school, maybe I do need to try and stop it before this whole town becomes overrun by non-Norms and creatures out of Other. And then my parents kill me for not telling them that a witch just happened to move to town. Yeah, oh by the way, she goes to my school and I just didn't think it was important enough to say anything. And also, there's this guy from the Silver Realm, you know, where all the Fay come from, and he'd like me to help him retrieve the cursed book he just happened to leave in the town library.

The powers that be have already made excuses for all the odd things happening at school, but I know my mom must be at least a little suspicious. When it comes to anything having to do with me, she seems to see conspiracy everywhere.

Crap! I need to find a way to fix this before she starts to dig into it.

CHAPTER FOURTEEN

There's an incessant buzzing in my ear. I swat at it and the alarm clock hits the floor. I roll across the bed to see if it's still working, emitting a pained groan when I see the time. After tossing and turning all night, I had finally fallen into a kind and gentle slumber. That was less than forty-five minutes ago and now it's full-on morning. I stuff my head under my pillow and will the sun to change its course and fall back below the horizon. For the millionth time, I wonder about Jeryd and Bree and that book she found in the town library.

How had it stayed hidden for so long? I'm not really buying the whole forest for the trees excuse. At some point, someone would have noticed this thing, if only a librarian removing old books from circulation, right? And if it's really so evil, what am I supposed to do about it? I shudder at the thought of actually working with Jeryd. There's more to his interest than what he lets on.

After all, the stuff I googled last night was pretty clear about the Sidhe or Fay or whatever you want to call them and their habit of tricking humans. Based on my research, I'm guessing Jeryd is part elf. He's too pretty to be almost anything else. But even the elves I read about aren't all wisdom and kindness like the ones in J.R.R. Tolkien's books. They're charming, for sure, but they're also arrogant and tricky. And, just like Papaw warned me, most of them are apparently con artists and sociopaths. I sit up in bed and freeze at the thought. How many of them are hiding among the human population?

I picture him, his silver-gray eyes, dark skin and fine-boned face, and feel my body warm. "Ugh! What the hell?" I leap out of bed and head for the bathroom and splash cold water over my face, forcing my brain to take control of my traitorous body. It doesn't matter how good-looking he is, he can't be trusted! He's half Fay for cripes sakes. And all Other, part of which is I don't even know what. Besides, good-looking boys, human or not, can't be trusted. Just look at what happened with Joey.

My eyes begin to burn and I splash more cold water on my face.

* * *

The lunchroom is loud and crowded. But, as usual, my corner is empty, except for me and my brown bag containing carrot sticks, celery, veggie chips and a PBJ. The scent of grilling burgers wafts from the kitchen behind the serving line, mixes with the odor of corn chips, spilled soda, and overcooked vegetables. I look at my lunch and realize there are more things that set me apart than just my DNA. It's pretty humorous that my mom and dad are practically vegan, that I rarely eat meat, even though a part of me is clearly carnivorous. But even in wolf form, as much as I want to chase down prey, small mammals like fluffy little bunnies, I don't really want to kill and eat them.

Most of the time.

Although, I think as I see Bree sashay into the room hanging on Joey like a parasitic growth, *there are things I would happily bite.* I glare at them when she sees me, waves and begins guiding Joey over to my table.

"Hey, 'Rissa," she coos, "mind if we join you?"

Before I can respond, Joey gives her a googly-eyed look and pulls out a chair for her right across from me. He stands behind her, stroking her hair. Bree reaches up, curling her fingers around his wrist and pats the seat beside her. Joey sits, staring at her with a stupid look on his face.

"What do you want?" I rub my bleary eyes and try not to grind my teeth. I take a deep breath to help me still my anger and something burns my nostrils. It smells like Other, but darker, like fire and ash, or singed Other on burnt toast. I try breathing through my mouth, but now I can taste it, and it's worse than any school cafeteria food I've ever eaten.

Bree shrugs. "I just wanted to see how you were doing. You look so tired," she croons. Her face is a mask of concern, but her eyes burn through it, a dangerous mix of curiosity and cleverness that reminds me of Jeryd.

I straighten up and peer closer at her. "Why do you care?" I try to make it a question, but the exhaustion in my voice makes it come out more like a groan.

A flash of confusion sweeps across her face, gone so quickly I almost miss it. Ire flashes in her eyes, even as she pushes her lip out into a pout. I can practically smell the malice on her. "What did I ever do to you that you hate me so?" she says in a slighted tone.

I can hardly believe my ears. "Me? Hate you?" I begin to shake with laughter. *Oh, crap! I'm so tired I'm getting hysterical.*

She nods. "Yes," she says, "all I want is for us to be friends, but you just give me glares and hate on me. Doesn't she, Joey?"

Joey nods his head; his eyes never leave her face. He looks like a drooling idiot, but without the drool. Well, minimal drool, anyway. Ugh. How did I ever like him?

I start to snarl, but the odd smell emanating from Bree's bag causes my nose to burn and I have to cup my hand over my face to keep from sneezing.

"What is it you really want from me?" I ask, trying not to inhale too deeply. The stench makes me want to retch and I wonder if it's the book, or something else I probably don't want to know about. I just really hope it's not her lunch.

"Just a little favor," Bree purrs. Her lips are curled into a smile, but her eyes have a strange light in them.

"And why should I do anything for you?" I ask. My words contain more growl than I'd intended and I look around to see if anyone else heard. But the general noise in the cafeteria appears to have masked our discussion from potentially prying ears.

Bree fake-pouts again, her lip stuck out so ridiculously far it almost makes me laugh. "Well, if you won't do it out of friendship, then maybe you'll take something in trade."

I start to grab my food and begin stuffing it back into my bag, not bothering to rewrap what's left of my sandwich. "Like you have anything I want."

"I thought you wanted him." Bree nods at Joey. He's still staring at her with that enraptured gaze. If he were a wolf, his tongue would be lolling out ready to lick her face.

I glance at Joey. "It appears he's already taken. Not interested in a do-over, anyway. Thanks." I try to sound nonchalant, but my gut is twisting and my words trail off. He's such a jerk. Why does seeing him with her like this feel so bad? I drop my eyes to the table. My hand is a smear of peanut butter mixed with grape jelly and I fumble for a napkin.

"True," she says. "But that could change as easily as this." She snaps her fingers and Joey shakes his head, blinks twice, sees me and a broad grin splits his face.

"Hey, Merissa." His eyes sparkle and he smiles his crooked smile. "You look great today. How've you been?"

I stare at him. It's like he just woke up and suddenly noticed I was there.

I'm stunned into utter silence.

Bree smiles at me and snaps her fingers again. Joey's gaze falls back on her, the goofy love-stare back in his eyes.

"What the . . ."

"You see?" she says. "I do have something you want."

I stare at her. I know my mouth is open, jaw hanging wide in surprise. I must look like a dazed fish. She's done something to him, cast a spell on him or given him a potion. He's not lovesick. He's been spelled.

Her eyes narrow and she licks her lips. She seems nervous and for just an instant it looks like she's flickering, like a double exposure, one Bree layered over another, but they're not quite identical. "You do want him, don't you?" The flickering is gone, as if I've imagined it.

My mind is a whirligig, thoughts chasing themselves like hounds after elusive prey. I suddenly realize that I don't really want anything more to do with either one of them, but there's something else going on here, something important that I want to understand, need to understand, but can't quite grasp.

Her eyes go icy and her lips make a thin straight line across her face. "Maybe he should just drop off the face of the earth, then. Or step in front of a speeding car. Is that what you'd prefer?"

"What are you talking about?"

"Well, if you don't want him, I certainly don't have much use for him anymore." She shrugs and gives Joey a sneer. "And he's beginning to be more annoying than fun."

I can't believe what I'm hearing. "No use to you?" A sick realization hangs in my stomach, swinging like a pendulum. She's admitting she spelled him, but not because she likes him, because she wants to use him.

Against me.

My hands tighten into fists and I realize I'm still holding my lunch bag with the leftover food in it. I let up before I squeeze PBJ all over myself. "You don't even like him?"

"Boys are just so, ugh, male." She smiles and shrugs, but her eyes are filled with an iciness that makes me want to bare my canines. Would she really hurt him? From what I see, she could make him do pretty much anything, lie in the gutter or, like she said, walk into traffic.

It's not that I want him to like me anymore, not like I want to date him again, not really, but I think about how much it would suck to be under someone's spell so completely that they could make you hurt yourself against your will. No one deserves that. Not even him, dammit. "What is it you want?"

"I want you to play fetch for me."

Great.

She smiles, but it isn't a nice smile. She's mocking me and it makes me want to grab her by the throat, the way I did Kandi in the Coffee & Cues. But what might she do to Joey?

I look at his goofy smile, the dimple that no longer seems deadly. I don't owe him anything. Not after the way he left me hanging in the Coffee & Cues. But I can't let her hurt him because of me, either.

It takes a few seconds before I can answer in an almost-calm voice. Meanwhile, Bree is humming the Jeopardy song under her breath. "Fine," I finally tell her. "What is it you want me to *fetch* for you?"

"Oh, just a little something that's been tucked away for the longest time. A bauble, really."

I feel my brow wrinkling in confusion. Why does everyone suddenly act like I'm their personal retriever? "You want me to get some kind of ornament for you? Why?"

Her lip curls up, but then she breaks into a smile. "Because it's rightfully mine and I want it back." Her voice is thin and sugary, but with an underlying hint of impatience.

I'm not buying it, but this coming right after my meeting with Jeryd makes me curious. I can't help but wonder how much of what each of them is telling me is truth and how much is lies. I wish I could sniff out the facts, but I just can't read either

Bree or Jeryd. They both seem to believe most, if not all, of what they're saying. "I don't mean why do you want it. I mean, why don't you just go get it yourself?"

"I'd retrieve it myself, but that would be messy and . . . complicated." The timbre of her voice has grown deeper with a rasp I've never heard before. Her face seems to fade, like she's moving underwater and I blink, trying to clear my vision.

Joey looks over at me, and for a moment his eyes are filled with pleading. He looks trapped. Helpless.

"What is this *bauble* you want?"

"A small trinket." She reaches into her messenger bag and pulls out the stolen book, placing it in front of me. She opens it and the burnt, metallic stench grows, rising from the old tome like a thick cloud, and I have to cover my face to keep from gagging.

"This." Her finger taps the page, pointing to a hand-drawn image.

It's some sort of jewelry, a necklace or a bracelet in the shape of a snake. I try to read the writing below it, but the letters are strange. It's familiar somehow, but definitely not English.

"What is it?" I ask.

"Let's call it a family heirloom," she says, slapping the book shut.

"If it's yours, your family's," I say, "why do you need me?"

"I told you. It's complicated," she says between gritted teeth.

The crash of breaking glass makes me jump.

There's a momentary hush in the lunchroom, then an eruption of applause. A screech of staff voices mixes with kids cheering for whoever dropped something, or by the sound of it, a lot of somethings, in the kitchen.

"Fine. Whatever. Just tell me where it is and I'll go get it."

She sighs and licks her lips. "There's one little problem," she says. "I'm not exactly sure where it is at the moment."

"Then, how am I supposed to get it?"

"I didn't say I don't have any idea where you should start looking."

CHAPTER FIFTEEN

The ancient fountain with the satyr statue on the top of it sits off at the northwest corner of the park near the old apple orchard and has been bone dry for as long as I can remember. It's far enough away from the crowded area and large enough, I hope, to block anyone's view of what I'm about to do.

I take out the piece of chalk I brought with me and draw a circle on the pavement and then draw two intersecting lines through the circle, one north to south and the other east to west. I slip my shoes off and place one inside the other and set them inside the circle where the lines intersect. I glance around to be certain no one can see me. Even if they don't know what I'm doing, it's going to look strange. With one quick shake to make myself forget how foolish this feels, I begin walking around the outside edge of the circle in a counter-clockwise direction, whispering Jeryd's name. I say it over and over until it becomes a chant. With quick measured steps, I circle my shoes exactly three times.

And nothing happens.

I stare at my ragged sneakers inside the circle and shake my head. I should have known it wouldn't work. I'm leaning in, reaching for my shoes, when I hear a muffled laugh behind me.

I spin around. Jeryd is sitting on the top tier of the fountain, not five feet from me. I can smell him now that the breeze has shifted and he's no longer downwind from me. That odd yet appealing tang of growth and decay seems to settle in the air around me.

"It worked," I gasp.

He rolls his eyes at me and smirks. "There are easier ways to communicate. And they don't wear out your socks." He leaps down from his perch, landing as graceful as a panther. He's grinning at me, and chuckles as he picks up my shoes and hands them to me.

I blush, looking at my shoes. I hadn't known what might happen to them in the process, so I'd dug out my oldest, rattiest pair, not wanting to lose my good ones in some weird hellfire or bizarre Other exchange program. I know it's silly, but now I'm embarrassed by my crummy old shoes.

"Go ahead, put them on," he says with a laugh. "They won't bite. Or make you walk into the Realm. Or–"

"Make me dance until I drop?" I watch him out of the corner of my eye as I sit on the lower edge of the fountain.

"They're just shoes," he tells me in a voice so quiet and honest that I think it must be true.

I slip my feet into my shoes, but I tie the laces loosely, just in case.

"So, what made you change your mind?" he asks.

I stare up at him. He's standing in the middle of my stupid chalk circle in a Peter Pan stance, legs spread and fists on his hips. A halo of sunlight illuminates the outline of his body, making him appear to glow. I look away. Probably some sort of glamour he's trying out on me. And I'm not falling for it.

"So you haven't changed your mind," he says slowly. "Then, what is it you want?" His demeanor has changed as quickly as a shadow passing before the moon, and he seems sincerely interested in my response.

He looks so vulnerable, so . . . charming. I feel warm and my hands tingle as if they're asleep. For a moment, I'm afraid to speak, afraid my voice will crack and give away my discomfort of being so near him. I scrape my shoe across the pavement, drawing circles with my toe. I need his help. But I'm not sure I can bring myself to say it. "I wanted to ask you something," I say so low I almost can't hear my own voice.

"A favor?" His eyes glitter. With a shiver, I remember who, what actually, I'm dealing with. What is wrong with me? Why is it that a boy, any boy, can have this kind of effect on me? Until I started going out with Joey, I'd never felt like this. Now, ever since the first time we kissed . . . I remember another kiss then and I feel myself blush in embarrassment. I turn away, willing my body under control. I inhale, taking in the scents of the park, focusing on the smell of the oak and tupelo trees, the aroma of bark and young leaves all pale mossy greens and browns.

Footsteps approach me from behind and I whirl around. He's too close and I back a few steps away, slip into a cautious stance.

"You're fast," he says, his eyes sparkling with humor. "And alert."

"It's best to be on guard. Especially when dealing with your kind."

His gray eyes flash dark and his smile grows tight. Less a smile than a grimace. "Tell me what it is you want with *my kind*, so I can be on my way."

His tone makes me bristle. For a second, I want to ask him if my calling him has compelled him to be here, but I'm not sure I want to know the answer. I swallow. "There's an object I need to find."

He quirks an eyebrow.

"In Other . . ." I whisper it as if I'm afraid merely saying it will cause some great calamity.

I'm not sure what kind of reaction I'm going to get from him. He's so difficult to read. His emotions seem flighty, elusive. And for a while, Jeryd just gazes at me. He doesn't stop staring until I start to look away.

"What kind of object?" he asks, warily.

"Some kind of talisman."

His forehead wrinkles, but only for a microsecond. Then he smiles, flashing his pointy teeth. They're not quite as sharp as an animal's, but not smooth at the ends like a human's, either. It makes him look truly Other, yet it doesn't make him less attractive. Although, I wish it did. Life would be so much easier if I didn't find myself pulled toward good-looking boys like the moon is pulled by earth's gravity.

"A quest." He takes that Peter Pan stance again, and makes a small bow from the waist. "It will be my honor to accompany you, m'lady." His tone is only slightly mocking as he looks up at me from beneath the lock of hair that's fallen across his eyes, but it's enough to make my hackles rise.

I bite the inside of my lower lip to keep from saying something nasty.

"Thanks," I mutter.

"There is a condition."

"I should have known." I steel myself for what he's going to ask in return for his help. In fairy tales, these things never go well.

"You already know what I want," he says.

"Fine. I'll help you get your precious book." I sigh, feeling like I just bumped the first domino in a long winding train of them. I just hope what tumbles over at the end isn't worth more than I can afford.

CHAPTER SIXTEEN

It's late Thursday night and I'm lying in bed waiting for my parents to be sound asleep. I'm shaking so hard the headboard is rattling. I have never snuck out of the house before. I've never even considered it, but Jeryd insists this has to be done at midnight, so I'm lying under the covers, fully dressed in a dark, long-sleeved t-shirt and jeans. Waiting. And trying to quell the coiling snake of panic inside me.

Actually, I've been trying not to freak out about this for two whole days, since Jeryd said he couldn't take me into Other until tonight. Something about the last night of the waning moon. I couldn't help but wonder if that's true or not, but who am I to argue the importance of the moon?

About thirty minutes ago, my mom turned off the

TV and padded down the hallway, her slippers scuff-scuffing on the hardwood floor. She dragged the tips of her fingers across my door as she passed, just like she has every night since I was a baby. I don't know what it means, but I've always found it comforting. Especially when we've been fighting. No matter how mad she is at me, she always slides her hand along my door as she goes to bed each night. I don't even know if she's doing it consciously, but I'm afraid to ask. No matter how angry I get at her sometimes, there's something reassuring about the gesture and I don't want her to stop.

Speaking of making Mom mad, if she catches me sneaking out of the house in the middle of the night, I'll be totally screwed. I'm starting to sweat, but I don't want to toss off the covers until I'm sure my parents are both sound asleep. It seems like it's taking forever, but I can't risk getting caught. I lie still, watching the digital clock on my nightstand appear frozen in time.

Finally, quiet settles over the house. With Dad home from a trucking run, Mom has in her earplugs, so, barring any loud noises, I am home free.

Hah. I smile weakly at my Freudian pun.

I slip out of bed, tug on my old running shoes, and slide open my bedroom window an inch at a time, my heart pounding against my ribs so hard, I'm surprised none of them crack. I pause with the window open. Wait. But the only sound is Dad's snoring, which is so loud it practically shakes the walls at a Richter-scale-registering level. Now, I understand why Mom wears shooter's plugs to bed, instead of the regular little foam ones they sell at the drug store. She always said I was a heavy sleeper, but I'm honestly amazed I can sleep through the racket my dad makes.

Come on, focus, or you'll never get out of here, I tell myself.

I stick my head out the window where the cool night air slides against my face. The neighbor's lights are out and the neighborhood seems to have settled down for the night. At least the people have. The sweet scent of early poppies mixes with the musk of small mammals and carries on the light breeze, luring me. Before I realize it, my shoulders are outside and I'm almost tumbling out head first. I check myself, duck back inside and quietly place my desk chair under the window. Then I step onto the chair and stick my legs through one at a time until I'm sitting on the window ledge.

I have to twist around so my stomach is on the window sill and my legs hang out and down. It isn't far to the ground, but I don't want to drop down and make a sound my mom might hear. Unlike Dad and me, she's a really light sleeper, which is another reason she needs the earplugs.

I try to shimmy myself down quietly, scraping my abdomen on the ledge. A gasp escapes me as I slide out of the house and into the back yard. I drop down into a crouch and wait, listening over the sound of my thumping heart for any sign that my parents may have awakened. But the night remains undisturbed, both inside and outside the house.

It's dark with only the last tiny sliver of the waning moon overhead.

Crouching in the shadows, I give my scraped skin a tentative touch with my fingertips. Crap. Not a good start to my first unlawful foray. I've been hurt worse and I do heal fairly quickly, but it's a good thing it isn't swimming weather yet, or I'd have to find a way to hide the abrasion. Maybe, I should have opted for the one-piece swimsuit during last year's clearance sale, after all.

It would be faster to run on all fours, but I don't think I've ever changed this far from a full moon. I don't even know if it's possible. And even if I was sure I could manage it, I would never risk changing here. Dad may not have "the family gift," but Mom is super-sensitive to all my moods and changes. So, even asleep she might sense something if I changed too close to home. I can't help wondering about that for about the zillionth time. She and Dad and even Papaw, who always seems extra reserved around her, insist she isn't of a shifter bloodline, but when I've tried to dig, they all clam up.

I sneak across the yard to the fence and follow it to the back corner where Dad stacks the firewood. Soundlessly, I climb the heap of logs, grabbing the fence when a loose piece of wood shifts and the whole pile feels like it's going to collapse. I hang on until the logs settle and I can breathe again. I swear at my klutziness and pull a splinter from my finger. I would have tried jumping the fence, if I thought I had any chance of doing it in silence. And without breaking my neck.

As it is, I lower myself into the peach orchard behind our house and pause again, ears perked. A dog barks on the other side of the neighborhood and a field mouse skitters over the irrigation ditch and hurries off into the night. But my own house remains silent and I breathe a heavy sigh.

Adrenaline rushes through my veins, hot energy zinging through me. I still can't believe I'm doing this. I stare back at my window, tempted to just go back inside, crawl under the covers and completely forget about ever being out here in the middle of the night. But then a gentle breeze rubs against my cheek and the memory of running on all fours and the earthy scent of the forest lights up the inside of my brain. And, without another thought or backward glance, I'm crossing the orchard, heading for the east meadow in the forest where I agreed to meet Jeryd.

Thinking about seeing him again sends a shiver across my skin, and I immediately feel stupid. I should have better control. Especially knowing who, what he is. And what about Joey? Isn't that why I'm doing all of this? To get him away from Bree?

Starlight filters down as I jog between peach trees, leafy and pungent. The sweet peach blossoms have mostly fallen and new fruit the size of peas clings to the branches like small clusters of dark green pearls. A mother bird rustles nervously on her nest as I pass by, settling protectively over her eggs only when she's certain the threat has passed.

My heart is still pounding, but it's no longer adrenaline firing through me, it's the spring air and a sense of belonging to the night that's filling me with a strange heart-buzzing joy.

The night air is a lure and once more I consider trying to make the change, even though the waning moon whispers that it's not the time for it. Besides, I'm not out here to run. I'm meeting Jeryd and I need to be in this form—fully human and fully clothed—to do this.

The cool night embraces me as I run. I pick up speed, finding that when I'm not working so hard to stay in control, not holding myself back, I can leap over the irrigation ditches without stumbling or losing my balance. For the first time in this form I run with a joy I've only ever felt before as a wolf. And then only in those moments where I've forgotten who I really was. For once, I'm truly in my element without being in my Other form, and I revel in this feeling. It carries me all the way to the woods before I realize, once more, that I'm breaking every rule my parents have ever laid down for me, not to mention what I'm about to do goes against everything Papaw ever taught me.

I walk into the meadow, no longer elated, but with a sense of guilt and foreboding that makes my limbs weak. The clearing is hushed and empty. Pale wildflowers stare up at the sky like ghostly reflections of the glittering stars. I walk into the middle, gulping in the sweet smell of earth and flowers. For a moment, I forget why I'm here and the open sky hugs me like a blanket. Then, I remember. "What am I doing here?" I whisper to the sky.

"Looking for me, perhaps?" Jeryd's voice comes out of nowhere and I jump, quickly scanning the meadow. I can't see or smell him and my skin prickles.

"Where are you?" There's a shiver in my voice that I can't contain.

"He's here, he's there, he's everywhere." His voice echoes around the open space and bounces from tree to tree.

I spin around, trying to locate him, my anger surging, replacing my initial nervousness and the tinge of fear that washed over me.

"Don't get all paranoid on me." His voice stops ricocheting off trees and I turn in time to see a shadow drop from a branch high in an oak tree and land in a crouch among the silent wildflowers without making a sound. The shadow rises up and comes toward me, becoming Jeryd's square shoulders and lithe figure. The moonlight seems to gather itself around him, limning him with light. For a moment, he appears both beautiful and frightening. Then he moves closer and he's just Jeryd.

I let out the breath I've been holding and some of the tension drains away. "Nice trick," I snap.

He shrugs and I can see his lips turn up in that charming smile he wears. The one that's usually so winning, but not tonight. Tonight, I'm not in the mood for winsome. Right now, I need to get this over with and get back home and into bed before my parents discover I'm gone.

"Let's get going," I say.

He bows low, sweeping his arm out. "Your wish is my command." His fairy tale words would have made me happy when I was a four-year-old obsessed with princesses and castles, but now they're only grating reminders that, while fairy tales have some basis in truth, they are ultimately lies. Most of the stories don't end happily ever after. At least, not for the Norms, and any outsiders, who become entangled with Others. That's one fact Papaw made sure I understood. "Don't ever trust anything that comes out of Other," he told me over and over. "And especially don't believe the words that come out of the mouth of anyone, or any*thing*, from Other."

And here I am about to trust an untrustworthy, Fay creature who can't be trusted to guide me through a place that can't be trusted. *Crap!*

He extends his hand, palm up. "All you need do is to place your hand in mine," he says, "and we'll be on our way."

I grit my teeth, figuring it's probably another one of his jests, but he waits until, finally, I put my hand on his.

I'm not expecting the electric jolt I get when our palms meet. My skin tingles all the way up to my scalp, down to my belly and out my toes. It's worse than when I kissed Joey. Worse, and so much better. Like when Bree kissed me.

The shock makes me almost let go, but Jeryd's hand is gripped tight around mine. The tingling eases and I realize my eyes are closed. I blink them open and gasp. The entire meadow is shimmering with light. It looks like the aurora borealis has suddenly come south and descended on this spot.

"Like it?" Jeryd asks. He's smiling and his silver-flecked eyes reflect the colored lights that dance and swirl around us.

"It's amazing," I say, "but what if someone sees it?" I'm suddenly worried. Nervous that someone might come to investigate and find us here. What will I tell my parents? "You'd better make it stop."

He tilts his head, a questioning look on his face. "No one can make it stop. It has ever been thus."

"What are you talking about? I've never seen the meadow do this. Make it stop!" I realize we're still touching and wrench my hand from his grip. The lights continue to dance, lighting up the meadow like the main stage at an outdoor concert.

Jeryd lets out a burst of laughter. "You don't really think you're still in Kansas, do you Dorothy?"

"What?" I take a step back. The trees are perceptibly taller than I remember them and the flowers seem to capture the lights, rather than reflecting them. They glow, actually, changing colors as if they contain rotating L.E.D. lights or something. And the fragrant odors emanating from them practically glow, as well. "This is Other?"

Jeryd spreads his arms wide. "This is one entry point to what you call Other, what some call Faery, Avalon, or Tír na nÓg, the Youthful Land. These days, it is generally called the Silver Realm. Although, most simply call it Natif, which to us means home." He lets out his breath in a sigh that seems to hold a thousand thoughts and feelings all swimming together in conflicted emotional somersaults.

I stare around at the sparkling scenery, trying to see what Jeryd sees, but beneath the light and shimmering scents it's the same green glade, only as if I am looking through an antique window, with thick and thin spots that warp my view. "But how? You didn't do anything."

"Of course, I did. I brought us through the gate."

"But there was no chanting, no casting, no . . . no ritual." I'm still staring.

He sighs. "Humans generally make everything so much more difficult than need be. Especially when they have trouble believing in something. And perpetuating the myth of rituals and special days for the opening of gates helps to keep out trespassers and . . . riff-raff." He shrugs. "The gate opens more easily for those who are of the blood and for those who have traveled here before. But the only real magic is in knowing where the gate is, and believing it exists."

There has always been something about this meadow that drew me, but I never knew it was because there was a doorway here to Other. "How would I know that?" I say. How would I know that rituals are only to help humans believe, when all I know is what little I've been told? Especially since my parents have never told me much of anything. And what Papaw told me most often didn't make any sense. Except all the warnings, and those he generally left unexplained, which is so not helpful now. "And why make me wait until tonight?"

He looks away for a moment, as if considering his answer.

"And no more bull," I say.

"I needed to be certain the meadow would be . . . available."

"Available?"

"Yes. There are certain . . . rites that take place here and it's not a good idea to disrupt them. Besides, it's best no one else know you are here." He gives me a meaningful look.

If I had more time, I'd dig deeper into these things he's talking about, but I suddenly remember why we're here. "We need to get moving," I tell him. I only have a few hours before I need to be home. Otherwise, I'm going to be in big trouble.

"Where would you like to go first?"

"What do you mean?" My voice is sharp with uncertainty. "I have no idea. I thought you knew your way around."

"I do," he says in a calm voice. "But this land is vast, much larger in fact than your own world in many ways. What I mean is, are there no clues to where you would search?"

I only know what Bree has told me. That and the stupid riddle she gave me. Riddle but no answer. Maybe Jeryd knows what it means, but I don't want to share it with him. I still don't know why he's helping me so readily. Is that old book really so important? Or, maybe this thing Bree wants is something Jeryd wants, too. What if I tell him the riddle and he disappears and goes after this thing himself, leaving me stranded here? I can't risk it. I don't even know what the stupid thing can do. And Joey. What will Bree do to Joey if I don't bring her this "bauble" she wants so bad? Coward or not, it's my fault he's involved in all of this.

I need to find out what Jeryd knows about the talisman.

I've never been a flirt and I don't think I'm particularly charming, but maybe if I pretend to like him, Jeryd will tell me what he knows. Not that I have to pretend too hard. He's almost too attractive.

"I thought you would know where to look," I say, stepping a little closer to him.

Jeryd raises an eyebrow and leans closer. He raises his left hand and places his fingertips lightly against my cheek.

I can feel my body heating up and try to ignore it. Flirting with him is supposed to affect him, not me, dammit. I try to relax and smile. After all, he may be a born con artist, but two can play at that game, right?

Jeryd's eyes grow smoky and my breath catches in my chest, but I hold my ground. "Other, I mean Natif, is your world," I say. My voice sounds thick, but all the better to win him over, I suppose. "And you clearly knew about this talisman before I described it to you, so why don't you just tell me where it is?"

"In the first place, this isn't as much my world as you might think." There's a bitter note in his voice, but his eyes remain unchanged, focused on mine.

Jeryd strokes my cheek with his fingers and a rush of electricity zings across my skin. His lips turn up at the corners. "In the second place, if anyone here knew where to look, the talisman would have been found long ago."

He leans closer and I can feel his breath on my face. He smells like a forest in spring, greens and red-browns with just that tiny edge of black.

"And third," he says in a wistful voice, "if I knew where it was hidden and was intent upon keeping the talisman hidden from you, there is nothing you could do to dissuade me from doing so. No matter how enticing you attempt to be." His hand falls away from my face.

I blink and feel myself swaying, as if I've lost my balance, but his words hit me like a bucket of ice water.

"I don't know what you're talking about," I lie.

"I assume you have heard the saying, 'don't try to kid a kidder?'" He winks at me.

It's clear he knows I was trying to play him and, for some reason, I'm mortified at what I've done. What was I thinking? Conning and manipulating people is not who I am. And just because it's who he is, doesn't justify my doing it to him. Or trying to, anyway. I'm not sure I know who I am anymore, but I don't think I like who I might become if I don't get myself extricated from Bree's mechanisms. Suddenly, I find the ground at my feet very interesting. "Whatever," I mutter. "Let's just go. It isn't like I have all the time in the world for this little adventure."

"I merely wait on your pleasure," he says, clearly mocking me.

I can't believe how fast I can go from attraction to annoyance with this guy. "Fine. There is a clue, but I have no idea what it means." My thoughts are rushing, my brain a vortex of fears, hopes, ideas. I don't want to give him the riddle. I'm sure he'll run off at the first opportunity and take this talisman thingy for himself. Maybe I can just give him the first line or two. "I'll tell you the first part, but first I need to know you won't leave me stranded here. No matter what happens."

"My word."

"I'm not sure that's good enough," I tell him, thoughts reeling. "I need something a little more . . . binding."

His eyes narrow and for a moment I see real anger on his face. But an instant later, the light is back in his eyes. "You don't trust me? I'm hurt." He places his hand on his chest as if he's actually wounded by the idea. "What can I do to put you at ease?"

His question catches me off guard. He's right. I don't trust him, but I have no idea how to ensure he'll keep his word. I think back to every fairy tale and story I can remember. There must be something, some hint of truth, some thread that winds through them that can help me. What would make a resident of this realm have to keep his or her word? But there's nothing, not without a trade. A bargain is the only common thread. The only thing that is consistent in nearly every story. There has to be a tradeoff. And there is nothing I can think of that I have to trade. Nothing that Jeryd would value enough.

Or is there?

"Would you be willing to make a bargain?" I'm not sure this is the smartest thing I've ever done, but considering that I have now lied to my parents by omission, gone against Papaw's training, and made a bargain with a witch, it probably won't turn out to be the most stupid, either.

Jeryd's eyes glitter with genuine interest. "What kind of a bargain?"

"An exchange," I say a little nervously. "You promise, no, you *guarantee*, not to leave me stranded in Other in exchange for something from me."

"Like what?" He tilts his head and tosses the hair out of his face.

"I don't know." He's being dense and difficult and I'm sure it's on purpose.

"You mean, like you'll give me your firstborn child?" He winks. "Or your hand in marriage?"

I open my mouth to tell him where to stick it, but I don't get the chance.

"Or maybe just a kiss? A priceless kiss." His smirk makes me want to bite him.

"How about I don't turn wolf and eat you?" I snarl.

His laughter at my threat only makes me angrier, and I bare my teeth at him. Suddenly he's not laughing anymore. His own anger is almost a physical presence. "If my word isn't good enough for you, what makes you think I'd keep any bargain?"

Suddenly, I'm confused. "I don't know," I tell him. "I just thought bargains were binding here."

He shakes his head, but his anger seems to have dissipated some. "You've read far too many fairy tales," he says. "Stop trying to be clever and use your common sense instead." He looks around, then shakes his head. "The beauty here is real, as is the danger. And there are some that will play at riddles and trickery, attempting to manipulate, using language as a game. They do so out of boredom and mischief, out of a need to feel superior, and some just because it amuses them. But there are those for whom a word given is an oath of promise."

"But how do I tell the difference? How do I know whom or what to trust?"

"The same way you do in your world, by learning discernment." His eyes grow hard and bright. "And by first and foremost trusting yourself."

I hang my head. Trust myself? How am I supposed to do that? I'm not even allowed out near the full moon without a leash. Even my parents don't trust me enough to tell me everything, to share the secrets they're obviously guarding. And the one time I decide not to tell my parents something I know I should have, when I decide not to tell them about Bree, my whole world begins to unravel.

"'Neath glittering dome of woodland home/The sparkling hiss at evening's kiss," I tell him.

"What's that?"

"The first lines of the riddle. The first clue. Do you know what it means?"

He wrinkles his forehead and stares at the ground for what seems like forever. Then, he looks up at me with a flicker of a sad smile. "I think I know exactly what it means."

He steps close, and begins to whisper something in my ear. He's close, his lips nearly touching my skin, his breath a tickle inside my head, as if he's afraid the breeze might carry away his words, unless he places them directly in my ear.

We're standing in the meadow, almost touching when the lights begin to flash brighter than before. Jeryd curses and steps away, glancing quickly around.

A sense of dread coils inside my chest. "What's happening?"

"Company is coming," he says. "We need to move."

"But I didn't understand what you said," I complain.

He grabs my wrist and pulls me to the edge of the meadow, yanking me down behind a thick flowering bush that smells like fresh mushrooms. I sniff the air and wrinkle my nose. The pungent odor fills my nostrils, a dark chartreuse, and I can't smell anything else.

Jeryd glances over at me and nods. "That's the idea. Hopefully, it will do the trick and cloak our presence."

"Cloak us? Why do we need it to cloak us?"

"Oh, did I perhaps forget to mention the penalties

for unlawful entrance into Natif?"

"If there's a lawful way to enter, then why didn't we get permission?"

"Too much red tape. Among other things."

"What other things?"

He puts a finger to his lips and stares out at the meadow.

The lights grow suddenly dim, then flare up so bright I have to avert my eyes. When I look again, I'm still seeing spots. Through the shadows in my vision, the spots resolve themselves into a strange collection of creatures milling nervously about. The fairy stories do not do justice to the odd diversity of fairies, goblins, monsters, and I don't even know what all.

At the center of the group stands a tall woman with what looks like antlers growing out of her head. Her antlers are draped with gold and silver mesh that sparkles with colored gems. A black leather corset cinches her body above a long flared skirt of red silk. The sleeves of her matching red blouse billow out just above her wrists, tapering into lace cuffs that drape over slender fingers, on which flash rings of gold and precious stones. A cloak of black velvet drapes her shoulders, the hem and borders embroidered with gold and silver threads in a pattern of swirls and symbols. She turns in our direction and I hold my breath. My gaze is pulled to her pale face. Her mouth is cruel, her eyes black holes that suck in the light and reflect nothing back.

The creatures around her bow low as her gaze

sweeps over them. "What is that unholy smell?" she demands.

Her followers sniff the air, turning their heads to and fro, eyes darting around the meadow. Their movements are sharp and frantic, fearful, but none respond to her query.

She raises her left arm and sweeps it down and across. The company falls back, exposing one of their number, who looks like a faun, except instead of the brown hair and dark skin I would expect, his skin is mossy green, his slicked-back hair jet-black. One horn, his left, is broken off in a jagged line, as if it's been partially torn away. He shivers under her gaze, eyes cast downward, frantically avoiding looking into her eyes.

"Mantos," the woman hisses.

"Yes, m'lady." His knees shake as he bows at the waist, eyes glued to the ground, but his deep voice resonates across the meadow.

"Did I not ask a question?" Her voice is low, an almost caressing tone, but there's malice behind it. The meadow has stopped swirling and dancing with bright jewel colors. Instead it has taken on a dark hue thick with fiery reds and deep purples.

"Yes, Lady Andarra." He's still bowing, and his shoulders hunch, as if he expects something bad to happen at any moment.

"Then, why is it that my loyal subjects do not deign to answer me?" Her lips turn down in a childlike moue that only serves to make her appear more frightening.

"I . . . I . . . cannot say," the dark faun stutters,

his voice no longer strong.

"You cannot say?" She tilts her head as if rolling her eyes, but there is no change in the blackness that fills her eye sockets. "Then let me help you." She turns around to look at each of the creatures in turn, black cape sweeping behind her. Where it passes, the flowers have faded, no longer glowing with the absorbed light of the meadow, but now a sickly ochre.

When she faces Mantos once more, she reaches out her hand toward him and touches his face with her fingertips. Her gesture mimics Jeryd when he touched my face and I feel my blood quickly warm again, but then, just as suddenly, I go cold. The faun straightens like a puppet yanked upward on a string, eyes staring straight ahead as the side of his face begins to blacken.

"Something has entered the Silver Realm by our back gate," the woman says through gritted teeth.

Mantos gasps as smoke curls from his cheek.

"Something unsanctioned."

The faun's eyes bulge and his tongue lolls out of his mouth, his breathing is shallow and ragged.

"I want to know who has allowed an interloper into our domain." The woman pulls back her hand and Mantos collapses onto the ground, moaning. The scent of burned flesh scorches my nostrils. "And I want to know now!" Her hand clenches and she drops her arm. The faun's limp form lies at her feet. No one moves to help him. Instead, the creatures scatter.

Jeryd pulls me away into the dense forest.

We're running. Jeryd has me by the wrist, pulling me with him as he leaps and ducks, twisting a path through the trees and lush foliage. If I was alone, trying to navigate the forest in this form, I'd be stumbling and making so much noise, the entire countryside would know where I was. But with Jeryd in the lead, holding my hand, I'm able to move though the landscape quickly yet quietly. It must be his Fay blood, but I wish it was trick he could teach me.

We halt at the base of a huge tree and Jeryd lets go. I rub the spot, still warm from his hand. It feels tender, bruised from his grip. He leaps high and disappears into the leafy green above me. For an instant I panic. Is he leaving me here? After making such a big deal about giving his word? But then his head appears and he reaches down. "Jump up and grab hold," he hisses.

The distance is huge, even with my wolf strength.

I jump. And miss.

He reaches lower. "Come on!"

I don't need the urgency in his voice to tell me we're running out of time. I can hear the sound of searchers closing in on us.

I jump again. This time, my fingertips brush his.

The sounds of breaking branches and rustling brush are so near they'll be on us in a moment. One more huge effort and our hands clasp. In an instant, Jeryd has pulled me into the leafy branches of the ancient tree. He points to an opening in the trunk of the tree, a large crack that wasn't visible from the ground and I ease my way in.

He presses his body in behind me and whispers in my ear. "Quiet."

I shudder. Between the adrenaline running through my veins and his closeness, my body is humming. I can feel his lips near my cheek as they curve into a smile and I find myself wanting to turn my head, move my mouth closer to his. Only now there's a whispery hiss as the hole in the tree begins to close.

My body jerks toward the opening in an involuntary effort to be free, but Jeryd holds me in check. "It's okay," he murmurs. "Red Oak is a friend."

My breathing is ragged and I have to shut my eyes tight as the hole disappears completely. I've always been claustrophobic. Even as a little girl I couldn't stand enclosed places. I can't even bear to have my blankets tucked in too tight. I know it's the wolf's aversion to being imprisoned, but no matter how much I tell myself it's only a feeling, no matter how my brain repeats over and over that I'm not really trapped, that escape is possible, the wolf struggles, freaking out and snarling inside me.

I open my mouth to scream and Jeryd's lips are on mine. For a moment, I continue to struggle, warring with myself. His arms wrap around me, one hand at the back of my head, pulling me into him. The closeness of the tree seems to fade behind the touch of his body, his earthy smell, the electric tingle of his lips on ,mine. Then I'm kissing him back, heat rising in my belly and the wolf all but gone.

There's no sense of time passing. But as the panic eases I suddenly remember where I am, who I'm kissing, and I stiffen and pull my face away. A small gasp rises between us and Jeryd places his fingers over my mouth.

Our bodies are still touching and I try to push farther away from him, but the inside of the tree is too small. There's no room to move and nowhere to go. My eyes are open, but in the complete darkness that surrounds us, they might as well be closed. I can't see a thing, but somehow I know that Jeryd is smiling and I'm certain it's a wicked smile.

It seems like forever before I hear Jeryd's voice. "They're gone," he says in a low whisper.

"How do you know?" I manage to squeak out.

"I told you, Red Oak is a friend."

I nod, but I don't really understand, and of course he can't see my head moving in the utter darkness.

"We'll wait a bit longer before we move on, but I think we can have a little light and air now." As soon as the words leave his lips, a thin strip of starlit sky appears and grows as the opening in the tree reappears.

The fresh air is a relief, but Jeryd is still pressed against me and my heart beats so hard, I know he can feel it slamming inside my ribcage. I put my hands on his chest and push him away from me. There still isn't much room, but at least now there's a small gap between us, and I can breathe normally again.

It seems to take forever for Jeryd to decide the coast is clear. When he ducks through the opening, I'm right behind him. "Wait here," he tells me.

Riiiiight, I think as I follow him outside. There is no way I'm staying inside this tree for an instant longer than necessary. Not with the fear of being trapped in here gnawing at my nerves. Jeryd gives me an angry look, but I don't care. Being outside is such a relief I want to shout for joy. Only, the memory of what happened to the dark faun and the possibility of discovery keeps me silent.

"I want to have a look around," Jeryd says.

"Not without me," I tell him.

He shakes his head. "Weren't you paying attention back in the meadow? She knows you're here and she's got her flunkies out searching for us. If you think what she did to Mantos was bad, just wait till she gets her hands on you. Or me," he adds, and the bitterness in his voice is powerful, almost venomous. "You have no idea . . ." his voice trails off and it sounds more like sadness and disgust than fear when he says it.

"Who is this horned woman and why is she such a psycho?" I try not to picture what I saw in the meadow, but the image has been seared into my brain and keeps replaying like a bizarrely looped horror movie scene served up by the creepy Doctor on that Video Psychotherapy website.

"Andarra is first cousin to the Queen and next in line of succession to rule the Fay. She's bad business."

"She certainly has anger issues," I say. "What's

her damage?"

"Politics."

"Great." Who knew politics could be any more ugly anywhere than in the human world?

"Anyway, we can't risk you sneaking around on the ground, scenting up the whole forest. At least not until we know it's safe. Andarra won't be the only one angered by our presence."

"What do you mean 'angered by our' presence. I thought it was me they're hunting."

"It's a long story. I don't have time to explain the politics of the Silver Realm right now." He looks out past the leafy forest surrounding us, as if seeing something I can't.

"What am I supposed to do while you're out scouting?" I bristle, but I know he's right. We need to know what's lurking out there before we move on. Not that he's bothered to tell me where we're going, which I'm trying hard not to freak out about. Tit for tat, I suppose. After all, I've only given him the first part of the riddle and he knows it.

He watches me for a minute, and I think maybe he's getting ready to say something. Something important. Something I need to know. But then his face closes down. "Just stay hidden up here while I have a quick look around. If need be, go back inside and Red Oak will protect you."

I'm not even going to give him a response to that. Nothing could make me want to go back inside that small enclosed space. I'd rather change form and take a bite out of the nasty horned woman then do that ever again.

CHAPTER SEVENTEEN

I crouch on the wide branch as far from the opening in the tree as I can without risking a fall. It's not that long a drop, but if I lose my balance and draw attention to myself, I'm toast.

A noise in the distance alerts me. Something heading my way. Have the searchers come back? Did Jeryd get caught and decide to lead them to me rather than suffer the faun's fate? I peer through the branches, but the layers of leaves are too heavy to see through. Whatever it is, it's getting closer.

Before I realize, I'm inching my way back toward the trunk of the tree, back to that dark opening. Large, heavy footfalls come nearer, but I still can't see through the thick foliage. I sniff the air, but everything here smells different than in my world.

Not to mention that I haven't actually seen a normal animal or person since I arrived. When I finally get a glimpse of the approaching creature, it sends me scurrying back inside the tree—so much for never going back in there—I keep both hands gripped over the edges in hopes that will keep it from closing.

The tree stays open and I breathe a sigh of relief, while simultaneously praying that whatever this creature is, it can't scent me up here and will simply pass by.

It plods along, closing in, all musk and bitter herbs, a scent so strong it overpowers all other smells, including mine.

I hold my breath as the creature shambles beneath the branch I'd crouched on earlier, waiting for it to pass. Instead, the pounding of its heavy footsteps ceases. I squeeze my eyes shut, wondering if I should let go, ask the tree to close me in.

The snuffling of the animal below is all the motivation I need. It's snorting and sniffing the ground at the foot of the tree where I leaped up to grab hold of Jeryd. I can't wait any longer.

I let go, folding myself inside the tree trunk, arms gripped over my chest to keep my pounding heart from bursting out.

Nothing. The opening remains unchanged as I press my back against the inside of the trunk. Do I have to say something? Touch something? Damn Jeryd! He told me the tree would protect me, but left me here with no operating manual.

The branches rustle. Something begins to climb.

Can the beast I glimpsed through the leaves actually climb? I'm about to plead with the tree to help me when I see a hand grip the side of the opening. A strong coffee-and-cream-colored hand attached to Jeryd's muscular arm.

I open my mouth to scream at him, to tell him what a jerk he is, but he shakes his head. "No yelling," he says in a low voice. "Someone might hear you." There's a glint of humor in his eyes and his mouth is quirked up on one side.

I know he's laughing at me, enjoying the way he frightened me. I clamp my jaw shut and try not to give him a death glare.

He offers a hand to help me out of the tree. To hell with him. My harshest death glare is all he's getting. I duck through the opening. My knees feel rubbery as the adrenaline in my body drains away, but I manage to keep my balance and wobble-step out onto the wide limb. "So, did you see anything on your scouting trip? Are we safe here?"

"Have you forgotten where you are?" he asks. "Nowhere is safe. Not here. Especially these days." He's wearing that distant stare again and I can't help wondering what he's thinking. "No. We need to move on. The sooner, the better."

"Where are we going? Don't you think it's about time you told me? What if something happens and we get separated? I mean, you left me here inside a magic tree with no idea how to engage its mojo. What good would it have done if it hadn't been you climbing onto the branch when you did?" I cross my arms. "A little information sharing is in order."

He holds his hands up, gesturing for me to stop. "Enough. In the first place, Red Oak would have hidden you from any danger because I asked him to." He gives the tree a pat. "In the second place, I'm not planning on us getting separated."

I open my mouth to disagree, but he cuts me off.

"In the third place, how would you find the place we're going, even if I did tell you where it is? You don't know your way around and there aren't any corner gas stations or quickie markets where you can buy a map or ask directions."

"In that case," I counter, "telling me can't hurt. So, there's no sense in keeping it a secret."

"Fine." He shrugs and jerks his head to the side to flip his hair back out of his eyes. "By that logic, you can stop withholding the rest of the riddle."

"How does that make any sense?" I snap. He starts to answer, but I don't give him a chance. "The correct answer is, it doesn't."

"You are never going to trust me, are you?" he asks.

"Why should I?" I counter.

"Because I brought you here at great personal risk," he says. "Because I protected you from the searchers." His gray eyes dig deep into me. "Because you want to."

"Hah. Nice try," I say, but I know he's right. I do want to trust him. The trouble is, I know I can't. Then again, if this bauble I'm after is hidden so well it hasn't already been found, then I'm going to need him to help me find it. Not to mention getting me home, afterward.

"May I suggest an exchange of information, then?"

I pretend to stifle a yawn, as if I'm bored with the whole trust/don't trust game. "You first."

"We're going to the Crystal Palace." Sounds awesome to me, but Jeryd says it like it's something abhorrent. The way someone else would say "ew" when stepping in a fresh, nasty yard bomb.

"You mean there's actually a palace here that's made of crystal?"

"No," he says. "There isn't."

"Then tell me where we're really going." I stamp my foot, but my shoe slips and I have to grab hold of a nearby branch to keep from falling.

Jeryd sighs. "There's no Crystal Palace . . . not anymore. But once upon a time," he says it almost reverently, "there was. Believe it or not. That's where we're going. To what's left of what once was."

"Seriously?" My imagination spins off, creating a web of sparkling walls and turrets, the image of what a castle made of crystal might look like. Then, suddenly I'm seeing just how dangerous the jagged ruins of such a place might be.

"Seriously. Now, it's your turn."

I think about the lines of the poem, the weird second verse. So much of it is meaningless to me, but Jeryd seemed to understand the first lines without any trouble. Then again, Jeryd knew there was such a place as a Crystal Palace. Or used to be. I begin to recite,

"*'Neath glittering dome of woodland home,*
The sparkling hiss at evening's kiss.

Forever clasp of jeweled asp
Rejoins the fight of dark and light."
Jeryd's face stiffens, and I pause for a moment, hoping I'm remembering it right, wishing I had just brought the sheet of notebook paper with me, rather than deciding it would be safer to memorize it. For a moment, I worry what might happen if I get any of it wrong.

Eyes bright with expectation, Jeryd waits for me to resume. Looking at him makes my chest tight. I close my eyes, grip the tree tighter and continue,

"One soul, one heart, one magic art.
A gate of worlds behind the words.
His soul reborn to slay the morn
And make the realm a shadow's dream."

I open my eyes and glance at Jeryd. He's holding his breath. I rush to finish reciting before I forget any of the words,

"The three forsworn at dark of moon,
An open gate the triad's fate.
The serpent blade a debt repaid
When traitors' seed unmake the deed."

I'm having trouble wrapping my brain around it. It's so dark and feels less like directions, more like a prediction. An ominous one. "I thought it was just a clue for finding the thing Bree wants," I say. "But it's more than that, isn't it?"

Jeryd nods. "It sounds like prescient singing," he says.

"Prescient singing? What's that?"

"Have you ever heard of prescient dreams?" he asks. "When someone dreams something and then it comes true, but not always exactly. Just in a way that they're certain that's what the dream meant?"

"Not really," I say, "but it sounds like some stuff I may have read about online."

"Prescient singing is for Fay, like prescient dreaming is to humans. Only it happens to us when we're awake."

"And the words come out in riddles?" I snort.

"Not riddles, exactly," Jeryd says. He reaches up and pinches a leaf gently between his fingers, and rubs it like a worry stone. "More like a hint at what will come." He lets go of the leaf and gives me a half smile. "The only trouble is, it's impossible to know when these things will happen and exactly how they'll actually manifest when they do. And since a lot of the information tends to be symbolic, they can't really be taken literally,"

"What does the poem mean?" I ask.

"Song," he corrects me. "And what it means is that we need to get to the site where the Crystal Palace once stood and find that charm. Sooner, rather than later." His voice is light, as if he's trying to be jovial, but it's obvious he's almost as freaked out as I am. It's also just as clear that he isn't going to tell me what it means. It's possible, I suppose, that he doesn't know.

Possible, but I wouldn't bet on it.

"How are we going to get there?" I ask.

Jeryd smiles and wiggles his eyebrows. "I thought you'd never ask." He points down at the ground below us.

I sidle over and look down. Beneath the tree a

large animal is quietly cropping the grass. It looks like the offspring of a horse and a hippopotamus, fat stumpy legs and wide body, with a huge head and fat nose.

"What the hell is that?" I ask him. From below me, the overpowering smell of animal musk wafts up.

"Your carriage, m'lady." Jeryd nods his head and holds out his hand to me, again.

I look down to where the beast is still tearing up hunks of grass as if it hasn't a care in the world. "Sporty. You really went all out," I say, letting the sourness I feel toward him slather my words. "But you might have splurged on a little air freshener."

"It's a bark-bull. We need to cover our tracks, and the scent of that . . ." Jeryd says in a matter-of-fact tone, while pointing at the beast below us.

He's clearly pleased at this apparent method of combined transportation and path covering.

I look back down at the huge animal and wonder how I'm going to ride it. I've never even ridden a horse, and this thing has no saddle or bridle. Not to mention it's the size of a baby elephant.

Jeryd sees me eyeing the animal. "Don't worry," he tells me. "I'm an experienced rider. All you have to do is hang onto me." He's wearing that smug satisfaction, again.

It makes me want to explode. But instead I pretend it doesn't bother me. "Lead on, McDuff."

He tilts his head in question.

"It's Shakespeare," I tell him.

"No," he says, "it isn't."

157

Before I can ask, he swings down from the tree and lands on the animal's back in a fluid movement so quick and graceful I can't help but admire it. His actions are liquid, like a performer in one of those circus acrobatic shows.

He guides the beast to stand directly below me. All I have to do is slip off the branch and drop down onto its wide back. Simple. For someone with some kind of coordination. But not for me. In an awkward collection of jerky motions, I manage to end up stuck, draped over the tree limb on my stomach, feet dangling. Below me, Jeryd snickers.

"Don't you dare laugh at me," I grumble, grabbing hold of the tree and inch myself off the branch.

I lose my grip, cursing at the sting of the bark scraping through my shirt as I slip off the branch.

But instead of tumbling to the ground, I find myself gripped by strong hands and sliding into a sitting position in front of Jeryd, legs straddling the girth of the animal's neck. Jeryd's arms are around my waist and he leans into me. His warm breath tickles the back of my neck through my unruly hair and all I want is to lean back and let him nuzzle my ear.

What the hell is wrong with me? It's like once I kissed Joey some switch got turned on, and now I can't turn it off.

I sit up straight. "I thought you said *I* would be holding onto *you*," I grumble.

"I think this works much better," he murmurs into the back of my neck. "And it's safer this way." He chuckles. "We wouldn't want you to fall off and scent the ground so Andarra's hounds can pick up our trail."

I place my hands on his and force him to loosen his hold. "I prefer a little breathing room, if you don't mind," I snap.

"Actually—"

"That last part was rhetorical," I growl before he can finish his thought. "I honestly don't care whether you mind or not."

He shifts backward a few inches, so he's no longer plastered up against my back. My relief is tempered with regret at the sudden absence of his warmth against me, but I keep that annoying thought to myself.

Jeryd slaps his hands gently against the sides of the animal and the bark-bull picks up its large hooves and lumbers deeper into the shadowy woods. I expect it to jounce up and down, but instead it rolls from step to step and side to side. Riding on the swaying back of this animal is weird. The rolling gait of the beast makes the entire upper half of my body rotate and sway like some demented belly dancer. Actually, it'd probably look graceful, even sexy, if a belly dancer was doing it, but I'm sure I look like a circus clown imitating a spastic hula hoop twirler.

The forest smells rise up as we pass, the scenery grabbing my attention, as the odors overwhelm. Even over the musky scent of our transport beast, loamy soil mixed with strange flowery perfumes and unusual new scents and colors hit my brain, a cascade of colors bursting in my head, demanding to be logged and catalogued. But there are so many new smells that I can't identify, I feel like I'm on ADD overload, like a computer with too much input and not enough processing speed. I finally close my eyes and try not to breathe too deeply, letting the rocking of the bark-bull zone me out.

I dream of being at sea. A ship rocking on an azure ocean, a pale sky above. The distant line of the horizon drifts nearer, then farther away. All is calm, but my gut roils with fear. Out on the teal water a white spot appears. It starts small, a tiny spout of water blown by an errant gust of wind. But it grows, rising rapidly out of the water to tower over me, morphing into a huge genie with muscled arms and a Titanic-sized chest. I try to scream, warn the captain to turn the ship, head back the way we came, but the genii has spotted us. He grins and reaches for us, huge hands and long fingers ending in cracked yellowed nails. His eyes are on me and I can't look away. They're white, the irises covered over with pale tissue, like a blind person's, but I know he can see me.

I gasp and jerk awake. It's no longer night and a light breeze tickles the leaves overhead. Rays of sunlight melt through the shadows, speckling the forest floor with dancing spots of brightness. The bark-bull has stopped moving and calmly crops the grass below me. Jeryd is standing about three feet away, his hands on the trunk of a tree, his face a mask of contemplation.

"Aren't you taking this tree-hugging business a bit far?" I ask, stretching to ease the stiffness in my back.

Jeryd's lips twitch, but his eyes remain closed for another moment before he turns my way. For an instant, his eyes appear to have no irises, just like the horned woman in the meadow. My heart catches. It's like I have a runner's stitch, only in my chest instead of my side. But the dancing blobs of sunlight flitter over his face and his irises look normal again. Was it only a trick of the light? I squeeze my eyes shut, then rub them with my fingers.

"You slept well?" Jeryd's smile is too friendly.

I check my face for drool, relieved to find my chin dry. The dream is fading, like a phantom in the light of day.

"Wait." I look around. "It's daylight."

"Very observant," he says.

"No. No, no, no. It can't be." Panic sprouts in my gut, spreads through my limbs.

He wrinkles his brow. "Why not?"

Head throbbing, I twist around to face him. "Because, if it's morning, I'm dead."

"You look quite healthy to me." He gives me a smoldering look.

"You don't understand." Hysteria makes my voice tight. "My parents. They are going to destroy me."

"Ah." Jeryd nods, like it's no big deal.

I am freaking out and he's being completely calm about it. Of course, he's not the one who has to answer to two totally structured parents, one of whom is paranoid of my being outside after dark without a chaperone.

He holds up his hand. "Time passes differently here. Did I not mention this?"

"No, you did not mention this! But you'd better explain it right now."

"I can't," he says.

"Can't? Or won't?"

"It's not a thing that can be explained. Time merely passes differently. You might be here for a day and discover the outside world has not moved at all. Or . . ."

"Or?"

"I think your most popular story would be Rip Van Winkle."

"How will I know?"

He shrugs. "You'll know when you return."

"That's just craptastic. Thanks so much for the heads up."

My body aches, and my legs tingle like they're going to sleep. I raise one leg up and over and begin sliding off the bark-bull, but Jeryd is at my side in a flash, keeping me from dismounting.

"You can't do that," he says, pushing me back up on the thing.

"But I need to get off this thing." My butt feels like I've spent all night skating and landing on my backside more than staying upright. "If this is the price of staying safe, I'm ready to face whatever comes."

Jeryd's eyes turn hard. "You wouldn't say that if you had any idea of what might come."

The fear that rose up during my nightmare, sidles back up to me. "Sorry. But I really need to get off this thing. Now."

He raises an eyebrow and looks thoughtful. "Wait." His gaze drifts over the ground, up into the trees, and back down again. Then he shakes his head and kicks off his boots. "Put these on," he hands them up to me.

I'm not the most hygienic person, but the idea of wearing someone else's shoes is not appealing. And Jeryd's boots are scuffed and worn. They've obviously spent a lot of hours on his feet. Boy feet. I wrinkle my nose. "Are you serious?"

"My boots, my scent. This will mask your presence. If you want to dismount, this is the only way." He holds out the shoes. "I won't give up the advantage we've gained, small though it is."

I stare at the boots for another minute before nodding. Removing my own shoes and putting on his, while straddling a two-ton riding beast is more than my coordination-challenged muscles can handle. It finally takes both of us to get my tennis shoes off and his boots slipped onto my feet. When I finally slide off the bark-bull, my own shoes tied together by the laces and slung over one shoulder, my legs are so wobbly I almost fall over.

Jeryd reaches out an arm to help me, but I swat his hand away. "I'm fine," I growl, still teetering as I walk out the stiffness. The blood finally starts flowing into my legs, pricking my muscles to life, and I take a good look at the woods as I stumble-walk around the small clearing. I've never seen such greens before, each leaf glows with new growth, pale and so full of potential it vibrates.

Even the grass sends out energy, as if I can actually feel it growing. Where I've walked, the grass has sprung back up as if I never stepped on it. I'm still staring when I realize Jeryd is studying me.

He smiles when he sees me notice him. "It's beautiful, isn't it?"

"It's amazing," I say and I don't even try to hide the wonder in my voice. "It's so . . ."

"Alive," he finishes for me.

I nod.

"It's Fay magic. Otherworldly powered, you might say. But to us this is not Other. It is the only land. The Glistening Realm. Our own Mecca. Most who live in this land have never traveled outside it. Those who have, long for the feel of life your world lacks. Sometimes to the point of fading away forever. Your iron and manmade stone has no energy, no life. Nothing to compare to this. Not even all of the gas, steam and electrical power you create can compare with the potential contained in a single blade of grass here." His face goes hard. "That's why so many work to protect us from the interlopers from your world, why the penalties for bringing humans and other outsiders here have become so . . . harsh."

I stop walking, listening to his eloquent words, his obvious love for his land, and his bitterness when he speaks of harsh punishment, which replays the scene of the horned woman and the faun in my head. "Are all of the people here like the horned woman?"

Jeryd shakes his head. "Yes. And no." He nods

toward the bark-bull. "We need to get going. I want to reach the Hallow Mere before midday."

I shake my head. "I can't," I say. "I can't get back on that thing."

"I'm not used to going barefoot." He points at my feet. "And it's much too far to walk. Besides, I thought you were in a hurry. Time may not pass the same in your world as it does here, but pass it does."

I look down at his boots. I'd forgotten I was wearing them. "No, I don't mean I want to walk all the way to where we're going. I just mean I can't ride anymore. Not right now." My face flushes, heat prickling up from my neck into my cheeks. I don't know how to tell him my bladder is full and getting back on that riding beast is probably going to burst it.

His brows knit together. "You don't want to walk and you say you can't ride. But without causing a major disturbance, that leaves us nothing else." He spreads his arms. "It is lovely, I know, but we can't stay here. As enticing as that sounds." He gives me his most charming smile.

"That is so not what I meant," I tell him. "I just have to, you know . . ."

"What?"

"My back teeth are about to float and I need to relieve myself," I blurt in frustration.

Understanding dawns. His eyes open wide and a hint of color rises in his cheeks. Good. At least I'm not the only one who can be embarrassed.

"That may be a problem." He glances around the

clearing, eyes darting furiously from tree to grass to leaf, then catches on something. "But I believe I have a solution." He's looking at a steaming pile of bark-bull dung. "Just the cover you need."

I wrinkle up my nose in disgust, trying to picture myself straddling the stinking mess. "I am not peeing on that!"

Jeryd rolls his eyes. "Of course not. You'll just use it to cover your, um, tracks."

I close my eyes for a minute, wondering if I can just hold it, but I know that sooner or later I have got to do this. "Fine, but you stay here and look the other way." I go off into the trees and find a secluded spot with good coverage. If I can't see Jeryd or the clearing, he can't see me. After relieving myself of about a gallon of water, I snap off a twig to mark the spot and find a good-sized branch that has a sort of fork in the end that I can use to scoop up some of the bark-bull dung. I pile enough of the dung on the spot where I peed so that I can spread it around. It's nasty work, and smells ten times worse than the animal does, but when I finish I know nothing will be able to sniff out that I've been here. "That should cover my passing," I tell Jeryd. I grin when he groans at the horrible pun. He groans again when I give him back his boots, now spattered with bark-bull dung. I have to work to hide my own smile.

We spend the rest of the morning galumphing along through the most amazing forest I've ever seen. This place makes Papaw's tract of land seem like an old run-down park. The number and diversity of the trees and flowers and fungi is incredible. At one point, we wander along a shallow river that passes through a narrow canyon. Rock walls rise up along both sides of the flowing stream, which sparkles and shimmers in the morning light. The rock wall beside us is completely shaded, its entire surface covered in an array of fungi like I've never seen before. Their colors range from a glowing white to reds, greens, blues, purples and oranges. Colors so vivid, they look like fresh paint that hasn't had time to dry.

I'm so fascinated, I reach out to stroke a cluster of hot pink bulbs each of which is the size of a baby's finger. They're soft-looking and shimmery, almost iridescent, and I just want to touch one. When my hand gets close they begin to sway, as if my movement has caused a breeze. Just as my fingertips near, Jeryd swats my hand. I start to give him a piece of my mind, but as he sweeps my hand away there's a popping sound and the cluster of mushrooms is now a mass of pink pulp with fierce-looking barbs sticking out. Tiny, but dangerously sharp.

I pull back, surprised to see such danger lurking beneath the attractive beauty.

"Not everything is as innocent as it seems here. Just as is often the case in your world," Jeryd says. "Hunters often attract their prey through disguise."

I consider his words and nod, thinking about high school cheerleaders, Joey's crooked smile, the dusty old book Bree found in the library. I think about Jeryd's charming ways, his glittering eyes, the undercurrent of danger in his demeanor, and the way he says things that make me want to punch him. "Not everything about this world seems innocent," I say.

He doesn't reply.

We finally stop again as the sun reaches its highest point. My stomach rumbles. I haven't eaten anything since last night's dinner. I should have planned better. I should have asked how long this little journey was going to take. I should have checked to see if there were snack bars along the way.

Jeryd dismounts and leads the bark-bull to a spot between two large trees that look like pine trees, only every branch sparkles like it's been sprayed with silver glitter. The ground beneath the glittery pines is covered in some sort of clover, emerald green and spotted with moisture. The bark-bull lets out a happy sigh and begins to rip up and rake in huge mouthfuls of the stuff, which makes my stomach grumble even louder.

"If we're going much farther, I'm going to need to eat," I twist left and right, trying to ease my aching muscles.

"Aren't you afraid?" he asks.

"Of what?"

"Oh, I don't know. Getting trapped here in the Realm for the rest of your life?"

I gasp. "Oh. I guess I thought all those stories were just fairytales."

"There is always some truth woven into the stories," he says. Then he laughs. "But not that.

The real problem with eating the food here is that the most attractive and appealing plants are often the most deadly."

My stomach rumbles and I cringe, hoping he didn't hear it. "Great," I say. "I'm so hungry even the grass looks good."

"You could try it," he says, "but I don't recommend it. Hard on the digestion, if you know what I mean."

I'm not sure I do, but then I think about the Bull Bark's manure and decide I don't want to find out. Jeryd tells me to wait and goes off into the thick shadows, returning with a very unattractive handful of green blobs and pale yellow fungi. I sniff once and cover my nose to block out the acrid odor. "That smells remarkably foul," I say. The grass is looking more and more appetizing.

"Tastes better than it smells," he says. "It will fill your belly, and should also eliminate the necessity of having to loan you my shoes." He looks meaningfully at his poor dung-spattered boots.

I pinch my nose with the fingers of my left hand and pluck a green blob from his outstretched palm. I begin to chew and my mouth puckers up. "It's like eating a moldy lemon."

Jeryd shakes his head. "Try eating them together," he tells me. "They complement each other."

I try to give him the evil eye, but my face is so squinted up from the sourness in my mouth, I probably look like Popeye on drugs. He shoves his hand toward me. So, I grab some of the fungus and stuff it into my mouth. It bursts with a sugary sweetness, like cotton candy melting in my mouth. It mixes with the sour and I open my eyes in surprise. Blended, they taste like ripe raspberries. I reach out and Jeryd drops a small portion of the berries and fungus into my hand. "That's it?" I say.

"A little goes a long way, at least until you get used to them." He pops the rest into his mouth and chews quickly before swallowing.

I look at the small pile in my hand, then eye him warily. "Doesn't look like you're very fond of them yourself," I say.

"I just don't like berries," he says with a grimace. "It's a texture thing."

I finish my berries and fungus. "So, what's this stuff called?" I ask.

"You don't want to know," he grins.

"Now, I have to know," I say.

"The green berries are Green Berries and the yellow fungus is called Ogre Snot." He laughs.

"Riiight," I say. "How about telling me what they're really called."

"Honestly," he says. "That's what they're called. I'm sure there is some ancient Fay name for them, but that's what they're called now that we speak the common language here."

"I don't believe you," I say, wiping my hands clean on my jeans.

"You will if you ever see an ogre's nose close up," he laughs.

CHAPTER EIGHTEEN

As we resume our trek, all I can think about is the Crystal Palace. What it once was. What it is now. On the other hand, a part of me is still having trouble imagining it. Although, I don't know why. After all, I already know Other exists, along with a multitude of strange creatures and unusual plants. I recall my near brush with the poison-barbed mushrooms and my hands clasp shut. But the Crystal Palace is more dream-like to me than any other story, fairytale or otherwise. It's more personal, somehow. Probably because when I was really young, I used to imagine I was a long-lost princess who belonged to a Crystal Palace, only I was kidnapped and carried off to a place where no one could find me and no one knew who I really was. So, now, as we lumber along through the forest headed toward the actual Crystal Palace, I'm shivery with fear and excitement, like a six-year-old waiting for her favorite holiday, feeling it will never arrive.

The forest grows darker as we move further north, the direction Jeryd tells me is where the ruins of the palace lie, and my shivers become less about emotions and more about the fierce chill that settles on the ground, clutching at the roots of the trees. Large shapes loom out of the darkness. Carved stones, cracked and broken, lurch up from the forest floor between twisted tree roots.

A dense mist rises from the soil, weaving tendrils about us, like long fingers stroking our arms, legs, and faces. The bark-bull whines through its nose and I feel Jeryd patting its heavy side, settling it down the way you would gentle a nervous horse.

A thread of mist has curled itself around my left arm and I shake it away, brushing it off with my right hand. It seems to let out a soft sigh as it tumbles down like a silk hair ribbon fluttering to the ground. "This mist is creeping me out."

"Try to ignore them. Hopefully, they'll get bored and leave you alone," Jeryd whispers.

"They?" I sit up straight, stiffening. "You mean this isn't just fog?" My voice is sharp but, muffled by the mist, it comes out as a tiny squeak.

"Shhhhh . . ."

"Don't you shush me," I hiss, turning my head as far as I can to get a look at his face. If he's teasing me . . . But his eyes are serious, his lips taut.

"What the hell are these things?"

"Remainders."

"Crap! You mean revenants? Ghosts?" I think about the stories I've heard about evil spirits returning to haunt the living, angry bitter ghosts of those who refused to depart.

Jeryd grabs one of my arms and speaks in a low firm voice. "Let go of your anger and fear," he says. "Find a place of calm inside yourself and go there."

The mist is denser now, covering the ground like a ghostly flood. The bark-bull raises its head above the fog, snuffling and rolling its eyes. Jeryd tries to calm the beast, but its fear is obvious. It kicks out in back, as if fighting a predator. I take deep slow breaths through my nose, but I can't release the tension knotting my neck and shoulders and pinching my forehead.

The mist continues to rise, long arms writhe about us, grasping. I feel myself slipping and grab at the bark-bull's mane, slick with moisture. Or is it the cold sweat on my palms? My senses are muzzy. I fall, flutter to the ground, as if I have become a piece of the mist, a writhing tendril, a part of the ghostly fog.

Without warning, the wolf rises, roiling inside me, wrenching itself free. For an instant, my hands scrabble at my throat searching for the shock collar that controls my animal, but my throat is bare. A triumphant howl bursts forth as I land on all fours, scrabbling for a foothold in the slippery detritus.

Cold arms reach for me, grasping, clawing. I run. Leap over fallen branches, skirt tree stumps rotted with age. Thick fog envelopes me, obscuring my sight. Scents, never quite familiar, fly past then rush back at me in an infinite déjà vu cycle.

I stop, turn uncertainly. No idea where I am. I raise my head to howl, but stop. Danger lurks and I'm lost. Fear shimmies up my back, raising my hackles.

Beside me, a gray shape looms up out of the mist, shaking and whinnying in fear. My lips peel back, fangs bared and ready for attack. Something grabs for me and I twist around, snarling and snapping. My teeth sink into flesh. Blood fills my mouth, not human or animal, but mixed with something that burns my tongue. I whine, open my jaw, rub my lips and jowls along the ground to wipe away the burn. The chill of wet leaves cools my face, but the burning in my mouth is undiminished. I flop down, wiping my paws down the length of my muzzle and whimper.

Beside me, twigs snap. Leaves rustle and I growl. A coaxing voice murmurs. A rise and fall of sound: calm, lilting, repetitious. My ears twitch as my brain deciphers the sounds and I begin to make out words.

"The wolf does not control you. You control the wolf."

I smell moisture. A cupped leaf filled with water is set before me. Drool leaks from the side of my mouth, as I raise my head, sniff at the leaf. I stick my tongue into the wetness, then lap it up quickly, and the burning begins to fade.

"Merissa?" Someone calls my name. I open my

eyes. Jeryd's face wobbles into view. "Welcome back." He smiles at me. His dark hair has fallen over his eyes and he looks at me from under it.

I'm lying on the ground, head in his lap, looking up into those smoky eyes. I jerk away from him and push myself up to a sitting position. Too fast. A wave of dizziness sweeps over me and Jeryd catches me by the arm to keep me from falling. "Careful," he warns.

My face flushes warm and I look down at my bare hands. I'm in my human form. I reach to cover my naked body, and touch fabric. I'm still clothed, but that's not right. I changed. I totally wolfed out. Without warning. Without getting undressed. My clothes would have been shredded. Only, they're not. "What happened?"

Jeryd's lips quirk up in that blood-warming half-smile, but his eyes remain dark and serious. "The revenants called to you," he says, "called to your inner being."

I begin to remember. Images swirl, faded memories. There's a bittersweet taste on my tongue and my mouth feels raw and tender. I jerk away and run my gaze over him. His left forearm is smeared with blood; an ugly bite mark visible just below the elbow.

He holds up his arm. "I'll heal. It could have been a lot worse."

Shame burns its way up my neck and face. "I am so sorry—"

"Not your fault." He shrugs. "I should have warned you. Revenants can be . . . mischievous and unpredictable."

I wouldn't call any of what just happened mischievous. More like vicious. I don't understand why Jeryd isn't angry. Although, it isn't as if my bite could actually turn him into a shifter. Even if he wasn't Other, I'm not a werewolf. My genetic disorder isn't communicable. Except to progeny. But there's something behind his smile that makes me uncomfortable. Like he has a secret and he's not going to tell me what it is.

This is all wrong. He's hiding something. I'm certain of it. I slip my arm out of his grasp, moving slowly so I won't get dizzy again, but making it clear I don't need his help. "It isn't possible," I tell him. "I must have just passed out. I can't have changed. My clothes . . ." I stop from saying what I'm thinking and try not to blush. If I had truly morphed, I would have been completely tangled in the tattered remains of my clothes—or, more likely, naked—when I woke up in Jeryd's arms. I need to breathe, to stop my traitorous heart from telegraphing my thoughts like a thousand jungle drums.

Jeryd steps back from me, gives me an assessing look, one eyebrow raised. "Things work differently here than in your world," he says, as if it explains everything. "If you're well enough to ride, we should probably move on."

I suddenly realize that we're not in the revenant forest anymore. At least, not in the thick of it. Rather, we're standing in the middle of a circle of stones, arranged a lot like Stonehenge, but much smaller in scale. And instead of being located on a vast open plain, this circle is in a clearing surrounded by forest. The trees have grown right up to the edges of the plinths, but their roots and branches remain outside the circle. Not a single leaf drapes across the invisible barrier that separates the circle from the forest.

"What is this place?"

Jeryd shrugs. "Another broken place," he says. His voice is a quiet monotone, but there's something behind his words. Something angry and sad. Something that catches my attention.

I can see what he means. Despite the scent of power that lingers, the giant plinths are cracked and blackened. Fallen lintels lie in heaps of rubble. "How?"

He snorts. "Someone threw a tantrum."

There's something about this place that makes me want to know more. A secret knowledge that seems to hover just out of reach, clinging to what remains of the circle that once stood here. "What was it before it was broken?"

Jeryd surveys the ruin, then drops his gaze to the ground. "A place of light in a darkening realm." He looks guilty and dejected, his shoulders hunched and head hanging low as if in defeat. But before I can ask why, a horn blares somewhere in the forest. Jeryd jerks his head up, eyes blazing with determination. "We need to go."

I hesitate and he grabs me by the arm and pulls me toward the forest. "Now."

"But what about the bark-bull? Or covering my

scent?"

He gives me a sour look. "Too late for that, after your little run. No. We'll just have to hope we can avoid them long enough to reach the grounds of the Crystal Palace. After that . . ." He shrugs. Then his eyes light up, as if he's suddenly thought of something. "Can you change?"

"Change?" I only have the clothes I brought.

His lips twist in annoyance. "Not your clothes. You. Can you make the change again? Right now?"

"I don't know," I say. "I've never tried to change so many times in such a short span. I've never needed to." I don't mention that all the training in control I've practiced has been to keep myself from changing. Also, I don't want to think about getting undressed and trusting him with my clothes. Although, if what he says about things being different here is true . . .

"Try now."

It's an order, not a suggestion and I give him a dirty look. "Why would I want to do that?"

"Because," he growls, "you move a lot faster in that form and I can travel the treetops. Maybe we can outrun them. With luck, we can reach the Crystal Palace, if you follow me on the ground at speed."

I think about all the times I have fought the wolf, how much I've tried to distance myself from that part of me. I shudder at the thought of losing control. Again. "I don't think I can do this," I whisper, my words charged with dread.

The horn sounds again and, rising behind it,

baying dogs and clamoring voices.

"If you aren't even willing to try, we may as well sit down and await our doom," Jeryd growls.

I scrunch up my face and think about the change, remembering the feel of it, recalling the day close to the full moon when I nearly changed at school right in front of Mr. Rajanni. How I had to hang onto myself so desperately and the way the full moon always pulls at me. But there is no full moon here. And without the push of the revenants, the wolf slips away from me each time I get close.

The baying and yelling is nearer now. I can't make out the words being shouted, but the voices are coarse and hostile.

"Now, would be good." Jeryd's voice is grim.

I'm suddenly cold. My hands shake. I clench my fists to steady myself, try to force my breathing to slow. But my breathing only grows faster, more rapid. I focus on the good parts of the wolf, the freedom of loping through the forest, scenting and chasing game, the graceful feel of lithe muscles and silken fur ruffled by the wind. I remember running all out beneath a full moon and I smile.

A strange sensation swallows me and for a moment I tense in panic. Then, I find myself relaxing, lulled by a powerful energy that emanates from the stones surrounding me. With a rumble, the ground suddenly shifts below my feet and I feel myself falling. I drop to my knees, catching my weight on my hands.

Or, rather, paws.

Startled, I look at my legs, covered in fur and for

an instant worry that I've forgotten to shave. Then, as the ground stops wobbling, I realize I've done it. I've shifted. Without the force of the full moon. I've made the change. I sit up and raise my muzzle to howl in triumph, but before I can utter a sound, I hear a familiar voice calling.

"Over here," Jeryd shouts. "This way." He's standing on the broad limb of a giant ash tree, waving at me, signaling for me to move.

The clangor of the charging creatures is loud in my wolf-keen ears and getting closer. I lope toward Jeryd, who leaps across tree limbs. He catches hold of a branch and swings himself across a wide space and into another tree. I follow him, leaping out of the stone circle and into the underbrush as the charging gang of creatures bursts out of the wood on the other side and comes to a sudden halt at the edge of the circle. I turn in time to see several creatures, including an indigo-colored centaur, pushed from behind, tumble between the standing stones and into the circle. They scream and writhe, kicking and clawing at the others to let them out, desperate to escape the strange power that still emanates from the broken stones.

Jeryd calls my name and I scurry to catch up to him. I put on speed, aware that the creatures are circling around the stones to follow us. Jeryd moves faster, bounding across open air, dancing on tree limbs, and swinging from branches I wouldn't believe would hold his weight. But they do, and I begin panting as I rush to keep pace. The sounds of pursuit are still behind us, but growing dimmer. I can't tell if they're tired of yelling or if we're actually beginning to outdistance them.

There really isn't any time for me to figure it out. I'm forced to run full out, dodging and leaping over and under fallen trees and thick undergrowth, all while keeping one eye on Jeryd, who practically soars from tree to tree, barely touching the tip of one branch before he lands on the next. He moves as if he's part squirrel. Mad squirrel. My panting tongue lolls out at the silliness of the thought, then I realize I too must look like a crazed circus animal, zipping headlong in and out and through and over any and all obstacles that appear in my path. I've never run this fast before, this heedless of my surroundings. I nearly stumble at the thought, then pull myself back in and focus on running. Before long, my lungs begin to burn, as do my legs, and my feet—not used to tearing across ancient forested land—hurt in a thousand places. There's no longer any sound of pursuit and I'd bark at Jeryd if I had the breath for it, signal for him to slow down, stop, give us a rest. But he continues to drive forward. Mad squirrel indeed, I think. But now it's no longer amusing.

I watch as he disappears from sight, then reappears again, farther away and high up in the branches of a swaying conifer. Then, suddenly, he drops, plummeting down and out of sight. I slow for a moment, waiting for him to reappear, but there's no sign of him. No more death-defying, mad-squirrel leaps. Has he fallen to his death? Or was it a trick of my vision? With a burst of speed, I rush forward, fear and shock warring within me. It's not that I care about his Fay carcass, I tell myself, but I need a guide. Without him, I have no idea where I'm going.

Or how to get back to the meadow, I realize with a start. Not after napping on the back of a bark-bull, not to mention the detour the revenants caused the wolf to take.

I focus on the tree where I last saw Jeryd and increase my speed. My lungs feel scorched and my legs and feet ache with the brutal full-out running I've been doing, but now adrenaline powers my limbs and I close in on my target with rapid strides.

As I near the place where I saw Jeryd fall, I lose sight of the tall evergreen. The forest is denser here and trees close in on all sides, blocking out the sunlight and hiding the way forward. I begin to slow, as I find my way blocked by thorn-encrusted hedges, huge gnarled roots, and great tumbles of fallen trees.

I smell danger, but before I can react, I'm snapped up.

Dangling.

In a net.

CHAPTER NINETEEN

I tell myself not to struggle, but instinct overpowers my brain and I snarl and gnaw at the ropy trap. The net flexes and swings with every movement. My left back leg is caught in the mesh and I can't get any leverage. Spurts of giggling erupt from below. Not the happy giggling of innocent children, but the ugly giggle-laughter of three creepy little creatures.

They stand on the ground beneath me. One, a little shorter than the not quite three-foot height of the other two, holds a long stick and stretches out to prod the net, causing it, and me, to spin around until I'm looking directly at them.

I snarl and the one with the stick jumps back. The other two turn and laugh, pointing at their smaller companion while holding their stomachs.

He grunts and comes back at me with the stick, jabbing it up into the net. He misses me, but I manage to grab the stick in my teeth and give it a shake. The creature on the other end lets out a squeal as he's raised up into the air a few inches before letting go of the stick and falling back to the ground in a tumble of arms, legs, and bright colored rags. He jumps up and curses at me, baring his sharp teeth and shaking his small fist. Ire blazes in his yellow eyes.

His companions, doubled over with laughter, have trouble catching their breath. The smaller one, face red with fury, runs over and starts kicking them. Their laughter increases, becoming great choking guffaws, until the short one lands a kick in a very tender place. The offended creature curls on the ground with a groan, then reaches out, grabbing the small guy by the ankle and tripping him. The third one has stopped laughing, and leaps on the short one and all three are suddenly rolling about on the ground, wrestling and clawing at one another.

With a start, I realize I should be trying to find a way out of my predicament, not watching a miniature Otherworld wrestling event. I search for a weakness in the net, a thinning of the ropes, a way out.

I gnaw at a section of knots that appears to have been repaired and retied. My canines tear at the twisted hemp-like ropes, and it starts to give. From the corner of my eye, I glimpse the creatures below me. The three of them are tangled together, grunting and swearing, each attempting to get the upper hand, but their movements have slowed. They're tiring, and I don't have much time before their attention will be back on me.

The knot gives and I feel my weight shift as a small hole opens in the net. I risk a look in the direction of the fighters. They're still in a heap, but the full-out battling has ceased. They kick and slap half-heartedly. I need to hurry. I pick another knot and begin to gnaw, grinding with my back teeth. This section is tougher and I worry at it till my jaw aches. Below me, the midget wrestlers continue to shout curses and land sporadic blows.

Finally, I manage to saw through the last strands of fiber. The rope gives and the net drops about a foot, then jerks to a stop. The hole in the net is big enough to stick my head through, but I can't manage my shoulders. I scrabble at the ropes surrounding the hole in the net, trying to loosen them, widen the hole, but they're all knotted tight. A growl of frustration forms in my throat and begins to escape before I realize.

The sudden silence below me, jerks my efforts to a standstill and I strain to see what the bully boys are up to, but with my head stuck through the hole in the net, I can't tilt it to see down. I pull my head back inside to get a better view of the ground. Two of them are lying on their backs, staring up at me, pale eyes wide with fear. The third, the little one, is sitting up, looking around, dazed. He's clearly taken the worst of the beating.

I hang in the air above them, the net creaking as it sways. The ropes pulling at my legs, feel as if they're tightening. I struggle and catch my breath as, with a sudden lurch, the net drops another foot. Once more I'm jerked to a stop, but now I'm barely above their heads. I move my weight up and down, straining at the ropes to get some leverage. Another shift. Another drop. Just a bit more and I'll be at eye level.

The two prone creatures jump up and run over to their companion. They begin slapping his face. I think they're trying to clear his head, but he just looks more and more confused. And more and more angry.

In a burst of rage, he leaps to his feet and begins to pummel the others. Shorty is a wild man, wind-milling his arms and hurling curses like they're bullets. The target of his ire falls to the ground and Shorty pulls back his leg to kick out at him, but before he can land the blow, the other one rolls away, jumps up and runs off into the underbrush.

The third creature has just been standing there, staring. Shorty rounds on him and the taller one decides it's not worth any more damage. With an angry curse, he scuttles after his buddy. Shorty looks around, stamping and huffing like he's ready to take on an army. When he sees there are no more enemies to fight, he swings back his leg and kicks at a baseball-sized rock, sending it skittering into the trees.

The net gives way again, and I drop down another foot or so. I'm suddenly eyeball-to-eyeball with the stormy anger of a three-foot tall, Otherworld wrestling champion.

He snorts and I growl back at him, remembering the stick that was shoved through the net. I lunge forward, trying to get my teeth on him, but the net still holds. He backpedals a few steps, pauses and stands with his hands on his hips, laughing at me.

Wrong. Thing. To. Do.

I'm so angry now, the wolf gets away from me, becoming a snarling mass of teeth, claws and fur. The violent lunge forward breaks the last of the rope strands holding the net to the tree branch above and it all comes crashing down with me in the middle. I hit the ground in a thump of net and snapping jaws. In a fury, I fling the remaining netting off my back and hurl myself at the puny creature, knocking him to the ground. Front paws on his chest, I bare my teeth in triumph.

He squeals, then lies still, big eyes round with fright. His fear feeds the wolf, but startled at my own ferocity, I wrench myself back under control. I focus my mind and shift. The creature's eyes bug out of his head as he watches the big bad wolf on his chest shimmer into a teenage girl in blue jeans and a t-shirt. Thank goodness Jeryd was telling the truth about things working differently here, or this creature would be staring at one very embarrassed naked girl.

I continue holding him down, giving him my best triumphant grin. "Not so much fun when the tables are turned, is it?"

"You . . . you not supposed to be here!" He

squeaks. "Not allowed."

"But I am here," I say, glancing at the pile of ropes lying on the ground beside us. "And you and your little friends gave me a really warm welcome, didn't you?"

He trembles. "Not allowed. Big trouble."

"I'll give you big trouble," I say, wondering what I should do with him. "How would you like it if I trussed you up in that net, hung you from the trees and poked at you with a big stick?"

He shakes his head, eyes still wide.

Apparently, Jeryd wasn't lying about me breaking some sort of taboo by coming here. I need to know what this creature and his friends know about me and what they might do next. "Tell me where your friends ran off to."

He shakes his head again. "No friends."

"Don't lie to me. I saw them. Where did they go? Those other . . ."

"No friends," he repeats. "Brothers."

Great. I search the clearing guardedly, pricking up my ears for any sounds of approach. If they're family, they'll probably come back looking for him, once they realize he hasn't followed them out of the clearing.

"What are you? And how many others are out there, including your *brothers*?" I lean forward, putting just a bit more pressure on him. "No lies."

He gets a quizzical look on his face and then tries to shrug, which is difficult with me holding him, but I get the gist. "Goblin. And many, many, but not so many as once."

"What the hell does that mean?"

He shrugs again.

I should probably hang the little creep in the net and leave him swinging, but I no longer have Jeryd to guide me and I don't know how to get to the Crystal Palace from here. I narrow my eyes at him and give him my sternest glare. "Where are we right now?"

"In forest?" he says in a frightened voice.

I blow out my breath in frustration. "Let's try again. What do you know about the Crystal Palace?"

"Nothing. Know nothing." His voice is shrill. His eyes dart from side to side as if he's contemplating escape. It's clear he knows something. It's also clear that what he knows frightens him. A lot. Great. He's totally freaked out about the one place I know I need to get to.

"Don't even try. Just tell me what you know about the Crystal Palace ruins."

He trembles, but says nothing.

"Fine." I reach over to grab the ropes, dragging them closer. "I'll just tie you up and hang you in a tree. Then, if someone, or something wanders by and feels like poking at you with a stick or claw–"

He squeals in terror and tries to wriggle away, but my knees are on his chest and I grab him by the throat. He continues to squirm. "It's clear you know about the ruins and I'm willing to bet you know the way. So, how about we make a deal?"

He stops squirming. His eyes are still wide with fear, but he's listening.

189

"You show me how to get to the Crystal Palace, and I will let you go." It's a gamble, but I'm betting he won't want to get too close to the place once he shows me where it is. And, he probably won't be in a hurry to tell anyone that he helped a trespasser find her way around their precious Silver Realm. I consider for a moment what the punishment would be for aiding and abetting a taboo breaker. After what I saw happen to the faun in the glade, I'd be willing to bet the penalty is severe. My conscience makes me consider what might happen to this poor creature if he gets caught helping me, but I push the thought aside. The little creep didn't seem to have any issues with catching me in a net and poking me with a stick while I dangled in mid-air. Besides, I need to find this artifact and get it back to Bree. Despite everything that's happened, I feel responsible for what is happening to Joey, and I can't help feeling like there's more at stake than what Jeryd says. After all, why else would he bring me here and risk having that Andarra woman pissed at him. And Bree, book or no book, would never have glommed onto Joey, if I hadn't liked him.

I need to get the artifact and get the hell out of this place before anyone catches me, or we're all in a world of trouble. Of course, if what Jeryd says is true, we're in for trouble either way. I hate damned-if-you-do-and-damned-if-you-don't   situations, dammit.

The goblin is eyeing me, his little brain clearly calculating. I grab the pile of rope and begin to untangle it, searching for a piece short enough for my purpose.

His eyes go wide. "Yes!" He nods his head rapidly up and down. "Show you. No hang in tree."

I stop what I'm doing and smirk. "Good," I say, as I continue to unravel a piece of the net. I make a loop at one end of the rope, tie it in a couple of places, and slip it over his head and shoulders, forcing him to stick his arms through as he kicks and squirms. His arm lashes out and smacks me on the chin and I sit back on my heels. We both stare at one another for a stunned instant, then he leaps to his feet and makes a dash for the forest. I grab the end of the rope and yank. The makeshift halter pulls him up short and he falls back, landing on his butt with a yelp.

He lets out a high-pitched shriek. "No hang! No hang!" He scrambles to his feet and tries to run again, but I hold fast, the rope wrapped around my fist for good measure. "I show. I show." He collapses on the ground and begins kicking and squalling like a toddler throwing a tantrum.

"Shush!" I tell him, searching the area for signs of the little brat's bigger brothers. "I'm not going to hang you in a tree. But I'm not letting you out of my sight, or off the leash," I give the rope a yank, "until you show me where the palace is."

He sits up and turns his bulging eyes on me. It's clear he's working this out, deciding which fate is worse. He shakes his head from side to side, as if he can't make up his mind, then looks at me once more. This time his eyes are pleading. "Crystal

Palace, bad place," he whispers. "Bolgi no go." He drops his head. "Better to hang Bolgi for brothers to torture."

"Bolgi?" I say and he looks up at me. "Is that your name?"

He nods, once, then hangs his head again. He looks so sad; I feel kind of sorry for the little guy. But I need to get that artifact and get the heck out of here. And I need a guide to do it.

"Bolgi," I say. "If you take me close to the palace, and you don't try anything tricky along the way, I won't make you go inside." He stares at me in silence, looking like he doesn't believe me.

"Would you rather be left hanging in a tree to be tormented by your brothers?"

He shakes his head. His fingers drift to the rope harness, then he nods once, clearly unhappy. "Bolgi show."

CHAPTER TWENTY

We trek through the forest, one end of the rope wrapped tightly around my wrist, Bolgi on the other end, guiding me. We seem to be heading in the direction Jeryd was taking me before he so inconveniently disappeared. If I ever see him again, I am so going to let him have it. Or maybe I'll just bite his face off. That would be a lot more satisfying. I picture his face, his crooked smile, his lips, and feel a heat rise in my gut. Ugh! Why does thinking about him do that to me? He's a total jerk and thoroughly untrustworthy. Joey may be a bit of a bad boy, but Jeryd is, well, he's Other. And all the wrong kinds of Other. It's ridiculous that I might have even considered liking him. I guess all the lectures adults give us about raging hormones have some basis in fact, after all. Maybe that explains why I want to go around kissing everybody I meet. I glance at the goblin tethered at the end of the rope. Well, almost everyone.

I shove thoughts of Jeryd and kissing aside and concentrate on where Bolgi is leading me. He scampers around gnarly tree roots, climbing over deadfall and ducking under low branches, as if it's completely natural. His short stature and stubby limbs belie the grace of his movements. He's surprisingly stealthy. "Bolgi," I say. "You're very good at keeping quiet. I can't hear your footsteps, even when we walk through dry brush."

He glances at me over his shoulder, his yellow eyes serious. "Practice. Hiding from brothers, and other . . . dangers." His head moves from side to side, checking for lurking monsters, or maybe relatives.

"You hide from your brothers?"

"Not always." His voice is angry. "Sometimes Blik and Skrog find Bolgi. Make big trouble and hurt for Bolgi. Then not hiding."

I think about this for a while. Being an only child, I always wondered what it would be like to have a brother or a sister. I always thought it would be fun. But for this poor creature, having siblings is a torment.

We walk in silence a while longer. Then, Bolgi stops, listening. His body tightens. With slow measured steps, he backs up, inch by inch until he bumps into my leg.

"What?" I whisper, scanning the forest in the

direction Bolgi is staring.

He shivers and plucks at the harness. With a sudden movement, he grabs my hand and yanks me back, pulling me toward the base of a large tree.

In the distance branches rustle and twigs crack.

Something comes out of the forest. Something covered in leaves and cloaked in darkness. Bolgi gives a squeal of terror, then spins around and kicks me hard in the shin.

I let out a yelp and jerk on the rope, but Bolgi has looped the slack around my arm. He falls to the ground in a heap of dead weight, yanking me down with him.

The dark creature keeps coming, uttering a string of guttural noises. Whatever it is has Bolgi in a fit of terror. He squeals and it comes whistling out of his nose and from between his teeth, high-pitched and ear-piercing.

I need to change. I fight better in wolf form, and maybe changing will startle him into letting go. I yank hard on the rope, pulling Bolgi up to standing.

The creature continues to approach, making those odd sounds and I back away, preparing to make the change, but Bolgi pulls the rope tighter around my wrist and digs in his heels. Then, he suddenly falls to his knees in a heap. Small noises emanate from him, but they're muffled because his face is planted firmly in the dirt.

I'm poised to drop to my hands and knees, hoping there's still time to change, when the creature steps out of the darker shadows. It takes my mind a moment to recognize Jeryd. He looks taller, and sort of regal, cloaked in an aura of forest and night. What at first appeared to be leaves and branches is a multi-colored cloak woven to look like a part of the forest.

He steps into the clearing and glares down at Bolgi. "What do you here?" he commands in an arrogant voice that seems to emanate from the trees.

Bolgi whimpers, raises his head a few millimeters off the forest floor. "Nothing, Lord. Nothing."

Lord? I'm confused. Why is he calling Jeryd Lord? "Jeryd, what's—"

Bolgi looks at me, shock and surprise in his yellow eyes.

"Nothing? Would you lie to me?" The words snarl out of Jeryd, cutting me off and hurling toward Bolgi with enough force to knock the small creature's face back onto the earth.

"Forgiveness, Lord," Bolgi squeaks

"And why would I do that?" Jeryd's eyes flash dark with cruelty.

"I bring gift." Bolgi turns his head to send a quick glance my way. "The trespasser."

Lord. Trespasser. Gift. My head buzzes like a thousand ants are crawling inside it as his words sink in.

"A gift? For me?"

"For Dark Lady. Andarra. Bolgi brings trespasser to Lord's mother." Bolgi sweeps his hand across the ground in the semblance of a bow.

The Dark Lady? Jeryd's mother? The woman from the glade? The forest sinks away from me, fading into a murky fog as my mind wraps itself around the concept and I realize I've been tricked. "I knew I shouldn't have trusted you!"

Jeryd stares at me, a hardness in his eyes, a dark glint, just like the one the Dark Queen—no, *his mother*—wore as she tortured that faun.

Bolgi's eyes flick back and forth between us, fear and confusion clear in his gnarled features.

"Do not speak to me unless you are told to do so," Jeryd's voice is a deep command, and his lip curls. "You should be punished for your insolence."

I suddenly realize I need to get away. I drop to all fours, prepared to change, but Bolgi leaps at me and sinks his teeth into my arm.

I let out a scream as rows of needle-sharp teeth slice through my skin and sink into muscle. With my eyes still on Jeryd, I try to jerk free of Bolgi's bite, but his jaw is clamped tight and he's wrapped his long fingers around my wrist. I pull my arm back and his feet come off the ground, but he doesn't let loose and the searing pain makes me drop my arm till his weight is on the ground again.

The fire in my arm is blinding. I lose focus. A bitter taste fills my mouth and I roll to my side, as Bolgi lets go of me spitting and cursing.

"Nasty. Bad." He crawls a few feet away and spews into the blurry underbrush.

I know I should put pressure on the wound, and I try to grab my arm, but my muscles don't respond. I just sort of wobble in place. Then someone is next to me, grabbing my wrist and yanking my arm away from my body. It's someone I should know, but I can't quite place the face with a name through the gummy blur inside my head. Muzzy darkness surrounds me and all I can see is a faint shimmer of green and gold at the end of a long tunnel. It makes me want to laugh, seeing the light at the end of a tunnel like that, but I can't remember why it should be so funny.

A voice echoes down the tunnel toward me. "Merissa." And I think that might be funny, too, if I could just remember the joke.

"Merissa?"

I try to answer, but my lips and tongue have gone to sleep and they're begging me to follow them. Everything tingles, like when the dentist puts that mask over your nose and turns on the gas, and I can barely feel the touch of someone's hand on my face before everything goes black.

CHAPTER TWENTY-ONE

It's dark and warm and I don't want to wake up. I try to reach for the snooze button, but my arm is a tree trunk, and each of my eyelids weighs as much as a house. There's a bitter odor in the air, bitter and rank with a rotten mold smell, pea green and swirling ochre. Something skitters across my feet and I jerk my head up only to have it explode into tiny pieces and crash back down. I've never had a hangover, but I think this must be what one feels like. I roll onto my side and gag as my body heaves, trying to expel not only the contents of my stomach, but what feels like all the organs in my body, including my colon. There doesn't seem to be much in my stomach, so nothing comes out, which you'd think would be a relief, but the sensation of trying to heave out your insides with absolutely no results, turns out to be worse than losing your cookies, cake and ice cream, all at once. Not because it's frustrating, but because it's so intensely painful.

Once the heaving passes, I lie still, breathing in shallow gasps. The smell is worse than before and I'm being poked and pricked by something stiff and scratchy. Gawd! I'm lying in a dank room on a pile of moldy straw. I suppose it's some sort of dungeon. Stupid cliché! But what else should I expect in a place where they're clearly prejudiced against technology—and apparently basic plumbing—and live like they're still in the dark ages?

I don't know if that's by choice or because they're unable to use or develop some kind of technology, but at the moment this off-the-grid stuff just plain sucks. At least a modern jail cell would have a toilet and a sink. Not that I think I could stand up long enough to use either without my head falling off my neck and rolling across the floor. Wait a minute. I can't get up in this form, but my wolf is stronger, so maybe . . .

As soon as I attempt the change, searing pain burns through me. It takes a moment to realize the bloodcurdling scream in my ears is tearing from my own throat. My neck is on fire and I feel like I've been simultaneously electrocuted and scalded with boiling water. I wish I could pass out again, but no such luck. When I can control my hands again, I reach up and gingerly touch the metal band encircling my throat. Completely smooth without any fastening at all, but it must contain a powerful spell. It sucks to be me, imprisoned in Other and trapped in my weaker human form.

A loud racket erupts; running feet, raised voices. Light flickers around the edges of the door and then, with a loud groan, the heavy slab of wood swings open. There's a tall dark shape in the doorway, limned by the brightness of torchlight. For a moment, I hope it might be Jeryd, then realize that even if it is, he's done this to me. He's the enemy. If I could change, I'd claw his face off, but I can barely sit up without the dizziness and nausea hitting me like a professionally-wielded baseball bat.

The figure steps into the room, ducking its head to keep from hitting gnarled horns on the lintel. Horns. Not antlers like I first thought. Twisted things, like a sickly goat's. It's her. Andarra. The woman from the meadow. My throat tightens and my muscles tense.

"So, this is our dangerous intruder," she sneers. "A girl pup."

I hold my tongue, the memory of the faun's dark face as it choked on nothing playing over and over in my head.

"What do you here?" she demands.

I open my mouth to speak, and shut it again in confusion. Why is she asking me this? Doesn't she know already? Hasn't her precious son told her everything?

"Speak up," she snarls.

Maybe Jeryd was telling the truth. Maybe he's as

afraid of her as everyone else. Or maybe it's some sort of trick.

I weigh my options. Go with my gut. Save what I know in case I can use it later. "Who are you? Where am I?" I ask feebly, making my voice rasp even more than is warranted. "You, you have horns! I must be dreaming. Or delirious." I let out a sob. If I feign stupidity, maybe I can find a way out of this. Maybe she'll let me go. Send me home. A maybe isn't a lot to go on, but it's all I've got.

Her face is hard. The torchlight casts dark shadows across her cheeks and deepens the hollows of her eyes. It makes her even more frightening.

"Tell me, little shifter," she says, her voice brittle and icy, "how came you to the Silver Realm?"

"Realm?" I wipe my face with my grungy hands, hoping I look as pathetic as I feel. "Wait. How do you know what I am?" I make my eyes go wide. "And what are you?"

Her face grows pinched and narrow. "Those of your ilk do not blindly stumble through closed doors," she hisses. "Tell me how you came here." She raises her hand and I feel my throat tighten. "Who opened the door for you?"

"Everything is so hazy. I remember I was out jogging . . . in the woods . . . it was Tuesday night, no, Wednesday . . . I can't remember." I'm gasping for air, my hands suddenly at my throat, even though I know it will do no good. I can't breathe. Panic surges. I'm going to die. My eyes dart around the room, seeking rescue where there is none.

She drops her hand and I suck in air, as if I may never get a chance to take another breath. Which I may not.

"Try. Again." She enunciates the words like they're separate commands and, for a moment, I feel compelled to spill everything, every single detail, beginning with Bree and the book. But there's a clamor of warning in my head. Something tells me things will be worse for me if I give her the truth.

"It was Wednesday," I say in a panic. "I'm sure of it. I was jogging in the woods. Near the open meadow. I must have stumbled . . ."

She lets out a snarl of frustration. Her hand snaps up and my throat closes. Shadows swim in my vision, a kaleidoscope of sparkling color dancing on the edges. I can feel my eyes bulging and I know that if I could breathe right now, I would tell her everything down to the kiss inside the oak, but I can't even signal my willingness. My head wobbles on my neck and I feel myself slump over onto my side. For an instant, all I can think is how pretty the lights are, just before the world once more goes black.

CHAPTER TWENTY-TWO

I don't know how long I've been here. There's no way to measure time. The light that seeps in from below the door flickers like torchlight, and never changes, which tells me nothing. My throat is parched and sore from the horned woman's magic choke hold. And I feel feverish, like I'm coming down with something. I'm almost never sick, so it must be this place, or the collar. I reach up and tug at it again. Just a solid band. I let my hand fall away from it and see a curve of angry red marks on my wrist. The skin around them is tight and puffy, and my entire forearm is hot to the touch. It looks infected and is probably the reason I feel so bad. I try not to let out the sob that balloons inside me.

The cell has only the one door, which is solidly

locked from the outside. There's no way out. Even if I could change form, I'd still be trapped, but I need to get up, try to find a way—

There's a loud click and the door shudders open. A shadow fills the opening, a darkness against the flickering torchlight.

"You're awake." Jeryd steps inside, then turns and looks both ways like he's searching the hallway for something or someone. He closes the door, and comes farther into the room. "Are you all right?"

I scoot back on the pallet, pushing myself into the corner. "What do you care?"

"I care," he whispers.

"What do you want from me? Why did you bother with all that crap in the woods? Just to toy with me before turning me over to her? Like a cat plays with a mouse before it finally kills it?"

He's quiet for a moment. I can't see his face, but I can hear his shallow breath in the darkness. "I know what you think of me, but you're wrong."

"Then why am I here? Trapped." My hand reaches up and touches the band around my neck. "Collared."

He seems to shrink in on himself. "It's my fault you're here," he says, his voice low, like he's confessing a sin. "My fault the dark Vestige has gained power over a human. I just thought—"

"What? That you could lure a stupid girl—a stupid wolf—here. Like Bolgi said, I'm just some sort of twisted gift for your darling mother." My words come out with an ugly snarl. I can't believe I let him kiss me. That I liked it. That I kissed him back.

If I could bite off my own lips right now, I would.

"No," he says. "Never that. You need to believe me."

"You lied to me and you betrayed me. Why should I believe anything that comes out of your lying Fay mouth?"

"Because you're still alive," he says. "Because you have a chance to finish what you started. Because I need you to."

He shakes his head and that clump of hair falls across his eyes, making him look vulnerable.

Only, I've learned my lesson. Learned not to trust my emotions. "Screw you." My voice is low and threatening, my wolf showing through in a way it never has before. For some reason, it feels good.

Jeryd's shoulders slump and he looks as if he's genuinely sorry, and for a moment, I'm nearly taken in by his act. But then Andarra's toadies shove open the door. She stalks into the cell. Her eyes glint menacingly in the torchlight, and Jeryd swiftly turns and goes down on one knee, bowing low to her. "Mother," he says in a deferential tone, revealing his true colors.

I'd laugh if I weren't so terrified of her. I'm afraid of what I might do or say and once more I wonder why Jeryd hasn't told her how I got here. Did he purposely bring me here to deliver to her? Or was he just screwing with me and nearly got himself caught bringing the Outworlder into their precious Realm?

It doesn't really matter, I think. All that matters

is that I find a way to both stay alive and not tell this madwoman anything. I push myself back against the wall and pull my knees up to my chin. "I want to go home," I whine in my most pitiful voice. "Why can't I go home?" I work up some tears, too. Easy enough, because I really am terrified and feeling sorry for myself right now.

"Pathetic," Andarra grumbles petulantly. "Doesn't really have any sport in it, does it?"

Jeryd's head snaps up. "There might be," he says thoughtfully, "a way to get some sport out of her." He eyes me, looking me over, as if assessing everything about me.

I wrap my arms tighter around my knees and hug them closer.

"What are you suggesting?" she asks, her interest apparently piqued.

"I mean," Jeryd stands up and steps closer to her, "when was the last time you called up the Wild Hunt?"

Her lips twist into a salacious smile and she looks up toward the ceiling. "Ah," she intones wistfully, "the Wild Hunt has not risen this past hundred or more. Those were some of the happiest moments," she purrs, stroking her throat in a sensual manner. "I was the Hunter's beloved, then." She turns on him with a look of ire. "That was before your father." She spits the words out as if they're poison.

Jeryd drops back down to his knee, head bowed lower than before. "Your forgiveness," he says.

"I am not in a forgiving mood," she says with

vehemence. "Convince me why I should be. Especially when you speak of the Wild Hunt and bring these distant memories to my attention. Why make me think of your odious, deceitful father?"

Jeryd blanches. "I did not intend it, Lady-Mother. I only wished to suggest that perhaps, if there were some sport to be had, the Wild Hunt might ride again." He pauses, tilting his head to judge her reaction. "With you at its head, once more." His voice is a soft stroke of velvet against the skin. And I can see his words are having an effect on her. She is thoughtful. Then suddenly, without warning she is shouting to her troops, issuing orders. In a flash, I am grabbed, held tight, and bound hand and foot. I fight my captors and struggle against the bonds, but the knots are tight and unforgiving. The ropes cut into my skin. My hands and feet grow cold. My fingertips and toes begin to tingle. I bite my tongue to keep from whimpering or saying anything that might make things worse. Although, at this moment, I can't think of anything worse than this.

"My, my, this is your lucky day," Andarra purrs, stroking my cheek with her razor-sharp nails. "You'll be our honored guest for the first Hunt in many decades." She laughs as if she's just told an extremely funny joke, but once more, I don't get it.

Panicked, I look to Jeryd for some hint of what's going on. He looks away, refusing to meet my eyes.

"Take her to the hunting grounds and remove the collar. We'll want her in form." She turns her gaze on me. "You will be a welcome bit of sport," she says. "Much more diverting than questioning you to death." She's laughing again as she picks up her skirts and sweeps out of the cell. "And if you do not disappoint, I may deign to kill you swiftly."

Jeryd rises and turns to me, hesitating, as if about to say something.

"Come along, Jeryd," she orders over her shoulder. "You will attend me on the Hunt. You have much to learn and this is the perfect opportunity for a lesson." There's something threatening in the way she says it, an angry edge to her words that makes it clear this will not be pleasant. Not for me or Jeryd.

Jeryd stiffens. He gives me an odd look before leaving the cell, jerks his chin forward and tugs at his ear with his finger and thumb. Why is he so twitchy all of a sudden? I'm the one who's going to be hunted down by the Horned Lady and something called the Wild Hunt.

CHAPTER TWENTY-THREE

Two huge creatures—hobgoblins, I'd guess, by the warts and tusks and nasty smell I'm trying hard not to inhale, they certainly match the description I recall—dump me on the ground, grumbling between themselves. One pins me down, grabs me by the throat, and I think this is it. They've called off the Wild Hunt, or it was all a ruse to get me out here without a fight, and now I'm going to be strangled by a monster and left to rot in a dark part of Other. But then something snaps and the metal collar falls away from around my neck.

The other hobgoblin whips out a long knife and waves it in the air like a swashbuckler before slashing down at my feet. It slices clean through the rope bindings and the first one lets me sit up. I try to wiggle my poor numb toes, working the blood back into them. The knife-wielding creature swipes once more, swinging the blade across the ropes holding my hands tight. I try not to flinch, but this slash is not clean. I feel the sting of the blade and my left wrist begins to bleed.

I'm too preoccupied with the sharp ache in my hands, as the feeling flows back into them, to even growl at the clumsy monster. Besides, I should probably save my breath for what's to come. I move my hands and fingers, waking them and grimace at the pain.

The ugly hobgoblin with the knife waves it in my face and bares its crooked, broken teeth. "Change," it says in a nasal whine.

"Up yours," I tell it.

"Change. Now." The nasty thing huffs out a cloud of halitosis that could drop a bark-bull.

I'm still sitting there, when a horn blast sounds in the distance. The hobgoblins jump and begin to tremble. "The Wild Hunt comes." With a pig-like squeal one of the beasts turns and runs snuffling into the trees.

The one with the knife stands there for a moment, drooling and gnashing its broken teeth. Then it backs away, retreating into the forest. "The Wild Hunt comes," it growls. "Bleed well. You will be easy prey." Then it's gone.

A thunder of hooves echoes above the trees and I realize that if whatever is coming frightens the hobgoblins this much, I don't want to stick around to find out what it is. I rise to my feet, stumble and begin to run. This body isn't fast enough. I need to change, but if I'm caught mid-change, I'm doomed. Then I realize, I'm doomed if I'm caught in any form. But I don't have time to stop and concentrate on changing. Right now, I just need to get the hell out of the open. Panic seizes me. I can't help but think how much faster I would be on all fours.

The next thing I know, I'm changing in mid-flight. It happens so quickly, I almost miss the transition. One moment I'm in human form, the next I'm 100-percent wolf.

And running for my life.

CHAPTER TWENTY-FOUR

Pounding hooves echo behind me. My heart thunders inside me. Trumpets blare, and bellowing hounds scream for blood.

My blood.

I crash through the forest, tearing up the fecund earth, avoiding the oaks. Hoping the other trees aren't as communicative as the red oak Jeryd seems so fond of. Feels like I've been running for days. My breath comes in ragged gasps. My tongue lolls. Branches catch and scrape, clutching at my fur like vicious claws, but I know they're nothing compared to what chases me. The fell howling of beasts nearly freezes the blood inside my veins. If I wasn't already running, I'd be catatonic.

But I am running. Running and leaping. The way

seems too clear, like the trees are shifting to let me through. I feel like I'm being herded. Panic freezes my brain. The next instant, survival instinct has me scrabbling across fallen limbs and shoving my way through heavy undergrowth, trying to avoid following the path that seems to open before me. I bound over a tangle of fallen trees covered in thick vines and find myself tumbling down a steep embankment. The sound of roaring water rushes to meet me. I back-peddle. Try to stop before I reach the edge, but it's too late. My legs work, but there's nothing but air. Then icy water closes over me and I sink beneath the rapids. I struggle to right myself, to find the sky, but the crashing water tumbles me over and around. I've no idea which way is up. But the wolf continues to strain and thrash, panicked.

I'm out of air.

Then suddenly, I'm slammed into something hard. My last breath is knocked out of me. I suck in water. Choke. Scrabble against the hardness. Find purchase. Drag myself up and gulp in cold, crisp, beautiful air.

I'm back in human form, clinging to a log. Splashing down a swiftly flowing river. The sound of baying hellhounds and cold trumpets grows distant. I pant, though I'm no longer in form, trying to still my exploding heart.

My head throbs. My lungs burn. My hands and feet are stiff and cold. I'm covered in stinging slashes and cuts. Not to mention the bruises. My pummeled body feels black and blue. I'll be purple by tomorrow. The thought makes me laugh. My grip slips and I get dunked under water and come up sputtering. I grasp the log in a strangle hold and decide the idea of looking like a giant grape is no longer amusing.

I kick my legs, steer the flotsam to the far bank. I'm shivering in the freezing cold. I need to get out of the water before hypothermia sets in. Wouldn't Mr. Rajanni be proud to know I actually learned something in class last semester? It's getting harder to move, but I keep kicking, straining to angle across the current.

The log finally catches on something. I feel it jammed up hard, but I'm still yards from the riverbank. There must be a huge rock below the water. I kick and struggle, but the log won't move. With a growl of frustration, I shove myself away from my lifeboat and stroke with all my might toward shore. The current is still swift and I'm carried along at a rapid pace. It feels like I'm making no headway. But slowly, I find myself inching closer to land. My muscles begin to spasm and my right calf cramps so hard, I can't swim any more.

I thrash with my arms. Try to fight the cramping and feel myself sinking. The moon appears from behind a dark cloud, just before my face goes under. I stare at the disappearing orb, as I sink below the surface and my feet touch bottom.

I push off with my left leg. Bounce up above the surface. Breathe in and sink down again. I hop along like this until I can drag myself ashore. Crawl out of the water. Fall flat on the damp sandy bank.

I roll over and stare up at the moon.
My symbol. My curse. My light.

CHAPTER TWENTY-FIVE

I don't rest for long. Just enough time to rub the cramp out of my leg and catch my breath. I'm still shivering, but the night is warm and I'm alive. That's enough to keep me moving. I've escaped the Hunt for the moment, but all the stories I've read tell me I need to keep going. They'll pick up my trail again before long and I need to be as far away as possible by then.

The only problem is, I have no idea where I am or where I should go. I need to find a way out of Other, get back to my own time and place, but I have no idea how. The best I can do at the moment is to try and follow the moon's path and hope that my luck will hold.

Scudding clouds leap across the face of the

moon, blocking the light and casting weird shadows. Every breath is loud in my ears, every step a thundering crackle that makes me cringe. Expecting any moment to be tracked down, caught and killed, I try not to think about the things that would be worse than death. I know there are plenty, especially here, at the hands of Andarra, but I shoo them away, over and over. I need all my concentration to keep from making too much noise and continue moving in a straight line, rather than going in circles.

I'm still soaked and getting cold again, shivering in the dark as the night wears itself thin and morning begins its approach. Ahead of me, a thick stand of trees crowds together. Their leaves rustle in the wind, making a sound like whispering voices. My stomach tightens and I decide a detour is in order. No way am I marching into a stand of nosy trees, not when I know Jeryd may have friends among them.

I drop into a crouch and tuck myself between a large rock and some thick undergrowth. Hunched in the dark, I try not to shiver, keep my breathing as shallow and quiet as I can.

I wait for the clouds to pass in front of the moon again. Once the moonlight dims, I creep from my hiding place, sticking to the shadows like paste. It takes an agonizingly long time to get past the copse of whispering trees and once more I find myself wondering and worrying if they're alive like Jeryd's oak tree. Are they whispering about me? Can their voices travel across the open spaces to the next copse, the next stand of trees? And do they only talk to Jeryd, or will they gossip to any Fay creature in the realm?

I force myself not to think about it. What I need to do is concentrate on finding my way back to the glade where the door leads back to my world—back to my quiet, little town—and home. I'm beginning to think living in Fair Glen isn't so bad, after all.

The moon peeps out from behind the clouds and I duck behind a rock. Something glitters ahead of me. A tiny flash of light that's gone as quick as it appeared, but there's definitely something ahead. Something unnatural.

I peer into the darkness, searching for an open path to the right or the left, some way to go around the unnatural landscape. At the same time, my gut tells me I'm headed in the right direction, that I need to keep moving forward. I press myself against the stone, preparing to move again, but something makes me stop and turn. My hands slide along the stone's polished surface. It's smooth and flat, and hums with energy. I look up. It's tall with a jagged top. The remains of what was once a huge pillar of polished quartz. More broken pillars march away to the left and right. I can make out the remains of a fractured arch and what must have once been a soaring rooftop. I blink in the moonlight at what used to be monumental pillars, tall plinths, soaring lintels, now crushed and tumbled into ruin. And the broken bits and pieces glitter, reflecting the light of the star-filled sky.

I place both hands flat against the stone surface

and feel the resonance of energy humming against my palms. It surges and fades rhythmically, pulsing, like shallow breathing, or . . . a heartbeat. I jerk my hands away and step back. There's something creepy about the energy. Not evil, just not *right*. Like it's sick. Sick and struggling to stay . . . not alive exactly, but . . .

The moon reemerges from behind the clouds and the place brightens, reflecting shattered light from a thousand prisms.

In the center of the circle is what looks like a large altar stone. Only this doesn't feel to me like a place where blood sacrifices would be made. I don't know how I know it, but this feels more like it was once a place of illumination, of light. I take a breath and, as the clouds cover the moon again, step between the pillars and into the circle. Power rises up in flickering tendrils around me, fluttering like a tattered curtain in a strong breeze. The altar stone pulls at me, and before I realize it, I find myself slipping through the shadows toward it. It alone appears intact, a glass-like platform rising above piles of sparkling rubble.

Without warning, the crescent moon reappears, beams of light reaching down to glaze the center of the circle in creamy light that leaps back from the altar stone in fractured rays of glittering prismatic color. The altar stone isn't a stone at all. It's pure crystal. I step closer and feel the sadness wash over me. It isn't whole, after all. What was once a solid gleaming piece of dazzling crystal is now a cracked and broken puzzle of jagged shards. Something glints gold beneath the pile of glittering bits and I move closer. I kneel and peer through the slab of fractured crystal.

A long strip of metal and gems glints from inside. Jeweled eyes stare at me. A snake? The words of the riddle come back to me: *The sparkling hiss at evening's kiss. Forever clasp of jeweled asp* . . . It glimmers in the moonlight, begging me to reach for it. My hand moves, as if it has a mind of its own and slips through the stone. Pulsing heat thrums against my skin. My brain has trouble grasping what's happening, but my body continues to move, my hand reaching through what should be impenetrable stone. My fingers curl around the glistening item that seems not to belong in this heap of crystal bits and pieces.

When I pull my hand out, what's left of the huge pillars shudders. With a resounding crack, the last of the glittering plinths shift and crash to the ground, shattering into millions of tiny pieces that fly in all directions.

I fall back, shielding my face, hissing in pain as slivers of crystal pierce my skin, slice into my arms.

When the rumbling stops, and the rain of splintered fragments ends, I shake crystal shards from my face and hair. I hold the metallic snake up and peer at it in wonder. And it hits me. The ruins surrounding me must be the remains of the Crystal Palace, and the shiny serpent in my hand the 'trinket' I came all this way for. I've found it. Despite the fresh bite where the crystal shards have pierced my flesh, if I had the energy, I'd do a happy dance. Then again, I should probably be careful. There's no telling what sort of power this thing might hold.

It's small, not much bigger than a number two pencil. Emerald eyes shimmer in the fading light. I guess they're emeralds. They're green and multifaceted and shine as if the light is coming from inside them. The tiny stones along its back—diamonds and sapphires I think—make a zigzag pattern all the way to its tail. I lay it on the palm of my hand, stretching it out to its full length. It's so beautiful, it must be a bracelet, but I don't see a clasp. If it is jewelry, there must be one, probably something hidden on the underside.

I pick it up and dangle it by the tail, searching the underbelly for some kind of hook, but I can't find one. The eyes sparkle almost as if the thing is alive, turning the beautiful piece of jewelry into something creepy. Although, how much creepier could it get? I mean, if whatever has gotten hold of Bree wants it, it can't actually be good, can it? Then again, it's so pretty, I can't help but drape it over my wrist just to see how it will look on me, ignoring the sting as it slides over the fresh cuts. It feels cool against my skin, like a real reptile might. I hold out my arm to get a better look.

With a sudden movement, it snaps around my wrist, coiling tight, latching its teeth onto its own tail. I try to pull it off, but as much as I pinch and pull, I can't get the mouth to open. The metal tightens and begins to glow. My wrist itches like mad, but I can't scratch it, can't even move the bracelet or shift it. It's stuck in place, the body encircling my arm, the head and tail adhered to the inside of my wrist like someone stuck it there with super glue. Only super glue doesn't sting, does it? The itching grows hotter and starts to burn, like it's eating into my flesh. I want to scream, or howl, but I'm afraid I might alert the Wild Hunt and draw them to me. My jaw clenches and I grab my wrist with my other hand, try to pry the awful thing off, but it's no use. I can smell the skin on my wrist burning. I imagine it searing and smoke rising from the damned snake.

What if it doesn't stop? What if it burns to the bone? Or all the way through? The pain is so bad I think my hand is going to fall off. I wish it would. Oh, what the hell have I done? I should have stayed home. I should have told Bree no. Should have stayed away from Jeryd. Should have listened to my mom's lectures. Should have believed her.

My mom's going to freak out and then have an "I told you so" festival. Tears stream down my face. God, it hurts. I close my eyes and clench my jaw against the pain. The wolf wants to run from it and I nearly laugh. Too late, now. Running isn't an option. Nor would it help. Like the new age books say, wherever you go there you are, along with your cauterized wrist and appendage-severing bling.

The pain shifts, lessens, becomes a stinging buzz, like the vibrate setting on a cell phone, only sharper, more electric, and it's inside my skin. I force myself to look at my wrist. Shit! The snake bracelet is gone. Not gone exactly. More like so far embedded in my wrist that it looks like a tattoo. I gently run my fingertips along it. Holy crap, it is a tattoo! On the plus side, I have a really awesome, glittering, nobody makes body-ink colors that rich tattoo. On the minus side, it looks like I'm permanently stuck with it. Plus-plus side, my hand did not fall off. Minus-to-infinity side, my mom is going to kill me!

Once I know my hand isn't going to leave my body, I hurry away from the Crystal Palace before anything else decides to attach itself to me.

The rest of the journey back to the gate is a blur of running and hiding in the deep shadows. I'm not even sure how I found my way back, only that I'm standing just outside the meadow, beneath the tall trees. The normal world, as screwed up and not-really-very-normal as it is, is waiting and all I have to do is work some kind of Otherworld-Silver-Realm-magic-mojo to get there. The only barrier is figuring out how to open the door and get through to the other side.

I stand in the shadows waiting and watching. Wondering why there are no sentries guarding the doorway. Maybe it's because they know I can't get out. No, I tell myself. There has to be a way. If Jeryd can pass through the gate, then there must be a way for me to do it, too. Stars glisten between the scudding clouds, shimmering like the doorway that Jeryd brought me through, but the iridescent meadow sits quiet. And empty. I crouch down, turning my head this way and that. I squint my eyes shut. The light in the meadow reflects up from the faces of the glowing flowers, just like before, but no matter how I look at it, there is nothing to show me where the door is located. The meadow remains empty.

CHAPTER TWENTY-SIX

I slump against a white-barked tree, hoping it isn't one of the talkative ones, and try to think. I recall everything Papaw ever told me about this place, sorting through each lesson. I dredge my memory for every fairy tale and magical reference I have heard or read or seen in a movie or on television, but no matter how I wrack my brain, I cannot think of a way home. I let out a wry laugh, wishing I had ruby slippers.

Damn Jeryd!

Oh, hell. Of course! Jeryd.

He said that anyone who had been here before could use the door, all one had to do was know where the door was located and believe. I stand up and glance around the meadow once more, making certain I'm alone. Then I dash forward to stand in what I judge to be the exact spot I was standing in when Jeryd first brought me here. I close my eyes and make myself believe I'm standing in the field back home, back in my own world.

The tingling starts in my left wrist and for a moment I panic, thinking the serpent has decided to finish what it started at the crystal ruins and burn itself the rest of the way through my arm. But the tingling spreads out and becomes that electric zing I got when Jeryd held my hand here, when we came through the doorway. How many days ago was it?

I feel a chill roll over me. What if, instead of passing slowly outside the realm like Jeryd said it might, time passed by more quickly there while I was here in the Realm? What if my parents and friends are all old, or even dead? I shiver and open my eyes. The meadow is dark.

The meadow is dark! I'm back!

I quickstep out of the center of the open area, away from the magical doorway, afraid for a moment that I might fall or get sucked back through.

Overhead, the moonless sky looks the same as it did when I left, except that the stars have shifted. Is it possible I actually got back the same night I left? After what seemed like days in Other? No way of knowing until I get back to town, I suppose. My feet are moving before I finish the thought. No longer am I running for the joy of it, but for the fear of what might be waiting for me, and the desperate need to know what does.

* * *

When I get home, I find everything just the way I left it. I peer in through the window and, according to the clock on my nightstand, I've only been gone a few hours. What seemed like days has only been hours. That is, if this is still Thursday. I climb in through the window and hit the space bar on my computer. Bizarre. It really is still Thursday. Well, actually Friday morning, but who cares. It's the same night I left.

I strip off my filthy clothes. My brain is fuzzy and I know I need a shower, but I can't go take one in the middle of the night. Mom and Dad will know something's up. I glance longingly at my bed and my fluffy down pillow, their softness calling my name like a Siren's song, but I really need to at least wash my face and hands before I can let myself lie down.

I throw my robe on, then slip into the bathroom and let the water run while I stare at myself in the mirror. My hair is glommed to my head, my eyes red-rimmed and glassy. I'm sweating and shivering and look like I've been through, well, exactly what I've been through. Only I can't let my parents know. Part of me is elated that I survived—not to mention I managed to succeed in sneaking out of the house and back in again without my mom or dad knowing—but deep in my gut I feel bad. Not just the I've-just-done-something-wrong kind of bad, but the I-have-totally-betrayed-everything-my-parents-have-taught-me-mind-searing-guilt kind of bad. I look away from the mirror. I can just imagine my dad's disappointment.

Not to mention how pissed my mom will be. Not like she'd ever listen long enough for me to explain why I did all of this. Especially since I should have just told them about Bree in the first place.

But how could I? There's just too much they wouldn't understand. Too much I don't understand myself.

My hands are wrecked. I roll up my sleeves and look at my arms. I sure as hell can't go to school tomorrow, or rather today, looking like I do. A shower isn't going to miraculously make all these scratches, cuts and bruises go away. Nor, do I expect the new addition to my wrist to miraculously wash off.

Feeling dizzy, I lean over the sink and wash my face, rubbing the cleanser into my pores, trying to get the smell and feel of Other, of Jeryd, off me. The cold water seems to help clear my head. I end up scrubbing at my arms and legs with a damp washcloth until my skin is pink. All, except for the tender area on my wrist where the supernatural snake charm has magically taken up residence.

I stare at the bright colors, the sparkling eyes that look nearly alive. It really is beautiful, but Papaw is totally going to kill me when he sees it. Not only does he not believe in marking up a body—he has always been clear on that count—but I got this thing in the one place he warned me over and over to avoid at all costs.

Great. I've pretty much done everything possible to completely let down every single person who cares about me.

I throw on a t-shirt and sweat pants. Then search around my room for my favorite hoodie and slip it on. I pull the sleeves down over my hands and slide the hood up to cover my filthy hair. When I finally flop into bed, the clouds on the horizon are already turning a light pink and gold. I pull the covers over my head and scrunch down, curling myself into a tight ball. I think I may never sleep again after what I've been through, but then I feel myself drifting away and I let myself go.

The next thing I know, the alarm clock is screeching at me to wake up. I roll over with a groan and smack the off button so hard it sounds like I cracked the plastic case of the clock. I still have the covers pulled up over my head, but I'm shivering, as if it's a winter day and I had the windows open all night. Only, I didn't. I made sure of that. No way was someone sneaking into my room in the night and whisking me back to Other.

My body gives a mighty quake and I realize that I'm not only shivering, I'm sweating, too. Like I have the mother of all fevers. On the plus side, I now have the perfect excuse to stay home from school. On the minus side, I may have contracted some sort of alien Other virus. On the plus-plus side, I can stay in bed and sleep. On the minus-to-hell-and-back-side, since I almost never get sick, my mom is probably going to freak. At least I don't have

S. A. Skinner

to face Breanna and tell her about my charming new addition. *Yet*, I think as I begin to drift back to sleep.

I come awake with a start, realizing I can't fall sleep until after my mom goes to work. I don't want to be asleep if she comes in to check on me and have her somehow see the bruises and cuts on my hands and arms. My face survived relatively unscathed, aside from the dark hollows beneath my eyes, which could easily be attributed to being ill.

I hope.

When my mom finally knocks on my door to see why I'm not already up and dressed for school, I'm snapped out of a deep drowse. My head feels like it's filled with buzzing gnats and my body weighs a ton.

"Merissa," she calls from outside my door. "You're going to be late for school."

I try to answer her, but all that comes out of my mouth is a croaking sound. Ugh, if I didn't know better, I might think I'd been turned into a toad.

"Merissa? Is everything all right?" My mom opens the door a few inches and peers inside.

"No," I croak. "I'm sick." For a moment, I yearn for her to come over and sit on the edge of my bed and put her arms around me like she did when I was little, but I'm afraid if she does, she might notice something to give me away. Painfully, I slip myself deeper under the covers as she crosses the room, so that all that sticks out is the top of my head down to my eyes.

"You look awful." She reaches down and places

her hand on my forehead. "You've got a fever." Her voice carries a worry that I hope is normal-Mom concern and not Merissa-must-have-some-completely-abnormal-Other-freaking-illness worry. "I'll be right back," she tells me as she leaves the room.

I close my eyes and lick my lips. My tongue is covered in sandpaper and I feel like I've been crawling across the Sahara Desert for days. So thirsty. I reach for the glass on the nightstand, but it's bone dry, too. I drag my hand back under the covers at the sound of my mother's approaching footsteps.

She holds out the electronic thermometer and pushes the button, checking that the readout is zero. "Open your mouth," she says in a quiet voice.

I pull the blanket down to my chin and open my mouth for the thermometer. We both wait for the thing to beep. When it does, my mom takes it gently from under my tongue and checks the readout again. "One-oh-three," she says, relief clear in her voice. "Not as bad as I thought, but bad enough. Your father's gone on an out-of-state run." She frowns. "I'll call work and tell them I can't come in."

"No," I squawk. "It's okay. I'll be fine. You don't have to stay home." By the time I finish, my words are a raspy whisper.

My mother considers me for a moment, doubt clear on her face.

"I'm not a baby anymore, Mom," I say, knowing it could make her go either way, but hoping it will push her out the door. "I just need some water and some rest."

"Okay," she says finally. She sets the thermometer on the nightstand, picks up the empty glass from beside the bed. She returns with a full glass of water and reaches out to hand it to me, along with a couple of aspirin, but I shake my head. "I'm a little nauseated," I rasp. "I think I need to wait a few minutes."

She sets the glass and the pills down on the nightstand and scoots the plastic trashcan over beside the bed. "Just in case," she says. "Are you sure you don't want me to stay with you?"

I nod.

"All right, but call me if you start to feel any worse or if the fever gets higher and I'll come right home."

She starts to leave and stops at the door. "I'll be home to check on you at lunchtime," she says. "Just in case." She gives me a weak smile before she leaves.

I wait until I hear her car back out of the garage before reaching for the water. My hand shakes so hard the liquid splashes over the sides, but I manage to get it to my lips and chug the entire contents before I realize I haven't taken the aspirin. With a sigh, I swallow them dry, ignoring the bitter taste they leave in my throat as I drift into a deep sleep.

CHAPTER TWENTY-SEVEN

I reach out and try to push the heat away from my face, only slowly becoming aware that it's the late afternoon sun slanting in through the window. My tongue is thick and sticky and my mouth is a fiery desert, my throat a searing pit of lava. I fumble for the water glass and drink it dry, only afterward realizing my mom must have come home to check on me and filled it without waking me.

I drop back against the pillow and try to straighten the blankets. I've managed to kick most of them onto the floor while simultaneously entangling myself in the sheets, which are now damp with sweat. My hair is plastered to my forehead and my body is one giant ache. I hope it's just the flu and not some stupid disease I've contracted during my time in Other. I think back over the past few hours/days. I could easily have caught a cold or flu after being doused in freezing water and being chased across what seemed like the entire length of the Realm. Then there's my lovely new wrist ornament. Might that be causing me to feel this way? Or maybe whatever was in that nasty little goblin's bite that seemed to knock me for a loop is still in my system messing me up.

Or maybe kissing Jeryd gave me some kind of Fay mono. Ugh!

I roll over onto my side to go back to sleep and start awake at the thought of the Wild Hunt. A sudden chill washes over me and I'm no longer fever hot, but ice cold down to my toes. The clock says it's only 4:30, so my mom won't be home for another hour. I have time to get up and take a hot shower if I can heave my sore body out of bed.

I feel like an invalid, dragging my butt slowly up and across the room. I grab clean underwear and long-sleeved flannel PJs, slip my robe off the back of the door and head into the bathroom. The mirror tells me I look as bad as I feel. I have to sit on the toilet while the water gets hot for fear of falling over. Once the water warms, I climb in and sit in the tub letting the shower rain down over me. Scrubbing seems like the hardest thing I've ever done. My arms are like wet noodles, and my muscles ache, but the soap and hot water help to clear my head and wash away the ugly memories of where I've been.

By the time I get dried and into my clean PJs, I'm

so worn out I can barely make it back to bed. I consider trying to change the sheets, but I'm so exhausted the effort would be futile. Instead, I pull the covers back onto the bed and get my old comforter out of the closet and curl up in it on top of the blankets.

When I wake up the next time, it's to the sound of my mother murmuring my name. "Merissa?"

I groan and roll over to face the direction of her voice. My eyes are crusty and glued shut and it takes some blinking to get them open enough to squint at her.

"I brought you some broth and ginger-ale." She sets the soda can on the bedside table next to a coffee mug full of hot beefy broth. My nostrils flare at the scent and my stomach rumbles. It dawns on me that I can't remember how long ago I last ate. I pull my pajama sleeves down over my hands and push myself into a sitting position and hold still while a tsunami of dizziness crashes over me. It's all I can do not to fall out of bed, but I try to keep my mom from seeing that I'm doing twirlies inside my own head.

She stands by the bed, waiting patiently and it reminds me of the time I jumped off the tire swing and crashed into the side of Papaw's cabin. She sat by my bedside all day and night, reading out loud and talking to me to keep me from falling asleep because everyone was afraid I had a concussion. I don't really remember the book she read to me. Something of Papaw's about living in the woods, getting back to nature.

Mom puts her cool hand against my cheek and I suddenly want to tell her everything, confess to all that's happened, have her tell me it will all be okay. "Mom," I start. But her phone rings and I stop. "Thanks for the water . . . and stuff." Saved by the bell, I think as she heads out into the kitchen to answer her phone. I reach for the mug of broth and, forcing my hand not to shake, bring it up to my mouth and take a tiny sip.

By the time she gets back, I've downed all of the broth and most of the ginger-ale, and I'm curled up under the quilt, pretending to be asleep.

* * *

For the next two days, all I do is sleep and push myself to suck down every drop of liquid my mom brings me. Most of the scratches and smaller bruises are nearly gone, and the larger bruises are fading. Even the bite mark Bolgi left with his wicked sharp teeth seems to be healing. My left wrist—where the snake bracelet has taken up permanent residence—still itches like a healing scab, even though the skin feels soft and unblemished, aside from the slight raised area. But I manage to keep my sleeves pulled down and my skin covered. Not too easy when the fever keeps me constantly shifting from shivering to sweating.

In my short spans of full consciousness, I have time to worry about what Bree might be doing while I lie here in bed, but I'm in no position to do anything for anyone at the moment, so worry is all I can do and only for short bursts between bouts of dream-laden deep, drowning sleep.

On the fourth night since arriving home, my mom declares my fever broken. The way she says it makes me look twice at her. She looks worn out and older than I know she is. The relief that flows off her is almost tangible when she reads the thermometer and touches my cheek for what must be the fifth time in sixty seconds.

I expect her to announce that tomorrow will be a normal school day for me, but instead she tells me I should plan on staying home, whether I'm feeling better or not, and finish recuperating. I start to protest, but since I can still barely raise my head up off the pillow, I decide to listen to my mom, for a change. Besides, I'm still trying to figure out what I'm going to say to Bree about her evil little trinket and its new home. I'm pretty sure I wasn't supposed to end up permanently adopting it.

Dad is still on the road, but Mom has been coming home for lunch every day to make sure I'm okay and that I have plenty of hydrating fluids. It's actually been kind of nice to be fussed over. If it weren't for feeling like my body has been kicked and dragged up and down the length of a football field a few dozen times, I might actually be enjoying the attention. As it is, once I'm no longer freezing and frying, I have the urge to get my butt out of bed.

As soon as I can sit up, I ask my mom to bring me something to read. She hands me a stack of textbooks and papers. Apparently, one of my classmates came by to drop off our homework assignments. I ask who, but my mom doesn't know her name. Just that it's one of the girls in my grade.

Crapola! I hope Bree hasn't decided to do anything crazy. Although, if it was her, at least she must know I'm really sick and not just avoiding her. I open up my biology text and try to read the assigned chapters, but the words swim before my eyes and in a few short minutes, I give up and scrunch back down under the covers and fall asleep.

By Tuesday night, I'm practically back to normal and my mom declares Wednesday, official back-to-school day. I lie in bed and stare at my wrist, which no longer itches but still gleams with the brilliant colors of the gold and gem snake bracelet tattoo. I've tried hiding it with make-up, but it shows through the heaviest foundation. As pretty as it is, I'm going to need a long-term solution for keeping it hidden from my parents.

CHAPTER TWENTY-EIGHT

Bree is waiting for me outside school the next morning. Her face is flushed as if she too has a fever. "It's about time. Did you get it?" Her hands twitch like she's had way too many mochas. What is happening to her?

I nod. "I got it all right."

"Where is it? Give it to me." Bree sounds desperate. And something else, something underneath that. Fear. I can't help wondering if the fear belongs to whatever seems to have taken hold of her or if it's another layer of the real Bree showing itself.

"I have it," I tell her, "but it seems to be stuck where it is." I stick out my hand and pull up my sleeve, exposing the jewel-eyed snake. "If you want it, you'll have to figure out a way to get it off."

Bree grabs my arm and yanks it toward her, eyes bulging, fingers digging into my wrist.

"Ow!" I wonder if she's planning to rip my arm off in order to take ownership of the possessed piece of jewelry. "Preferably a way that doesn't involve tearing off any body parts." I pull back my arm, yanking it out of her grasp and rub at the red marks her nails have made on my skin.

"What the hell did you do?" she demands.

"I didn't do anything." Not entirely a lie. I only tried it on my wrist. "It just wrapped itself there and then burned its way into my arm. Which was not fun, by the way. Trust me. I wouldn't have done this to myself." Not that it's a bad looking tattoo. In fact, I kind of like the way it glitters against my skin, the colors so vibrant the gold even looks metallic and the jewels practically catch the sunlight like real ones.

Bree's face contorts with anger and her eyes dart around the schoolyard, like she's searching for something. Then her hand slips inside her bag and her face softens, becoming almost blank. "Not the end of the world," she mutters. "Changes things, yes, but nothing is incorruptible." She stops, looking up as if just realizing I'm still there. "Fine. We'll work around it."

She pulls out her notebook, opens it, and rips a page out and thrusts it at me. "Since you've gone and complicated things, there's another task you'll have to complete before we can move forward." Her voice sounds funny. Deep and thick, like she has a bad cold and there's something stuck in her throat.

"What the hell, Bree? We had a deal. I go get your precious thingamajig—which by the way you could have warned me was a living piece of perma-jewelry that would ultimately make me sicker than death at death's door—and you take your stupid love spell, or whatever it is, off Joey." I can't believe I kissed her, that I ever liked her at all. Probably some stupid spell she tried to put on me, like the one at the coffee shop.

"Funny. That's not the conversation I recall. In fact, I only asked you to do me a favor. I never said I'd do anything in return." She closes her notebook and tucks it back into her bag. "Some people just hear what they want to hear." She smirks. "Besides, you didn't really get that pretty little bauble for me, now did you? You kept it for yourself." Her face goes blank for a moment. Then, just like that, she's back again. "On the other hand, things might still work out," she purrs.

My anger rises and, with it, my wrist begins to tingle, as if the snake is writhing under my skin. I stare at my arm, but it looks normal. Except of course that there's a magical snake tattoo wrapped around it. The funny thing is that my surprise at the tingling has caused my anger to subside, and that in turn seems to have caused the tingling to stop. I don't have time to think it through, because Bree is still pushing the sheet of notebook paper at me.

"Tell you what," she says all sweet and friendly. "You do this for me, and I'll give you Joey." She blinks. "This time for reals."

"No." It sounds far too easy and I have to make sure I do this right. Apparently, dealing with Bree is as tricky as bargaining with fairies and . . . traitorous half-elves. "If I do this for you," I say pointing to the paper, "you will remove any spells from Joey Marsh and you will leave him alone from now on."

"Where's the fun in that?" she asks with a pout. "Wouldn't you rather I just give him to you?" Her eyes twinkle with evil mirth.

I knew there was a catch in the way she'd said it. Now I'm glad I thought this through. "What I want is exactly what I said. In exchange for me doing this last task, you will remove all spells, ensorcellments, compulsions or any other magical means from Joey Marsh. And you will leave him alone henceforth."

"Henceforth?" she laughs. "You're too funny."

I stare at her. Okay, so maybe the word choice was stupid. On the other hand, it makes sense to use archaic language when dealing with Others. Plus, bonus points for me for using my vocabulary. "That's the deal." I cross my arms.

"Okay, fine." She seems genuinely grumpy about it, so I think I may have worded things correctly, after all. At least, it sounds right and legally binding to me, in an Otherworld kind of way.

"I hope it's worth it." She shoves the paper at me again, a smile playing at the edge of her lips. "You must really like him." She shrugs, then runs her tongue over her lips. "Personally, I prefer a lot less tongue when kissing. And softer skin." She stares at my face, obviously hoping for a reaction. I feel my cheeks warm, but I'm not about to give her the satisfaction. Besides, I'm done with Joey Marsh, and soon I'll be done with her, too. So what do I care, right?

I take the paper between my finger and thumb, like it might be covered in poison. It's a hand-drawn map that looks like a tracing, and I wonder if it's something out of that creepy old book she's so attached to. Little rows of squares and exes march across the paper. Three odd symbols sit at the bottom of the page. One looks like a cross, but the arms are shaped like an infinity sign. The second is a circle with an eye in the center. And the third looks like a half circle with horns. In between the symbols are some numbers and lines, and to the right are what look like letters and an outline of what might be an eyedropper.

"What is this?"

"Directions." She leans forward. "You're going to need them."

"Not helpful," I tell her. "What do these little squares and exes mean?"

She looks at me like I'm an idiot. I probably am for agreeing to do anything else for her after what happened in Other. And with Jeryd. I can feel the heat rising up my neck and face and the stupid snake tattoo starts to tingle again. Crap. If that thing is going to act up every time I get a little emotional . . .

Not that it's Bree's fault what happened between Jeryd and me. It wasn't her idea to ask him for help. Although, I probably wouldn't have found my way into Other without him.

Or been caught. Or imprisoned. Or hunted like an animal, I remind myself.

"At least tell me where to start," I say, trying not to let my frustration get the better of me.

She rolls her eyes. "It's a cemetery," she says. "If I had to guess, I'd say it's the ancient one, outside the city limits next to the old church ruins. Just off the highway where that erroneous historical marker says it was the first church in the region and built by the town's founders. Wrong, of course. They just built their church over an existing sacred grove. Typical."

"Sacred to who?" I ask. Or should that be whom? I can never keep that straight.

"Don't you mean to whom?" she snickers, as if reading my mind. "I thought you were good at English."

"Whatever. Just answer the question."

She stands up. "Not part of the deal," she says.

I look back down at the map, wondering what ugliness is in store for me out at the old cemetery. "You need to give me a few days to get out there," I tell her, hoping to buy time, maybe find a way out of this mess.

"I don't think so." She shakes her head. "I'm not feeling very patient."

"I can't go before this weekend. My mom isn't going to let me go anywhere after school. Not after being so sick."

Her eyes narrow and I can almost see her

calculating in her head. "You have until Monday," she says. "After that I can't be held responsible for any . . . accidents."

I open my mouth to argue, but her jaw is set, eyes hard. "Fine."

She smiles, like she's won some kind of contest. "I have to admit this little town isn't as boring as I thought," she says. "In fact, it's gotten rather interesting."

Her words trail off and I'm suddenly wondering what she means. Then I look back at the drawing in my hand and the glitter of color peeking out from under my sleeve. Interesting isn't the word I would use.

CHAPTER TWENTY-NINE

The old landmark cemetery is three miles outside the town limits. I guess it's one of the main hangouts for the party crowd. Not that I've ever been invited—one of the negatives of being more or less invisible—but I've heard the whispers of juniors and seniors talking about meeting out at "the orchard" or "the rope swing" or "the old cemetery."

Saturday is chore day and my mom has plenty for me to do. You'd think she'd go lighter on me since I was so sick recently. But by the time she lets me off the hook, it's too late to head out, so it's Sunday before I get a chance to get away. Since I don't have a driver's license, and I sure can't ask my mom or dad to drop me off at some ancient historical marker, I have to resort to riding my old bicycle—another thing I'm not too graceful at. It's been forever since I rode the thing, so I have to pump up the tires first, which means a walk to the Bridge Station across town. It's early morning, and there's not a lot of traffic out, so at least I don't have to worry about that.

Good thing I brought along extra change. It takes me two quarters and a lot of air hose wrestling to inflate my bike tires to the proper pressure. Once that's done, I hop on and start peddling. The first few feet are pretty wobbly, but I get straightened out and hey, it's true what they say about riding a bike, you really don't forget. Of course, if you're no good at it to begin with, you sure don't get any better by not doing it. At least it's early enough that I don't have an audience.

About half way to the cemetery, I get a flat. Arrg. I should have just walked in the first place. Now, I'm stuck pushing this stupid lump of metal on the gravelly shoulder alongside the road. I'm tempted to just dump the bike in the bushes and walk the rest of the way, but if anything happens to it I'll get another one of Mom's fabulous lectures on responsibility.

It isn't that the darn bike is all that heavy for me, but it's awkward holding onto the handlebars and leaning across to push it. Plus, I'd forgotten the road to the old cemetery was uphill from town, which doesn't make it any easier.

I hear a car coming up behind me and I walk as far off the shoulder as possible, so I'm not in the lane. But, instead of just passing by, the car slows down.

"Hey!" The driver calls. "You need a lift somewhere?"

I'm about to say no when I turn my head and see that it's Volleyball girl. Kat. She's driving one of those mini-pick-up trucks. I hesitate, wondering what she'll think if I ask her for a ride to the cemetery. "That's okay," I tell her. "I'm just going up the road a little farther."

"Come on," she says, pulling ahead and driving the truck onto a small turnout. "Throw your bike in the back and get in."

A ride sure would make things easier. I suppose I can tell her I'm doing some sort of report for school. I push the bike over and set it in the back of the truck and get in.

She smells like soap and citrus—dark blue and mint green—and I stare at her dark hair.

"What?" she says suddenly, glancing in the rearview mirror. "I got something in my teeth?"

"No. No, you're fine." I look out the window so she can't see me blush.

"So, where are you headed?" She straightens the rearview mirror before pulling out onto the road.

"The old cemetery," I say, not wanting to tell one more lie.

"Really?

I don't know what to say, so I don't say anything.

"Not the happiest place on earth, but who am I to tell you where to spend your Sunday?" She glances at me then turns her full attention back to the road.

When we get to the cemetery road, she pulls over and shuts off the engine. The mile marker is obscured by tall weeds and the road is worn and rutted, but some of the old monuments are visible through the trees.

"Thanks for the ride." I hop out and unload my bike from the back of the pick-up.

"You sure you don't want me to take you back to town?" she asks. "It's going to be a long walk back pushing that flat."

"No thanks," I say. "I'll be fine." She shrugs and starts the engine, waving as she pulls away.

I stand there and watch her go, wondering for a moment where she's headed. Probably out doing something perfectly normal.

Unlike me.

It's suddenly chilly in the shade of the old walnut trees that line the highway.

Once her pickup is out of sight, I wheel my bike along the rutted road and lean it against the rusted gatepost. The graveyard is tumbled down. Brambles invade through the rusty fencing, grass and weeds obscure headstones. Whoever put up the state historical marker, apparently forgot all about it and never bothered to come back. No one has cared for this place in forever.

I stand just inside the gate and pull out Bree's map, surveying the ancient burial ground covered in wild growth mixed with decay. Trees and undergrowth have taken over the place and headstones tilt at wild angles. An angel with broken wings stares at me out of empty eye sockets and in a far corner a dark crypt yawns open-mouthed, its wrought iron door hanging crooked on rusty hinges. I read somewhere that places like this used to be considered memorial gardens and people would actually visit them and stroll between the headstones and even have picnics. But this place is creepy enough to play a starring role in some kind of horror film.

I try not to think about that as I unfold the map.

I turn the piece of paper around, trying to orient the marks with the scene before me, but with all the weeds and tumbled down markers, I can't quite get things lined up. Then I see it. The odd cross with the infinity sign for the crosspiece matches up with one on the wrought iron gate of the decrepit crypt. Great. A shiver runs up my spine and the back of my neck prickles.

I do not want to have to go inside that thing.

I scan the cemetery grounds, using the yawning crypt as a potential starting point, once more trying to align the map with the layout of the graveyard. There's a square on the map that appears larger than the rest. Maybe this is supposed to be the crypt.

I pace off the line of headstones, cross to the left of the crypt, and the last grave lines up exactly with the last square on the map. So, maybe the crypt is the starting point? But why couldn't Bree have just told me that? Stupid games! Or maybe she only knows so much. I rub my wrist. She didn't seem to know where the snake charm was hidden in Other. And she seemed completely surprised, not to mention pissed, that the damn thing decided to permanently embed itself in my arm.

I walk back over to the crypt and peer inside. It's dark and smells foul, like some kind of animal took up residence inside and then died. But whatever it was is so decayed, I can't even tell what it used to be. Holding my breath, I try to see inside. I really do not want to go in there.

Between the first two symbols on the map are the numbers 3E and 5N with a diagonal line between them. Without the letters, it sort of looks like the fraction number three-fifths. But that doesn't make any sense. I stare at the map for a while before it clicks. The highway runs north-south, so the cemetery gate faces east. I count three graves over and five back and end up standing in front of the broken-winged angel.

The hollowed-out eye sockets stare blindly out across the cemetery. Creepy, but at least I don't have to go inside that smelly crypt. I look at the map again. The next symbol, the circle with the eye in, it has me puzzled. The angel's eyes are empty. But this circle has an open eye drawn inside it. I move over beside the monument and look out over the cemetery, trying to see it from the blind angel's perspective, but there's nothing obvious. No eye-shaped markers or anything that remotely looks like something inside a circle.

Maybe I just don't have the right angle. If I can hoist myself up onto the pedestal beside the angel, maybe I'll have a better view. The pedestal is pretty high and the angel's robes cover most of it, so I have to leap up and grab on. My fingers catch at the broken wings, but the stone crumbles and I start to slip off. I have to grab for something else and I wrap my arms around the angel's head. When I try to adjust my perch, the fingers of my left hand slip into the angel's eye socket and I hear a grinding sound. The monument shudders and starts to move. The stone vibrates, rattling my teeth, and all I can do is hang on.

The statue rotates a full half-circle and stops. I wait till I'm certain the thing isn't going to start moving again. Then I reposition myself to look out over the graveyard. Cracked and broken grave markers, weeds, a couple of creepy monuments. Nothing that looks like the circle with the horns on top. Then I remember. The line after the eye symbol was an arrow. Pointing down. I look at the base of the angel monument and my heart sinks. There's a hole with steep steps heading down into darkness.

CHAPTER THIRTY

The stairs descend at a steep angle, heading deep into the earth, and my wolf side bristles at the confined space. I go slow, alert for any animals that may have made this their home, but there are no fresh scents, just stale air like you'd expect inside an ancient tomb. There doesn't seem to be anything down here. At least, nothing alive.

The whole place smells like it's been sitting undisturbed for eons, which makes no sense. The angel monument sealing up the entry can't be more than a few hundred years old, can it?

The little L.E.D. light on my house key isn't as bright as a flashlight, but it illuminates enough of the passageway that I can see at least a few steps in front of me. I'd have a better light source, if my parents would only spring for a cell phone . . . Although, I can't really argue with my mom when she asks who I'd call, anyway.

Stone crumbles beneath my feet and I stumble forward, losing my grip on the light. My hand scrapes on the cold wall when I reach out to keep from tumbling forward and breaking my neck. I have to get down on my hands and knees and feel around in the darkness for the keychain, and my only source of light down here. I promise myself that as soon as I have a few dollars, I'm going to buy a keychain with an actual little flashlight on it. My hands roam across crumbled stone and dust. A few steps down from where I stumbled, my fingers finally brush my house key. I grip the keychain and press the button to turn the light back on. It's so deathly quiet, I can hear the echoes of my breathing. The cold combined with the inhalations and exhalations bouncing back at me cause a shudder to run through my body. I don't know why I'm frightened. What could be down here?

Bad question. One I should probably not think about.

I continue my downward journey, deeper into the earth. The passage narrows and, although there is still plenty of room to move, the walls feel like they're closing in on me. The layer of earth overhead feels weighty, ponderous. It becomes more and more oppressive, the deeper underground I go. My breathing becomes labored, as if the air pressure has changed, the air becomes denser, even though that isn't scientifically possible. Is it?

The wolf is starting to fight me, hating the enclosed space, the lack of light and air.

I stop and look longingly back up at the tiny square of daylight high above. The sooner I get to the bottom of this thing and find the eyedropper or whatever it is, I tell myself, the sooner I can be back above ground. I force my feet forward, feeling my way as much as seeing the next step illuminated in the cold light from the tiny L.E.D.

After what seems an eternity, the stairs end and the passageway takes a sharp turn to the left. I take a last look up at the distant patch of sky above and behind me before turning the corner. The floor here is smoother than the stairs, like it's been worn down and polished by hundreds of years of footsteps and the ceiling slants upward, though the floor remains level. But even with the passage growing taller, the dark space above me opening up, it still feels oppressive. The walls here are smooth, polished. The lingering scent of incense and sweat clings to them, as if thousands of rituals have taken place down here. Whispers surround me, the echoes of chanting voices, repeating the same phrase over and over. But the words make no sense. They're in some foreign language, guttural and sing-songy at the same time. I try to ignore them. Pretend my brain is just toying with me.

My wrist itches and I'm tempted to go back, to get the hell out of this place. There's some kind of lingering energy down here, like the energy stored in a battery waiting to be released and I'm afraid what might happen if it is. But I picture Joey, that goofy look on his face, and he's stepping off the curb in front of an oncoming truck. Dammit! I shake myself out of the illusion. Beads of sweat form on my neck and forehead. I hurry forward, needing to get this over with so I can get the hell out of here.

The smooth passageway ends abruptly. There's no side passage. No door. Nothing. I press my hand against the wall in front of me and push, but it's no use. It's as solid and smooth as the side walls, except for a row of deep notches carved into the center of it.

I hold up the light and run my fingers inside the grooves. They're evenly spaced and sized, each one large enough for my balled-up fist to fit inside. Or— holding the light aloft, I look up—a person's hands and feet.

In the rock overhead, there's a metal grate covered in swirls and curlicues that turn into reptiles and snakes and dragon's heads. It looks thick and is probably heavy. Good thing I have the strength of someone more than twice my size and build. Too bad I'm not twice as tall.

It's awkward climbing the wall, using the stone notches and I have to stick the light in my mouth, pinched between my teeth, to keep it lit. When I'm high enough, I reach up and shove at one edge of the metal grille. It won't budge. Great. I shove harder, but there's something holding it in place. I feel around inside the decorative scroll work, reach between the bars and run my fingers along the inside edges, searching for a catch or some sort of mechanism, even a padlock I can try to pick—or more likely, break—but find nothing.

I drop back down and fish the map out of my jeans pocket and unfold it. I keep staring at the markings, but there's nothing on the paper that indicates how to open this grate or where the lock might be located. In fact, there's nothing on the stupid map to indicate there even is a grate.

I review the symbols on the map. The first one, the cross with the infinity sign, represented the crypt. The second one, the circle with the eye inside it, represented the lever inside the angel's eye that caused it to rotate. The third was the arrow that pointed down into this hole. So this fourth symbol, the one that looks like a circle with horns, must mean something. But what?

I shine the light overhead, running it along the ornate curls and swirls of the metal grate. Still nothing. I stare back at the map. Think, Merissa. Use that head of yours for something besides daydreaming about boys and girls and kissing . . . I look around the tunnel. The walls and floor and ceiling are polished smooth. Except for the layers of dust on the floor, the passageway is completely clear of debris. I turn and run my hands over the foot and handholds carved into the back wall. They're smooth too, almost polished, but it seems like I felt a rough patch when I was hanging on, like the top edge of the highest handhold was uneven. I climb back up, using one hand and shine the light inside. Maybe there's a lever, like the one inside the angel's eyes.

But there's nothing in the back of the cleft that's been carved into the wall. I get ready to jump down again and my fingers find that uneven spot again. It can't be a coincidence. All the other indents are perfectly smooth and polished. All but this one. I shine the light on the edge of the handhold and there it is. The half-moon shape that looks like horns, but instead of a circle at the bottom, there's a slot. A narrow slit carved into the polished rock. I push at it with my fingers, but it doesn't budge. This must be the keyhole.

I let the light go dark and using my fingers as a guide, try to slip the end of my house key into the slot, but it's too thick and it won't go in. What good is a keyhole if you haven't got a key? If it weren't for the fact that this whole place was so elaborately designed, I'd think Bree has sent me on one crazy-assed wild goose chase. I press my fingers against the slot again, feeling the shape and size of it. I wonder . . .

I slip my fingers into my pocket and pull out a quarter and drop it into the slot. It's a tight fit, and nothing happens. I sigh and reach to pull the coin back out, but my foot slips and I have to grab for a handhold. My fingers crush down on the edge of the quarter. It shoves deeper into the slot with a scraping noise, and a loud snick reverberates in the dead-end space.

As soon as I regain my footing, I reach up with one hand and give the grate a shove. It barely budges, but there's a creaking sound and chips of rust rain down on me. I cling onto the wall and shake my head, blinking my stinging eyes.

This time, I turn my head and keep my eyes closed, shoving against the grate without looking. It takes a couple of tries, but I finally hit the right spot. Something snaps and the grate groans open. I shake the grit and rust from my face before climbing high enough to stick my head up and peer over the edge.

It's pitch dark inside and just as silent as the underground passage. I have to let go of my handhold on the wall in order to hold the light up over my head and see around. The space is so small the open grille leans against one wall.

I start to stick the light back in my mouth so I can hoist myself up and climb inside. My wolf wants to howl and, once more, I have to fight the urge to run back up and out into the world. That's what it feels like in here. Like the world is outside and this place is separate. Not separate like a tomb, but apart from it in the same way that Other is. I can't quite bring myself to call it the Realm, anymore. Silver or not. It's too pretty a name for such a dark, messed-up place. Papaw brought me up calling it Other and that's what it is to me.

Anyway, I push down the claustrophobic fear that's choking me, grab hold of the edges and pull myself up to sit inside the hole with my feet dangling. It doesn't take any time at all to scan the space and see there's nothing there. The room is so small my head nearly touches the top. It's not polished stone, like the passageway, but roughhewn rock and dirt, like an afterthought that was never completed. I let out my breath in exasperation. I can't believe Bree could send me on a useless errand like this, that I came all this way for nothing! Grrrr. She's probably just toying with me, dangling Joey's freedom in front of me like a carrot, just so she can pull it back again.

I'm just about to leap down when the light glances off something pale in the dirt. Something that looks more like fabric than soil. At first, I think it's just a pile of rotten rags, but I lean forward and blow the dirt away. There's something there. With tentative fingers, I brush away the rest of the debris. An oblong bundle of rotted cloth lies resting in the dirt.

I hold my breath and pick it up. It's heavier than I expect. I stick the light back in my mouth and unwrap the bundle, unrolling the scraps of what's left of the cloth to reveal a knife in a leather scabbard. The leather is rotted through in places and I can see the glint of metal beneath. Slowly, I draw the blade out. It's shiny, polished, like new. The hilt is carved from some kind of bone, covered with strange letters and designs. It looks like something that should be on display in a collectibles store. Or a museum.

There's a low humming sound coming from somewhere. Suddenly, the snake tattoo on my wrist starts to squirm. The thrumming seems to be coming from everywhere all around me, and then it's inside me, filling my chest, rumbling my insides. My jaw aches, like it does when my teeth are beginning to morph. A growl rises in my throat

261

and along with it the urge to bite something. Not just bite, but rip and tear. I shove the blade back into the sheath and drop to the ground. The entire passage vibrates, echoing the sound. Dirt falls out of the opening above, raining down on my head. I run back up the passageway. The polished floor and walls are slippery and I can hardly get any traction. I feel like I'm in one of those cartoon nightmare scenes where the character is running, but the hallway keeps stretching longer and longer. It feels like eons before I reach the corner and skid into the wall, unable to make the turn because I'm running so fast. There's a huge sound behind me and a cloud of dirt begins to chase me, so I speed up, stumble, and chomp down on the light. It breaks against my teeth and I have to grab at my house key before I lose the entire keychain.

The humming has turned to a full-on rumble and the square of daylight looks like it's jiggling on the end of a wire. I can hear the crack of stone and the tumble of rock. My wolf is ready to tear the throat out of the mountain as I take the stairs two at a time. No thought for clumsiness. No thought for anything. Except escape.

The angel teeters at the top of the stairs. I put on a final spurt of speed and dash up and out of the entryway, stumbling forward onto my hands and knees as the monument crashes down. The angel's head scrapes across my back and what's left of her wings shear off in marble chunks as she dives into the hole. I cover my head with my arms, as an explosion of debris rains down on me.

CHAPTER THIRTY-ONE

The flat tire makes a whispery sound against the pavement as I wheel my worthless mode of transportation along the highway shoulder. I should probably be happy to be alive, but I'm mostly angry. Angry and sore. I wasn't fully healed from my lovely adventure in Other and now I'm going to have bruises on top of my bruises and my scraped-up hands and knees are raw and painful. I'm covered in dust and dirt and I've ruined yet another pair of jeans. Not to mention the huge hole I've torn in my good running shoes.

Of course, all of that is nothing compared to what I'd like to do to Bree for getting me into this mess.

Admittedly, I wanted something to happen to ease the boredom of living in a small town, but this is so not what I had in mind.

I suddenly wonder what made Bree's grandmother move here. I suppose it could be coincidence, but my gut isn't buying it. Doesn't matter, anyway. It's obvious now there must be a lot more Others out there then I ever dreamed.

It dawns on me that we aren't living in this town for no reason. I mean, I know my parents are actually hiding me here, but what made them choose a small town, and why this one? It seems like it would be easier to hide in a big city, blend in with all the other odd people, especially the ones like Bree. And me.

I could understand it if we lived closer to Papaw, but there are a ton of cities and towns closer to him than we are. And it isn't like he ever comes down here to visit. It just doesn't make any sense.

I've only been up to his cabin twice. The first time, when I was about seven, was like walking into a magical place, like a storybook fairyland or something. It was greener than anyplace I'd ever been, and not just the kind of green you can see, but the kind you can smell and feel, the kind that unfurls like a fern inside your head and fills it up with damp and earth and feathers and fur. I wanted to stay there forever, and I cried when we had to leave.

The second time, just after I turned thirteen, we spent a whole month there. It was the month of the first full moon after I hit puberty, and it was the most amazing and horrible month of my life. The moon seemed to take total control of me, and Mom was so afraid they'd lose me to the wolf, she never left my side for an instant. That's when my hair changed color, streaks of red and silver mixing with the brown, and the full moon called me for days and days before and after it actually appeared as a perfectly round disk.

Now, every time I ask to visit Papaw, Mom tells me that I'm safer at home. At least until I'm older and more in control. Her words, not mine. But sometimes, when the morning is fresh and the air fills with ripeness and new growth, my feet want to drag me north and east, up to those mountains where the colors and smells wash against you like cool silks and warm velvets—and I want to claw my way out of my own skin, and it's all I can do not to howl.

So, I think I get what she means, even though I really don't want to. Mostly, because I hate it when my mom is right, which is way too much of the time.

I drag my bike off the road into the shade of a huge walnut tree and lean it up against the sturdy trunk. My mouth is parched and tastes like graveyard dust. I should have brought water. I laugh out loud at the thought. Right. Along with a flashlight, a spare tire, a bicycle pump and a first aid kit. I pull the knife out from where I've tucked it into the waistband of my jeans and sit cross-legged in the grass.

My fingers trace the designs on the hilt, itching to pull it out of the sheath and try the blade on something, but I resist the urge. I can't prove that unsheathing the knife is what caused the tunnel to collapse, but I'd be willing to bet my college fund on it.

Tires hum along the pavement, from around the bend. I slip the knife behind my back as a pick-up truck passes me. The driver stops and begins backing up. It takes me a second to realize it's Kat. She must be on her way back to town from wherever it is she went.

She looks out the driver side window and her eyes get big. "Holy crap. What were you doing out there? Robbing graves?"

How does she know? I start to freak. "N-no," I stutter.

"Calm down," she tells me. "I was just joking. You'd think you actually were by the look on your face." She leans out the window. "But you definitely got trashed out there, whatever it was you were doing." Her smile fades and a look of concern flashes across her face. "You feeling okay?"

"Yeah. Fine." I wave her off. "I just, um, hit a rock on my bike and fell."

"Not a good idea to try riding on a flat tire." She shuts off the engine and gets out of the truck. Reaching behind the seat, she pulls out a small blue box with a red cross on it.

I realize it's a first aid kit and I almost laugh. "You don't happen to have a spare tire and a bicycle pump on you?"

"No such luck." One side of her mouth quirks up in a half smile. "But I can stop that bleeding for you."

"Bleeding?" I look down at myself and something

drips into my lap. I reach up, touch my fingers to my forehead, and they come away red and sticky. "Oh," I say.

Her eyes narrow. "You mean you didn't notice?" She drops to one knee in front of me and holds up her hand, three fingers extended. "How many fingers am I holding up?"

"Wow." This time I do laugh. "I didn't know people ever really said that."

"Yeah," she says, all serious. "They really do, and for good reason. How many?"

"Three," I say. "I'm fine. Honest."

She holds one finger up.

"One," I say.

She rolls her eyes. "I don't want you to count it. Just look at it and follow it with your eyes, but don't turn your head."

I do what she says and she nods. "You seem all right, but I'm giving you a ride back to town as soon as I dress this cut. And then you should have your parents take you to the doctor to get checked out. Just to be sure."

I start to argue, but shut my mouth and nod.

She opens the first aid kit and puts on a pair of thin rubber gloves before tearing open some gauze pads. She squirts something that reeks of strong medicine on the pads, then pushes aside my bangs. I try not to wince as she dabs at the cut on my forehead. Then she tapes a bandage over the cut and finishes cleaning the blood off my face.

"There." She closes up the first aid kit and pulls off the gloves, turning them inside out and rolling all the trash up inside them in a practiced motion. Her skilled bedside manner makes me smile.

"What?" she asks, her eyes narrowing.

"Nothing," I say. "It just looks like I'm not your first patient, Doc."

"I get to practice all the time on my little brother, Devon." She laughs. "Luckily, his injuries are never life-threatening." She stuffs the first-aid kit behind her seat, then comes back, grabs my bike and pushes it over to the truck.

While her back is turned, I reach behind me to make sure the knife is tucked safely into my waistband and pull my shirt down over it. "Wait a minute," I say. "I can help you with that."

"Nope," she says. "I got it. Doctor's orders." She opens the tailgate and hefts the bike into the back of the truck, slamming the tailgate shut.

Kat chats about her little brother the whole way back to town, only stopping now and then to ask me my name and what the date is. I answer dutifully, leaning awkwardly in the seat to keep the knife from digging into my back.

She lets me out in front of my house and gets my bike out of the bed of the truck. She pushes the bike back over to me, but before she lets go of the handlebars she leans forward to look into my eyes. "Are you sure you're feeling okay?"

"Of course." I shrug. "Why wouldn't I be?"

"The way you were sitting in the truck, looked like you might have messed up something in your back." She purses her lips together. "Plus . . ." She hesitates. "There's something different about you.

Something about your eyes. Only it doesn't look like any medical thing I know of. You really should have your parents take you to see a doctor."

"Okay, sure." I grip the handlebars of the bicycle and gently pull it toward me. "I'll go in and tell them what you said." *Yeah, right*, I think. As if I were stupid enough to tell my mom that, after being sick for a week, I went romping out to the old cemetery and dropped a gigantic tombstone on my own head.

Kat raises an eyebrow, but she lets go of the bike and I back up a few steps, not wanting to turn around in case the knife is visible. "Thanks again, Doc," I say. "For the ride, and the first aid." I give her a smile and watch her get back into the driver's seat and pull away.

CHAPTER THIRTY-TWO

Back when I was a kid, it bugged me that my parents worked such odd schedules and that my dad was away so much, but I've gotten pretty used to it and right now it's actually a relief when I open the garage door and see that the car isn't there. I lean my bike against the wall and hit the button to drop the door back down before digging in my pocket for my house key. Dad used to tease Mom about all the extra door locks, but now he just lets it go. I guess after hearing about "safety first" and "cautious isn't the same as paranoid" a bazillion times, he decided to roll with it. Although, he drew the line at getting an alarm system. "Beauty of small town life," he likes to say, but I think it has more to do with money.

I go into the bathroom and wash my hands.

Then, I gently pull away the tape and gauze that's now tinged reddish-brown with dried blood and stare at my forehead in the bathroom mirror. There's a jagged cut on my forehead and a small lump has formed under it, but it isn't bleeding anymore. Lucky for me, that means no stitches. Added bonus, I can pretty much cover the cut with my bangs, if I brush them just right. A touch of Mom's foundation on the skin that's starting to bruise, and I might just get away without saying anything. On the other hand—no pun intended— my palms are a mess of scrapes and cuts. I wash them off again with warm soapy water and squirt some antiseptic on them before patting them dry.

By the time my mom gets home that afternoon, I've showered, cleaned up and buried my torn jeans in the bottom of my closet. I had to stash the knife under my bed when she pulled into the driveway and the garage door opener whirred to life. I know I should make some excuse to get out of the house for a while, so I can deliver the blade to Bree, but my mind is still whirling from the whole secret-underground-tunnel-cave-in experience, and for some reason, I don't want to let go of the knife just yet.

Dad's home for dinner tonight. The big semi-truck and trailer parked along the street takes up the entire space in front of our house and most of the neighbor's. He's on an offload trip, so I guess the truck is empty. Normally, it would be cool to have him here, but tonight all I want to do is get back to my room and get on the Internet to see if I can find out anything about the knife that's tucked under my bed. I'd say I have homework, but I already told my mom I did it last night.

"How's school?" Dad asks, buttering a slice of whole grain bread. "You all caught up from being sick?" It's a harmless question, but there's an unusual tension in his voice.

"Fine. Absolutely." I reach for my glass, forgetting to keep my palms covered and wince when my mom grabs my wrist.

"Merissa! What happened to your hands?"

"Ow, Mom." I pull my hand back, trying to give myself time to think. "It's no big deal, I just, I got a flat tire on my bike and . . . you know . . . It's fine. I'm fine."

"And I suppose your head's fine, too?"

I jerk away as she pushes back my bangs to get a look at the cut on my forehead. I hope the make-up and the bandage I put over it, are doing their job, but I brush my hair back into place just in case.

"Why didn't you say something?"

"I didn't want you to worry again, after my being sick and all." It sounds lame even to me.

"Merissa, it's our job to worry about you." Dad reaches across the table to pat my arm.

Great. Just great. Like I couldn't feel any lousier for lying. A part of me wants to spill, tell them everything, but I just can't. They can't fix this for me. This isn't a little boo-boo they can kiss and make better. This is something I have to take care of myself.

After I finish my after-dinner chores, I end up

sitting out in the living room, listening to Dad talk about his most recent road trip. The story involves a cow and I think he says something about a circus truck. Usually I love my dad's road stories, but nothing seems funny tonight. I finally tell them I want to get a start on some research for an upcoming school project. Dad gives me a funny look, but he doesn't say anything as I escape down the hall to my room.

* * *

I've stacked a pile of books on the edge of the desk nearest the door, just in case Mom decides to peek in on me. These days, she usually knocks, but I'm not taking any chances.

Not with this.

Beside the books, the knife blade glimmers in the light from my desk lamp. Curving between the odd symbols, two snakes curl around the hilt, biting their own tails. I run my finger along the tattoo on my wrist, wondering how these two things might be connected. Then, questioning if I really want to know.

I tap in a description of the symbols on the knife hilt and hit enter. My web search isn't helpful. I come up with a lot of old pagan images, but wading through them takes forever. No matches, but apparently, reptiles and well-endowed naked women were all the rage a few thousand years ago. Other than that, the odd swirls and snakes with bird-like heads and beaks don't seem to connect to anything. The closest I get is the Mayan Quetzalcoatl that's supposed to be a feathered serpent god, but it just looks like a blocky snake to me.

I have no more ideas about this thing than I do about the awesome new tattoo that's attached itself to me. I push up my sleeve and turn over my hand. The snake that's clamped itself there has a kind of beak-shaped mouth. But otherwise, I don't really see any similarities, until I flip my hand back over and look at the back of my wrist. The swirling pattern on its back, the one made out of jewel tones, is the same as the pattern on the knife, only reversed, like it would be in a mirror. The only thing that doesn't match is that the snake on the knife has a bird's head.

There's a light tapping at my door and my mother's voice from the hallway. "Don't forget, it's a school night."

"Okay," I call, covering the tattoo up with the leather wristband leftover from an old Halloween costume. I go to switch off my computer and catch a glimpse of a shadow outside my window. I push a book on top of the knife and jump up, but when I get to the window, there's nothing there. Must be my brain playing tricks on me. I reach up and touch the small beige bandage beneath my bangs. The tender lump on my forehead feels as big as an egg.

I stare out the window for a few minutes, thinking about all the weirdness that's happening. Bree. The book. Jeryd. The thought of them sends a war of emotions running through me. His touch. Her lips. His betrayal. Her games. It's all too much and I want to scream and howl and run out into the wild. There's a sudden burning in my wrist and I grab it with my other hand and let go just as suddenly. Beneath the wristband, the tattoo stings. The snake writhes beneath my skin, as if it's trying to break free. I realize that, without intending to, I was about to change, to go wolf, with no full moon to force the urge on me. What is happening to me?

The tattoo calms, but a dull ache settles into my wrist. It's as if the snake acted like some kind of buzz collar, only there's no one monitoring it, no one with a remote pushing the button to bring me back to my senses.

I shiver, even though it isn't cold, and go into the bathroom to wash my face. In the bright light from the round bulbs over the medicine cabinet, I stare at my reflection. My eyes look glassy, like they've been locked on a computer screen for too long, or like I've been up all night reading.

That's it. I'm giving Bree her stupid knife tomorrow, and she can take her compulsion or her spell or whatever it is off Joey Marsh. And then I'm out. I don't want anything more to do with all of this. I think I liked things better before I knew so much about witches and Other and all of it. My parents were right, it's better to just keep quiet and maintain a low profile.

I go back into my room and stop dead. The window is open and the books that were piled on my desk have tumbled over, two of them lying on the carpet. The one that was covering the knife is now on my computer keyboard.

The knife is gone.

CHAPTER THIRTY-THREE

I rush across the room and stare out the open window. It was locked. I know it was locked. Mom is such a security freak she'd have a total nuclear meltdown if I ever left it unlocked.

I slide the window closed and shove latch into place with more force than necessary. It locks with a loud snick. Then I search the desk and the pile of books. I know it's fruitless, but a part of me can't believe the knife is gone. I risked my life for that thing. And I need it! I need it to get myself out of Bree's stupid games, to get Joey away from her. If it weren't for me, Bree never would have latched onto Joey to try and use him. Even if he is a coward and a poor excuse for a boyfriend, not to mention total fake—bad boy my ass—it isn't his fault Bree decided to use him against me. And no one deserves to get used like that. I remember Bree trying to get inside my head at the coffee shop and I get angry all over again.

But being angry isn't going to get the knife back. I need to use my head. No. I need to calm down and use my brain and my nose. The scent is so barely there, I guess I thought it had been on the clothes I'd crammed into the bottom of my hamper, but this is fresher, newer. The smell of Other, the elusive musk of flowers and decay—like spring and fall clashing with a hint of burnt blood—is unmistakable. I remember the movement I saw outside the window, the flash of shadow and light.

Jeryd.

For an instant, I inhale his scent and remember the feel of him near me, his lips on mine. What the hell made me think about that? He's a total bastard! I should hate him. I DO hate him. Suddenly, I want to rage, to tear around the room, pound the walls, scream. But I don't do any of those things.

Instead, I sit on the edge of my bed and try not to cry and wonder why it is that everyone I like turns out to be such an asshole. Are all boys jerks? Is this Bree's actual personality showing now and I just didn't see it before? Or is there something terribly wrong with me?

My face is wet. I'm losing the battle with my emotions. I want to curl into a ball and hide under the covers. But that's not going to do me any good. Not to mention that my anger is starting to win out over all my other emotions. Now, I understand why revenge is such a popular theme in books and movies.

Mom and Dad finally shut off the television. The light touch of Mom's hand against my door as she glides down the hall both reassures me and dishes up another heaping serving of guilt. A part of me longs to call out to her, ask for her help. But I can't do it. It isn't just that I can't bring myself to admit to not telling her what has been going on, the stories I've told about where I've been going and what I've been doing, and the sneaking out. No. This is my problem. I got myself into this mess, and I'm going to get myself out of it.

I shut off my bedroom light and wait, listening in the quiet of the night for my parents' murmured conversation to die away and Mom's steady breathing, and Dad's snores, to settle into the slow regular cadence of deep sleep. In the distance, a dog barks and the breeze outside brushes the tree leaves against one another in a white noise of shushing sounds that would normally lull me to sleep. But not tonight. Tonight, I'm wide awake, abuzz with a trifecta of anger, guilt and worry. The perfect storm for insomnia. And for ensuring I don't fall asleep before doing what I have to.

* * *

The meadow is empty. Just like the first time I met Jeryd here. But now, instead of pale wildflowers, the glen is wild. Berry brambles grow at the edges, clumps of ripening fruit filling the air with sweetness that fails to cover the now familiar scent of Other that clings to the meadow. That spring to summer mash-up of dead dry leaves and decay mixed with green buds, flowers and fresh turned earth. I stand on the edge of the meadow, searching the open area for a shimmer or any other hint of the gateway. Am I really planning to do this? What if I do manage to get back in? If I get caught, will I survive to escape a second time?

I can't stand here worrying about it. I need to do this, need to stop the forward momentum of events before I, along with everyone I care about, tumble into the abyss opening before me.

I take a tentative step forward, and catch it before I see or hear him, Jeryd's elusive but unmistakable scent. I step back into the deep shadows and prick up my ears. Needlessly, it turns out. Jeryd walks across the clearing, directly toward me.

He stops just a few yards away and stares into the shadows, exactly where I'm standing. "Wolves aren't the only ones with exceptional eyesight."

Smug jerk! After all I've been through, I'm way too tired to put up with this crap. I take a step forward and bare my teeth. "What the hell are you doing here?"

"Waiting for you." He holds up the knife. It glints in the starlight.

"I'm surprised you haven't already run back to Other and handed the blade over to your precious mommy."

"It's not like that." His gravelly whisper sends velvet shivers along my skin. His full lips turn down in a frown and I feel a catch in my throat. WTF?! He's a liar and a fake and my stupid chest hurts just seeing him. Am I nuts? Clearly, all that stuff they told us about in Sex-Ed is true. Or maybe—I clench my fists—he's trying to pull some of that Other mojo on me like Bree did outside the coffee shop. Well, screw that!

"I had to find a way to get you to talk with me and I knew you'd never agree to meet me without . . . Taking the blade seemed the best way," he says.

"Right," I sneer. "You took the knife from my room just to lure me out here into the woods to have a conversation."

"It's true."

"Liar! Why would I believe anything you say? You betrayed me." My words are harsh, even though my voice is quiet. A look of pain spreads across his face, but I know better. The anger wells up inside me, shoves all my other emotions aside. My wrist starts to tingle, but I ignore it. "You tricked me into trusting you, into liking you." Fury shakes me. I want to wipe the memory of his kisses from my lips, erase the feel of his warmth. "But I won't be fooled again."

"How can I make you believe me?" he asks.

I need that knife, need to finish what I started, need this to all be over. I weigh my options. Measure the distance between us. Calculate the amount of time it might take me to change, and wonder if my wolf could take him in a fight. Not likely. Instead, I say, "Give me the knife."

"Not until you hear me out. Let me explain."

"There's nothing you can say that will ever make me trust you again, so why bother?" The words come hurling out of my mouth. "If all you took it for was to get me to talk to you, mission accomplished. Now, give it back."

He holds the knife up and examines it, like he's considering it for the first time. "Do you even know what this is?" he asks. "Why she wants it?" He looks at me, his gaze burning across the space between us.

"I don't really give a rat's ass," I tell him, crossing my arms.

"You might," he growls, "if you knew anything about the world around you. If you cared about anything that happens more than three feet outside your own ego."

"Wow. That's funny." I laugh. "*You're* accusing *me* of being self-centered?"

"Open your eyes, Merissa. Do you not see the things that are happening? Can you not feel the darkness that is rising up? You may think you're human, that none of this affects you, or your parents, but what is coming won't care if you're shifter or Fay or human or witch. And the humans in this town, they'll be the first to succumb."

"I don't know what you're talking about. And I don't care."

"You might," his voice drops to a dark whisper, "if you knew what he plans to do."

"He, who?"

He looks back down at the knife. Cradles it in his hand, like it's alive. "It wants blood. You know. You held it. You must have felt the hunger."

I shudder, recalling the urge to morph and attack something when I first held the unsheathed blade. The compulsion to change. The desire to be the animal and nothing more. "You're just trying to scare me." I curl my upper lip. "And it's not working." But I'm worried and I'm wondering how he knows. Even if he'd managed to follow me into that tunnel without my knowing, there's no way he could know how I felt.

He unsheathes the knife and runs a finger down the blade. Something dark drips from his hand onto the ground. I smell blood. Jeryd's blood. The heady earth and fire of his essence. I can sense the way the enchanted ground soaks it up, as if it's returning home.

Jeryd is watching me, like he's waiting for a reaction. But all I do is shrug. "So what is that supposed to prove?"

His eyes narrow and he tilts his head to the side, like he's trying to see me from a different angle.

"It's not that I haven't had the urge to rip you a new one after what you did," I tell him. "But what would be the point? Besides," I growl, "as much as you seem to think otherwise, I'm not that kind of girl."

He opens his mouth in surprise, as if something has suddenly dawned on him. "You have it! You've got it on you!"

He comes closer and I step back without thinking and bump into a tree. "I don't know what you mean." But even I can hear the lie.

"I wasn't sure," he says, his voice full of awe. "I only hoped." He wipes the blade on his sleeve and slides it back into the battered leather sheath. "Show it to me." His words are less a demand than a plea.

No way am I going to let him see what this thing has done to me. No way is he going to gloat over what he's caused to happen. I tug at my sleeve. A mistake. His eyes dart to my left wrist and he stares at it, like a starving man stares at a steaming hot meal.

I snarl and slide my arm behind my back.

He's totally alert now. All eyes and ears and curiosity. "I knew it. This is why I took you into the Realm, why I helped you." His eyes reflect the flickering starlight, glittering silver in the darkness. "It's chosen you, hasn't it?"

Chosen me? Is that what it's done? Why it's bored its way into my flesh, embedded itself under my skin? I bring my wrist out in front of me, push up my sleeve and remove the leather bracelet. The snake shimmers in the moonlight.

Jeryd gasps. A fierce smile lights up his face. That can't be good.

"What do you mean, it's chosen me?" My words are slow to form, like I'm thinking and talking in slow motion.

Jeryd wipes at his eyes with the back of his hand, as if they're watering. "Merissa," he says to me in hushed tones. "What Bree has found, that book. It's not just cursed or haunted. Yes, the darkness is coming from the book, but it's not the book that's causing it. It's what's inside. It's not really a book at all." His voice drops to a whisper so low only my extra strong hearing can distinguish his words from the light breeze that rustles through the grass. "It's a prison." He points to my wrist. "And you hold the key."

CHAPTER THIRTY-FOUR

"What the hell are you talking about?" I yank my sleeve back down to hide the glittering snake. If what he says is true . . .

"Bree sent you after the key to unlock the book because she's being influenced by the dark entity within it. All it wants is to escape back into the world and exact revenge on the ones who imprisoned it."

"And you want to help it?"

"No!" he says, his face a mask of disgust. "I helped you because I hoped I could stop it. That *we* could stop it."

"Oh right." My voice is slathered with sarcasm and I slap my forehead in a mock 'I get it now' gesture. "That's why you helped your sweet mother imprison me. That makes so much sense. I'm so dense. I don't know why I didn't figure it out sooner."

He frowns. "Fine. I know how it looks, but I was in a bad spot. If I had tried to get you away when one of Andarra's pet goblins could raise the alarm, we'd both still be stuck in Natif. Only, I'd be dead. Or, more likely, wishing I were."

"Sure. I totally get it. Couldn't piss off Mommy Dearest."

"Come on," he says. "Do you really think you escaped on your own? That the trees didn't turn you in because they'd fallen in love with you? That they guided you for their own purpose?"

Something about what he's saying nags at me, telling me there is truth in his words. But isn't that the way it works? A little bit of truth always makes the lie more believable? "What are you saying?"

"I'm saying that I helped you escape," he says. "I'm saying that we're on the same side."

"I doubt that," I grumble.

"We are," he says with certainty. "I understand if you don't trust me. But there is more at stake here than you know."

"Like what?" I don't know why I ask it, why I'm still standing here talking to him, but the question slips out.

"Like the entity escaping that book, ripping open the gate to the Realm and exposing it and this place, both your home and mine, to the Seekers."

"Give me one good reason why that means anything to me."

"Because it would also destroy your parents' ability to remain hidden from them."

"Who are the Seekers? And why would they be looking for my parents?"

"You don't know?" he asks, the look of surprise on his face so real, for a moment I almost believe he's being genuine.

"Okay," I say, curious what bald-faced lie he's planning to tell me next. "I'll bite. What don't I know?"

"That your parents are playing out the live version of Romeo and Juliet, or the star-crossed children of the Hatfields and McCoys." He looks at me pointedly. "Ironic in a way."

"Not even a good try," I say. "And here I thought you would come up with something original."

He shakes his head. "I just assumed you knew. That they told you. Why do you think they settled in this tiny town, so far from everything?"

"Romeo and Juliet? Oh, please," I bark. "I don't even like you."

His face hardens. "What makes you think I meant us?"

I'm stunned into silence, surprised by how much his words hurt.

"Bree is caught up in something she can't, or won't, control." He raises an eyebrow. "Bottom line, someone needs to do something about it. Someone needs to stop the vestige from escaping."

"Still waiting to hear why I should care." I cross my arms and glare at him.

"Because the Seekers will take their vengeance

on your mother for not carrying out her duty."

"What are you talking about?"

"They're supposed to hunt down shifters and their ilk, not fraternize with them." He places his hand over his heart. "Love makes fools of us all."

"You're full of it!" I snap. But there's something about what he's said. Something about the way my parents look at one another when they think I'm not paying attention. My body suddenly goes rubbery and the ground beneath me feels like it's shifting.

"And don't think your grandfather will be safe, either. Since it was one of your ancestors who helped imprison Metaphys, he's going to want revenge on your entire line." He pauses for a moment, as if gathering his thoughts. "I want to help you. I want to help get the book back, to stop Metaphys from escaping his confines and wreaking havoc."

There's something in his voice that tells me there's more, that there's something in this that's personal for him.

"Who is this Met-uh-fiss guy you're so worried about?"

He stiffens. "That's my business. Isn't it enough that he's a threat to all of us, including your family?"

"You want me to trust you, to believe my parents have been lying to me my whole life, and you want me to take all of this on your word?"

"That's pretty much it."

Doubt ripples through me, but one look at his

gray eyes and sharp teeth resets my resolve. "Screw you."

He flinches, but steps closer. "You may not like me or want anything to do with me, but for the time being at least, you need to accept that we are on the same side. Don't you know the saying 'the enemy of my enemy is my friend?'"

"I prefer the saying 'the enemy of my enemy is still my enemy.'"

"Fine," he says placing the knife on the ground as if it's something fragile. Or dangerous. "When you're ready to stop acting like a stupid wolf, let me know." He turns and walks away. As if he's stepping through a glittering curtain, he vanishes into a shimmering mist that dissipates as soon as he's gone.

I look at the place where he disappeared and there's nothing there. The knife is still on the ground, right where he left it.

I take a tentative step forward to retrieve it, glance around. Senses on high-alert, I bend down and pick it up with shaking fingers.

I don't believe it's real until I'm holding it in my hands. But there's something different about it. Something off. I inch the blade out of the sheath. It's glowing, just the tiniest bit, like one of those phosphorescent stars people put on ceilings, right before the light exposure reaction wears off and it blends into the darkness. And the anger I felt the first time I unsheathed it is dimmer than it was, less urgent. But there's no time to wonder about it.

I tuck the blade back into the sheath, get to my

feet, and lope through the woods. I have to get home. More than that, I need to get away from this place.

CHAPTER THIRTY-FIVE

Before I'm ready for it, the alarm goes off and sunlight slaps me in the eyes. I really want to roll over and cover my head with a pillow. By the time I got back from the meadow, it was past midnight and then I was hyper-tense for hours, ears pricking up at every tiny sound. When I heard Dad get up before dawn, I almost ran out into the kitchen to confront him, ask him if what Jeryd said is true, but I shoved my head under the covers instead and listened to the sounds of him making coffee and packing his cooler, which meant that Mom was on the afternoon shift again.

Stupid Jeryd! He's obviously trying to make me doubt everyone I care about. I just wish I knew why.

I shove the blankets off and make myself get up. Crud. As much as I'd rather keep all our meetings public, and even though I was awake for most of the night, I still haven't figured out how to get the knife to Bree without meeting her someplace private and off campus. I'd love to get this over with sooner rather than later, but I definitely can't bring a weapon on school grounds.

All the way to school, I worry. I've stashed the knife in the safest place I can think of, in my dirty running shoes in the back of my closet under a pile of laundry. But what if Jeryd breaks in and steals it again? I almost wish Dad would have agreed to let Mom install that home alarm system, after all. Then again, that would have made sneaking out a lot more difficult. Not that I intend to make it a habit. Not once this flipping mess is cleaned up, anyway.

School sucks. Everyone is on edge, anticipating the next disaster. I already feel fidgety, and the adrenaline level in the air isn't making things better. When I finally see Bree in the hallway, I suddenly get that feeling again, like I don't want to give her anything, especially not an angry enchanted knife that wants blood. She raises an eyebrow at me, then heads into the girls' bathroom, but before I can follow her, someone taps me on the shoulder.

I spin around and see Kat. "Hey," she says. "How's your head?"

I glance over my shoulder at the door to the bathroom. "My head?"

She gives me a funny look. "Yeah. You know.

That thing on your neck?"

I swing back around, my hand going to my throat. "My neck?"

"Are you okay?" she asks, starting to put down her backpack.

"Oh, my head," I say, reaching up to touch the spot under my bangs. "Sorry. Distracted." I let out a little laugh.

"You sure that's all it is?" She tilts her head. "Did the doctor say you're okay?"

"Doctor?"

"Yeah. Lady in a white coat who takes your temperature and checks out your head wound to make sure you don't have a concussion." She frowns. "Your parents did take you in to have your head looked at, didn't they?"

"I'm fine," I tell her. "I just didn't get much sleep last night. Up late, um, studying. I'm just a little tired."

I feel eyes boring into the back of my head and sneak a peek behind me. Bree is standing outside the bathroom, glaring, like if I were a witch *she'd* be burning *me* at the stake.

"I gotta go," I tell Kat just as the bell rings. "But thanks for checking on me." I turn to see Bree still throwing me the death glare. I give her a quick shrug before I rush off to class. Literally, saved by the bell, but not for long. Bree and I still have biology together, so—since I can't have her telling Joey Marsh to walk into traffic or jump off the West Corners Train Bridge—I had better either learn to be an incredibly good liar before biology, or else I'm going to have to hand over the knife.

As I head to English, I wonder why I feel like giving it to her is so wrong. And I can't help thinking there might be some truth to what Jeryd told me about the book, the power inside it.

There must be more to the story. More that Jeryd is hiding.

CHAPTER THIRTY-SIX

"Well?" Bree leans over our latest biology project and hisses in my ear.

I'm using a pair of tweezers to sort the tarsal bones from the carpal bones of a rat skeleton. At what point will humans get over their grudge with rodents? The substitute teacher handed out the packets of bones last week and our job is to assemble them. It wouldn't be so bad, but staring through the magnifying glass makes my eyes feel squirmy. I sigh and steady my hand as Bree nudges me for the umpteenth time. "Where is it?"

"I told you," I say between gritted teeth, "it's safe. I couldn't very well bring it on school grounds." Not without risking permanent suspension. And being grounded till I'm thirty.

She's all agitated tics and nerves, like she's had too much caffeine.

Outside, dark clouds have collected and the wind swirls dust, dirt and leaves across the school grounds. A streak of lightning flashes across the sky and a terrific boom rattles the windows. Another crack of thunder rumbles overhead and all the lights go out.

Cheering erupts in the classroom. No one can work on these stupid skeletons in the dark. I set the tweezers down on our lab table and scoot back onto the stool. The light coming in through the windows is a gauzy gray and the classroom is all shades of dark on dark. I reach over and rub my wrist, my fingers automatically tracing the line of the snake beneath the leather band.

As much as I think it's a bad idea to give Bree the stupid knife, at this point it might be worse not to. "I'll get it to you after school," I tell her for the tenth time.

"You better," she grumbles.

The substitute decides to give us a lecture on eyes while we sit in the dark classroom with the storm grumbling and flashing outside. What is it with science teachers?

After the longest biology class in history is finally over, school officials decide to cut us loose for the day. I grab my stuff and, with Bree tight on my heels, head for my locker. The lights come on in the hallway, and kids boo, figuring we won't get early release, after all. But then they flicker and go out again, followed by a rousing cheer. We're all moving by the light of the security lamps placed at intervals along the hallway. A few of the more daring kids are taking advantage, hiding in the shadows to grab a quick make-out moment. Bree's breath on my neck makes me shiver, and I pick up my pace to put some distance between us.

She stands beside me as I work the dial on my locker in the dim light. Her face is tight and she shifts her weight nervously.

"You can't come to my house," I say.

"Why not? You came to mine."

I feel the color rise in my cheeks remembering that day at her grandmother's house.

Bree's eyes glitter strangely in the pale glow of the emergency lights.

I stop myself from saying something I might regret by counting down from ten to one. "Because," I tell her, "my parents don't know about you." And I'd like to keep it that way. Although, I don't know how long I can keep her and her grandmother a secret in a place as small as Fair Glen. Especially with all the weird stuff going on.

Last night, I overheard my parents talking about it, arguing whether or not my dad should go back out on the road or stay home. They definitely know something weird is happening. How long before they figure out I'm in it up to my ears?

* * *

The junior high down the street is letting out early, too. Kids stream out of the school buildings.

Buffeted by the wind, they spill out across the lawn and onto the sidewalks. I'm waiting to cross the intersection when the tattoo on my wrist starts to buzz like a cell phone set to vibrate. I look up in time to see the school bus swing out of the parking lot and turn down the street. A car coming from the other direction just misses capping the front bumper and the bus swerves out of the way. Across the street there's a kid on a bicycle and suddenly, the bus is heading right toward him. I wave my arms and shout, but he's got his earbuds in and the wind tears my voice away. No one else seems to notice the looming disaster. They're all just herding along with their heads down, trying to keep from being blown over by the blasting gale.

For an instant, everything slows down. My head and heart pound. The air in my lungs seems frozen, crystallized. Then I'm moving, streaking across the sidewalk and out into the street, grabbing the boy on the bicycle, trying to change his course, knocking him aside. He can't keep his balance and goes down hard just as the bus motors past.

When things speed up again, there's a crowd gathered around the boy, who's lying unconscious on the pavement. I move forward, wading between bodies, trying to reach him.

Kat comes running up, pushing kids out of her way, dark hair whipping in the wind. "Get back." She orders, shoving me aside, her voice strained with fear and urgency. "Don't touch him!"

She bends over the boy. "Devon. Devon. Are you okay? Someone call 911!" she shouts, taking off her jacket and placing it over him like a blanket. She leans close and puts her ear against his chest. There's panic on her face. She places her hands over his chest, like she's about to give him CPR, but before she can start compressions, he coughs and lets out a groan.

My hands are shaking and I let loose a sigh of relief, scanning the road, but the bus is long gone.

Finally, EMTs arrive and push the crowd back to give them room to work.

All around me kids are staring and whispering, their voices buzzing in my ears. The blustering wind makes it hard to hear, but I can pick out a few words and phrases. "Crazy . . ." "Is he dead?" ". . . messed up . . ."

Messed up is exactly what things are.

The EMTs say the kid is going to be fine, but they need to take him to the hospital where a doctor can check him over, just to be sure. After the ambulance leaves, Kat stalks over to me. "What the hell were you thinking?" She screams in my face. "You could have killed him."

I'm confused. I can feel the blood draining from my face. "I was trying to help." I tell her. "The bus—"

"What the hell are you talking about?"

Kat's face is filled with anger, but there is also fear in her eyes.

"What do you mean? That kid on the bike. He was in danger. Didn't you see?"

"That kid on the bike, the one you just almost killed, is my brother," Kat says. "And all I saw was you slamming him into the curb." She gives me a shove.

What the hell is wrong with her? "I was trying to keep him from getting mowed down by that—"

"By what?" she shouts. "A stupid girl?"

What the hell? Didn't she see it? "The bus! It was . . ." The crowding students stare at me, like I'm insane. "Didn't anyone else see it?" My voice is raised, even though I'm trying hard not to lose my cool. The clouds open up and rain pours down, needle sharp and cold.

We've become the center of a ring of kids. They're hoping for a fight. Savage energy flows off them like a slap to the face. The snake on my wrist writhes.

My hackles are up and all I want is to rip off Kat's head. I step into her, but before I can do anything else, I see Bree's face over Kat's shoulder. She's standing at the edge of the school parking lot, a twisted smile on her face. My brain replays the scene and I suddenly recall the smell of sulfur that hung in the air almost, but not quite, obscured by diesel exhaust. It's enough to stop me in my tracks. I back away from the angry girl in front of me. The girl who bandaged up my face. The girl who helped Mr. Rajanni when he slipped and fell. The girl whose brother is right now on the way to the hospital. And not because of some freak accident, but because of Bree and that nasty old book.

"Kat," I say, taking another step back. It's raining harder now. My hair is sticking to my face. "I'm sorry about your brother. I really was trying to protect him."

She takes a step toward me. "Sure didn't look like it from here," she snarls.

I try to back farther away from her, but the circle of kids tightens around us. They're egging her on, telling her to hit me. Angry energy pulses off them as the rain streams down.

My wrist burns and my wolf is on alert.

Kat's fist comes forward and I block it with my forearm. Her knuckles catch on the leather band on my wrist, causing a sharp pain, as if the snake sank its fangs into my flesh. I let out a hiss and drop my arm. I'd think the idea was ridiculous, if I hadn't watched the damn thing worm its way under my skin in the first place. But I don't have time to worry about that right now, because Kat's taking another swing. I lean away and her hand glances over my nose, but manages to connect with my right eye. I duck down and spring back up, grabbing her by both wrists.

"You. Need. To. Stop." My eyes bore into hers. "This isn't you."

For a moment, I think she hears me, understands. She stops struggling and the tension starts to go out of her. I'm about to let go, when a steel-muscled arm grabs me around the neck and squeezes tight. The crowd erupts. So many voices yelling it's impossible to make out the words, but I know they're screaming for blood.

I don't need to see her to know who it is. I can smell the tan and pale yellow of horses and hay on her. Kandi Johnson has chosen this moment to get even with me. I want nothing more than to spin around and knock her on her ass, but all I can think about are the repercussions when my mom finds out. And there's no way this doesn't get back to her. Not with Kat's brother on the way to the hospital.

I pry Kandi's arms off me and duck away. I search for an opening in the crowd, but these kids want a battle. Despite the pouring rain, they're not going to let anyone escape till they get it. I have no choice but to fight, or take a dive, and I am not about to roll over for anybody right now.

I don't think Kandi thought I'd get out of that chokehold so easily. She probably figured a surprise attack while I was already fighting off another person would be a great gambit. Since there's clearly no escaping this, I try to stand my ground without letting on that I could have actually taken her in short order. Again.

Unfortunately, once she realizes I'm not going to bowl her over the way I did in the Coffee & Cues, she decides to get in as many licks as she can. I dodge most of her clumsy swings. She's muscular, but not all that fast. As I duck, her meaty fist whips by my head. One of the kids in the crowd gives her a shove, sending her staggering into me. I back away as she pinwheels her arms to keep from going down, but get tripped up by someone's size thirteen combat boots. In the time it takes for me to rebalance, Kandi manages to connect one of her red-knuckled fists with my left cheek. I'm too off-balance to swing my head away in time to keep my face from absorbing most of the impact and it stings like I just did a major belly-flop on my face.

I suck it up, but decide I've had enough. I telegraph a swing at her head and, when she reaches up to cover her face, land a hard punch in her stomach. She doubles over and gags. For a second, I think she's going to lose her lunch. Instead, she rushes forward, trying to head-butt me. I spin sideways and her momentum carries her into the crowd. The ring of teenagers falls back and the crowd splits apart. I take advantage and sprint toward the opening, only to be stopped by Principal Tyler and Officer Merlin, the school's security guard.

They're both drenched and fuming with anger.

Kids peel off and fade away. But I'm trapped. Caught. I am so screwed. My mom and dad are going to hear about this sooner rather than later. My right hand strays to the cuff on my left wrist. I squeeze the place where the tattoo is still tingling, wanting to scratch at it, dig it out. At first, I thought it was cool. It seemed to warn me, help me control my temper. But now I'm not so sure what it's doing. Helping? Hindering? Just plain annoying me for no good reason?

Principal Tyler gives me the eye and jerks her head toward the school admin office. I look around for Kandi, but she's managed to slip away with the rest of the kids. Officer Merlin ushers the last few stragglers off campus, as I follow Principal Tyler to her office. Kat is standing on the corner, looking confused. She sees me glancing at her and starts toward us. I shake my head at her. I know she started the fight, but I don't think it was her idea. As a matter of fact, I'm pretty sure Bree and her nasty little book were behind all of it, including the way things escalated so fast. The sooner I give her what she wants, the better.

CHAPTER THIRTY-SEVEN

An eternity later, I emerge from the Principal's office and head home. I've been sentenced to two weeks of detention. I could have gotten it whittled down to a single week, if I had been willing to tell her who I was fighting with. Turns out I didn't have to give Kandi up. Officer Merlin got one of the other students to spill. The only reason I'm not suspended is because I've never been in trouble before. And because someone told Officer Merlin about the bus. So, it looks like there won't be charges pressed against me for what happened to Kat's brother. Although, I'm not exactly getting a medal for it, either. Principal Tyler believes in second chances. Preaches it, in fact. At length. Apparently, that doesn't mean not calling my parents and scheduling a conference with them.

The rain has let up, but the thunder and lightning continue to flash and rumble their threats. Bree is waiting for me around the corner from school grounds. She takes a good look at my face and gives a little laugh. "You should see the other guy," she says. "Oh, wait. You *are* the *Other* guy."

I keep walking, trying to ignore her, but she swings around and matches my pace.

"You know," she says. "As entertaining as that was, I'd rather you just gave me what is mine, than to have to aim another bus at someone."

I stop and turn on her. "Excuse me?"

"You heard me," she says without stopping. "Next time, the bus will be aimed at someone near and dear to you. You have until midnight tonight to give me the athame," she calls over her shoulder. A bang of thunder punctuates her statement.

"The what?"

She scowls. "Bring. Me. That. Blade." Her voice is gravel under heavy tires, and her eyes flare. Then, she wheels around and stalks off, beneath the grumbling sky.

I watch her walk away, eyes boring into her back, biting my tongue to keep myself from screaming curses at her. Near and dear? Does she mean Joey? Or someone else? No matter. The sooner she gets her precious toy, the sooner I can get back to my boring, but safe existence. She can have the stupid knife and this whole damn town can go to hell.

As I trudge home, the tender skin around my eye

swells, filling with blood. It'll be black before I get to our street and my head already aches. If it hadn't been for the principal breaking up the fight when she did, Kandi would look even worse than I do. I don't think I could have held back much longer. As it is, the other kids finally got the blood they wanted when she fell into the crowd and smashed her nose into someone. I don't think she broke it, though. Double-edged sword that. I start to laugh and stop as the pain of my split lip brings me back to the world of real. As in my mom is totally going to have a meltdown. I just hope she doesn't call my dad.

The lights in our house are all out when I get home. I unlock the door and head for my room and drop my school bag on the floor. I dig the knife out of the back of my closet, unwrap the old jeans from around it and stuff it down into my bag before heading back out into the dark afternoon. There's no point even looking in the mirror. Make-up won't hide the damage to my face, and Principal Tyler already called my mom, so I'm doomed anyway.

Bree's waiting for me, standing on the porch of her grandmother's house. The plants have grown impossibly huge in the short time since I was there. A jungle of greenery wraps around the house.

The air feels calmer here, less electric, but there's an undercurrent of energy that hums through the soles of my feet, like walking on the face of a rock concert speaker. Bree is leaning against the porch railing, her eyes so dark, they look like patches of night in her pale face. I suddenly notice she looks thinner. Not in a teen on a diet way. More like there's a kind of transparency to her. The knife feels heavy in my bag, like it's trying to weigh itself down, keep me from crossing the yard.

I falter at the edge of the property.

"It's about time," she says, her voice as dark as her eyes. She glances up at the sky, then turns her gaze on me again.

There's something about her look that makes me think of curdled milk.

"What are you waiting for? An engraved invitation?" She looses a laugh that's filled with dark melancholy.

I don't get the joke, but I don't bother to ask. I take a step forward, then stop. Suddenly, I know in my heart this is no longer Bree I'm talking to. This isn't the girl who came to town a month ago and turned my world upside down. The girl who kissed me, and made me question everything I thought I knew about myself. This is someone—something—else. Something that has taken control of her, trapped her the same way Joey is trapped. "Why don't you let her go?" I ask, throat tight with emotion.

"Let her go?" Dark eyes shine at me from the shade of the porch. "And why would I do that, after all this time? And just when we're finally close to completing our compact?" This time the laughter that erupts from her is menacing. "And she is such a deliciously perfect vessel." She sniffs at the air, black orbs honing in on me. "I am so looking forward to getting the band back together."

Maybe I should just go. Maybe Jeryd was right. I can't give the knife to Bree, no matter what the consequences. But before I can leave, something drags at me, pulling me forward. I fight the need to take first one step, then another.

"Come on," she gripes. "Quit wasting my time. I've got work to do before the moon is full. And you don't want to make me angry. Your little boyfriend would be much the worse for it, if I don't get what I want. Now."

I reach the bottom of the porch steps and there's a hard tug on my backpack. It yanks itself off my shoulder and soars through the air into Bree's outstretched hand.

I manage not to gasp in surprise. "I'd like my bag back," I manage to say without my voice trembling.

Bree opens the backpack, reaches inside and takes out the knife, then tosses the bag at me. It happens so fast, it almost flies right past my head before I can grab hold of it.

She stares at the blade in her hands, a hungry look on her face.

"What about Joey?" I say, suddenly remembering what this was all for.

"Joey?" She looks up, but her eyes are unfocused.

"We had a bargain. Remember? I give you the knife and you take your stupid spell off him."

"Oh, right." She glances at the blade, then back up at me. "It requires some . . . preparation. Meet me in the forest, the Silver Meadow. At midnight."

"What?"

"Don't worry. Joey will be there."

She tilts her head to one side, then her eyes slide back to the knife blade as it slips from the ragged sheath. It glitters in the dying light, sending a flash of silver into my eyes, making me blink. And just like that, I know I've done a terrible thing. That Jeryd was right. The entity possessing Bree is going to destroy everything.

She disappears into the house, leaving me there on the walk, literally stuck holding the bag, as the sky slams open and dumps a fresh deluge on everything.

CHAPTER THIRTY-EIGHT

By the time I slog home, the rain has stopped and the weak sun has dropped behind the hills west of town. My mom is there and she's already started dinner. I smell broccoli steaming on the stove and for an instant it seems like things could be like they were.

"Merissa," Mom calls from the kitchen and the moment is broken. Her voice has that hard edge that says she's not happy. "Will you please come out here? We need to talk."

OMG. Here it comes. My skin tightens and my scalp feels like a wig that's on too tight. I scan the images that fill my brain, running through every lie, outright or by omission, every time I've snuck out. The visits to Bree's house. Jeryd. The meadow.

Other. I swallow hard and fill my lungs with oxygen before stepping into the line of inquisition.

She lets out a small gasp when I enter the room and for a nanosecond I think she's going to go all comfort-Mom on me and let me off the hook. But her shoulders stiffen and her mouth curves down and I know I'm doomed. My eye is swollen nearly shut and with my bruised cheek and split lip I must look like hell, but I'm getting no sympathy. Mom lays into me like a blazing cannonball into a pirate ship.

Mom's anger washes over me like a tsunami. First it's all about Principal Tyler's call and the fight. The way I, once more, risked everyone knowing "our" secret. Once she's worn through that canvas, she's onto everything else she knows.

That includes Bree, and, of course, the odd things happening in town. She's certain there's a connection. She's completely irate about the fact that I didn't tell her any of it, that she had to learn about all of this stuff second-hand. I think she suspects there's more, but thankfully she isn't sure. I keep my mouth shut. Beneath the leather band, sweat pools on my wrist. It makes me want to yank the stupid thing off, but the last thing I need right now is to have to explain my live-action tattoo. So, I try not to fidget with the cuff.

"Your father and I have worked hard to create a safe haven here. Not just for you, but for all of us." She paces the floor. Her face is tight and her left temple throbs so hard I can see it from across the room. She stops and turns to face me and there's more than anger in her face. For an instant, I think I see panic there as well, but it's gone so fast, I can't be certain. All I know is she is pissed off and completely disappointed in me. I have to admit, I'm disappointed in me, too. I hang my head, stare at my shoes, zero in on the scuffs on the toes.

"How well do you know this . . . girl?"

Her question surprises me and I jerk my head up and stare at her, trying hard not to blush. What if she knows about the kiss? What will she think of me? Will she be even more disappointed? We've had the talks. The ones about the birds and the bees. The talks about boys. Always about boys.

Suddenly, I'm angry, too. It's not my fault I was born with our family condition. Not my fault Bree and her grandmother chose to move here. And it's not my fault that all this stuff is happening in our, as Mom puts it, safe haven.

"Her name is Breanna." I try not to growl the words into existence, but it's hard to hold in my anger. Is it my fault that Bree kissed me? That I liked it? That I'm not only not a Norm, I'm not even a normal shifter? "I met her when she started attending school last month. She's in my biology class. I sort of liked her at first, but she turned out to be . . ." I stop, surprised at the disgusted tone in my voice.

"What?" Mom asks, her voice dropping almost to a whisper. Fear and concern show in her eyes. "She turned out to be what?"

My head pounds and the snake squirms beneath the wide leather wristband. "Not my friend," I say.

"She turned out not to be my friend." It hurts more than I thought it would to say it. Even though it simplifies matters between us. Although, it complicates things for me, too. How am I supposed to figure out whether I liked her because she was a non-Norm, or because I like girls? On the other hand, maybe it really was some sort of spell. I liked kissing Joey well enough before Bree came along. And Jeryd afterward. I feel the blood rising up my neck and toward my face. I push these thoughts out of my head. I can't deal with this now. I have way too much else going on at the moment.

My mom's face softens with what looks like relief. "Merissa," she says, her voice as soft as her eyes have become. "Your father and I only want to protect you."

Her words hit me like an arrow. My anger erupts anew. I stand up and face her, eye-to-eye for the first time in my life. "Protect me from what?" I ask. "All my life, all you ever worried about was keeping 'our secret' from the neighbors. Making me hide who and what I am. How am I supposed to even know what I like and don't like when I'm not allowed to be myself?" I'm yelling now, but I don't care. "Did you ever stop to think about me? How maintaining your safe little haven was affecting me?" Hot tears are ready to burst from my eyes, stinging the blackened one, but I fight them back. "All you ever cared about was looking like the all-American, small-town, perfect family."

"Merissa." Mom reaches for me, but I step back. She stiffens and her face goes pale. She looks like she's been slapped. I know my words have hurt her, but I just don't care. In fact, her reaction seems to punch a hole the rest of the way through my anger dam.

"Well, guess what, Mom. There's absolutely nothing normal about us. Or about me. In fact, I'm as far from normal as it's possible to be. And this whole stupid town would be better off without me in it."

"Merissa," she says, hurt and anger coloring her voice. "Don't talk like that. Your father and I . . . You have no idea what we've done, what we've had to endure . . ." Her hand goes to her mouth, as if she has to stop herself from saying something more. Then her arm drops and she's suddenly composed again. Her words come out sharp, hard-edged. "Everything. Everything we've done has always been to protect you."

"Right," I tell her. "Shock collars are such a hug!" I turn and run from the room, slamming the front door as I rush out of the house and away. I have no idea where I'm going. I only know that I can't stay here for another instant. I feel like I'll spontaneously combust if I have to spend one more second trapped in this house in this awful town.

"Merissa!" Mom shouts as she follows me to the sidewalk. "Merissa, come back here." The wind whips at my hair as another clap of thunder tries to drown out her words. "You are so grounded." Her voice fades as I lope down the street and head for the orchard at the end of our neighborhood. "Merissa. Get back here." Her words trail after me, so I put on speed and sprint through the trees toward the two-lane road that leads out past the town dump and away from Fair Glen. Once I hit the road I'm flying. I rip the leather cuff from my wrist and let myself go.

CHAPTER THIRTY-NINE

I wake with the pungent smell of wet forest surrounding me. I raise my head and stare down at my paws. Damn! When did I change? I remember the fight with my mom and running from the house, fiery anger nearly blinding me. Then . . . nothing. Crud. My mom is going to be so unbelievably pissed at me.

I wish things could go back to the way they were. That Bree had never come here. That I had never lied, never snuck out, never traveled to Other, the Realm, whatever the hell it is.

Never liked Joey. Never kissed *anyone*.

A few stars are barely visible overhead, then the clouds part and the brightness of the moon blazes down for an instant, almost as bright as daylight. I stand and shake myself all over, preparing to change back, but a shiver runs cold fingers over me as I realize I'm stuck. I can't make the change. I concentrate. Breathe deep. Try again. My wrist burns like I've been zapped by a Taser. But my hands are still paw-shaped. My nails still claws.

I snarl and try again. My left foreleg burns like I hit an electric fence and I yelp.

Trapped. I'm trapped in this form. That's it. I am so done with this thing. I bite at my leg in desperation, gnawing at the buzzing pain. I taste blood. Now I know what drives wild animals to chew off a foot to escape a trap. But the serpent only digs deeper, burning its way toward the bone. And I finally have to stop my useless self-mutilation.

I raise my head to howl at the full moon overhead.

The full moon.

How the hell did I lose track of that?

No wonder the change came over me like it did. I only hope I was safely in the woods before it happened. That no one saw . . . I glance up at the glowing moon.

Oh, no. The book. The entity. And whatever is happening with Bree.

It's happening tonight.

Before I realize it, I'm running toward the meadow, crashing through the underbrush, ignoring the pain in my leg. Branches grab at me, pulling out clumps of fur as I pass, but I keep going. I don't know what I think I can do, especially in this form, but I need to try and stop this. I need to try and keep things from getting worse.

I see the meadow ahead through the trees. There's a fire burning in the middle of it and Bree is there. I can smell her scent, twisted, mangled by the burnt smell from the curse. It smells like devastation.

CHAPTER FORTY

Bree holds the book and raises the knife. The blade flickers red in the firelight as she chants. Strange words drip off her tongue with a lilting hiss, like water droplets landing on a hot surface. Jeryd stands beside her, with Joey kneeling before her, wrists bound behind his back. Not that he needs to be bound. It's clear he's still under the spell Bree swore to remove.

My hackles are up and I have an overwhelming urge to leap out of my hiding place and attack them both. But Jeryd is fast and strong and who knows what kind of power Bree is drawing to her. Prickling magic swirls and ebbs around the glade. It pulses, and with each rise of energy there's a momentary aura of flickering multicolored light.

I suck in my breath as a tall rectangle becomes outlined. The door to Other, the entryway to the Silver Realm, begins to open.

Bree reaches forward and jabs the blade into the heart of the fire. There's a flash of blue flame and when she pulls out the knife, the sizzling flame comes with it. Dancing on the blade, it writhes like something alive. Bree thrusts the tip of the knife up toward the sky and the flame leaps higher, a blazing torch that lights up the entire meadow as if it's the high school football field on game night.

Thunder bursts overhead and a swirling wind whips the trees. The ground begins to quake. One by one, the trees at the far edge of the meadow drop their leaves and stand like stark skeletons against the dark, the blue light from the flaming blade illuminating their bony branches. Bree's hair has come undone and whips around her head like a dark aura.

A twig cracks and I spin around. Jeryd is there. In all the chaos, I didn't see him move away from Bree and Joey. Didn't hear or smell him sneaking up behind me through the trees.

I bare my canines at him, a low growl filling my throat.

"So," he says. "The Third has arrived." He holds out a black leather muzzle and wags it at me. "Here Merissa," he croons. "Nice little doggie. Time to get dressed for the party."

I step back, forgetting for a moment what's behind me.

Bree. Joey. The flaming blade.

I freeze. What did I come here for? What made me think I could do anything to stop this? I'm outnumbered and trapped in wolf form. My left paw is raw and bloody where I tried to chew the serpent tattoo away, rip it from under my fur and skin.

I can't believe I once thought the serpent was keeping me from losing my temper, from changing into the wolf. Instead, it was keeping me contained in my human form. Just like it's keeping me in wolf form, now. If I can only figure out how to circumvent the effects, I'd change in a heartbeat, but for the moment, I'm as trapped as I was when I was wearing that collar in Other.

Bree continues to chant, electricity charging the air around her, locks of her hair writhe like serpents. Joey kneels on the ground before her, still completely enthralled.

I keep my left front foot lifted up off the ground to avoid putting my weight on it. I'm not only outmanned, I'm not even at my fighting best, and Jeryd knows it. I can see it in his eyes. The way his mouth quirks up on one side.

Behind me, Bree's chanting dies down. The blue light fills the glade and pushes back the shadows under the trees. Overhead, lightning bolts crackle and lash against the darkness.

I have no chance. I can't face them alone. I prepare to dash into the trees, but before I can move Jeryd is on me, his strong hand gripping the fur at the back of my neck. I let out a yelp, manage to shake him off and roll away from him, but he's quick. He grabs for my bloody foot. I snap at his hand, jaws clamping shut on empty air.

We tumble over one another, wrestle for a moment. Then I feel the muzzle being slipped over my nose. In desperation, I try to open my jaws wide, but the leather strap is tightening, pulling my mouth shut. I heave my weight up and back, but Jeryd manages to curl away from me and hang onto the leather straps at the same time. I try to stand, but he yanks on the muzzle and kicks my right front foot out from under me.

I go down hard on my left paw and collapse forward with a yelp of pain. Jeryd twists around and tightens the harness. My jaw is clamped shut and all I can do is growl as he deftly winds a length of rope around my back feet.

"Funny," he says. "I thought you'd be tougher to heel." He drags me over to where Bree is still chanting. The flame dances on the tip of the knife and electric energy rises from the earth. My left foot burns with it, like it's absorbing the charge of it and I force back a whimper of pain. Instead, I growl deep in my throat, wanting to howl, but unable to open my jaws wide enough.

The look on Bree's face is fierce and ecstatic, filled with hunger. Her eyes are black holes that seem to absorb the light. There's no life reflected there. Jeryd leans over me, his face close to mine. I begin to struggle, but he grabs the strap of the muzzle and pulls my head back, holding me still and putting his mouth near my ear. He whispers something and my eyes go wide. He pulls away and looks into my eyes. There's something in that look that makes me want to believe what he's said.

Before turning away, he mouths the words, "Trust me."

But how can I, after all he's said and done?

I feel the strap on the muzzle lose tension. I want to leap up, run, but the rope around my feet keeps me in place, tensed and waiting to see what will happen next.

Jeryd stands and turns to Bree. "It's ready," he says, his voice a deep rumble against the background of hers as it rises and falls in that ominous ritual chant. She nods and takes a step forward and stops chanting. She reaches down and strokes Joey's head, the way you'd pet a big dog. "Hello, Merissa," she says it like we're friends who haven't seen each other for long time.

I growl.

"It didn't have to be this way," she tells me. "But you just couldn't play nice." She grabs a handful of Joey's hair and pulls his head back, baring his throat, and holds the burning knife beneath his chin. "But you wouldn't want anything to happen to sweet Joey here, would you?"

She promised she'd release him, gave me her word. I try to rise, a growl building deep in my chest.

"Ah, ah, ah." She slides the knife closer to his throat. The flame from the blade licks at his skin, but he doesn't even flinch. That stupid look is frozen on his face. "You're going to be especially nice now, and do as I tell you, aren't you?"

"Agree," Jeryd hisses.

My mind whirls. I fight the urge to bare my teeth and whimper instead. I don't know how else to convey I'm going along. For now.

"Good doggie," she says, and pulls the blade away from Joey's neck. "Let her up and let's get on with this," she tells Jeryd.

Jeryd unwraps the rope from my back legs and pulls me to my feet, I'm still limping on three legs as he guides me to a spot in the meadow just beyond the outline of the door. Then, he places himself equidistant from Bree and I. We're standing in a triangle with Joey and the doorway between the three of us. There's something oddly familiar about the place I'm standing. It takes me a moment to place the scent of Jeryd's blood from when he cut himself with the blade. Despite the recent rain, the ground is still ripe with it.

I don't have a chance to think about what that might mean, because the storm that has been whipping around the meadow becomes a screaming whirlwind that surrounds us. It forms a cone, like an upside-down tornado. The flame from the knife leaps to the top of the cone and we're bathed in a hot blue light.

Bree is chanting again. This time it's more guttural and ugly. A hungry energy licks at me. The static charge stands my fur on end. Power crackles up through the pads of my feet. It surges through me and stabs out the top of my head.

Jeryd stiffens. His body is wreathed in a blinding light. So is Bree's. Her head tilts back and flames shoot from her eyes and mouth. There's a crack of thunder and, across from the door to the Silver Realm, the outline of another door appears. This one is dark and deep, a bottomless pit, endless and empty. An eerie nimbus illuminates the edges.

The book lies in front of the door, limned in an ugly light, the color of dried blood. I can feel the darkness emanating from it, struggling to be free, feeding off the energy that rises up from the three of us. It crests at the top of the cone, then cascades back to the ground.

Suddenly, I know what I need to do. I sit on my haunches and raise my left leg high, reaching toward the flames.

The snake begins to writhe and crawl, then it's spinning around and around on my wrist, burning white hot. The searing pain makes me want to scream, drop to the ground and curl myself around it, but I force myself to hold on.

The dark door begins to open and behind the red light is a blackness deeper than an eternal abyss, the edges licked with red-gold flames. The words that Jeryd whispered in my ear, ring true. *The door he's trying to open leads to a dark place where others of his kind are trapped. Once loose, they will set him free from his prison. You have the power to stop this. You are the key.*

Bree is grinning now, her face a mask like the rictus of a withering skull. The book gives off heat, shimmering in the mixture of its own light and the black shadows coming from the doorway.

A howling erupts from within the opening, screams and groans, shrieks of madness and a cackling laughter that echoes around the meadow. Then I see them. Shades and grotesque shapes, and something huge and terrible reaching for the edge of the doorway, as if to pull itself through. Bree raises the knife high in the air, and reaches for Joey.

Fear grips my stomach. There's no reason the shift should work now, not when it hasn't before, and the pain will be unbearable. But I have to try. Have to stop this madness. Have to save the people I know and love. High school may suck. And this town may suck, but this is home, and I'll be damned if I'm going to let some pissed-off jerk of an evil entity destroy it all.

I force myself not to think about the pain. I picture the faces of my parents, of the kids at school, all our neighbors. I hold the image in my mind and make the shift. A white light envelopes me, wraps around me like a cocoon, warm and comforting. No searing pain, no burning agony. I'm simply human.

The snake jerks to a sudden stop, turns and spins the other direction, moving counter-clockwise on my wrist. Lightning streaks from it. I swing to face Bree, see Jeryd turn toward her, too. He aims something at her, something green and glowing, at the same time that I point with my left hand and a streak of white lightning flashes across the open space.

The whirling tornado dissipates, the wind moaning through the trees in what sounds like dismay.

"Nooooo!" The sound is coming from her mouth, but the voice is a deep rumble. For a moment, I think I see the face of someone else flash across her features. Then it's like a mask is being slowly pulled off. Suddenly, I can see in her eyes that it's Bree standing there. She looks at me, at Jeryd, then at the door. There's a hint of recognition in her eyes.

"Breanna," I shout between gritted teeth. "You have to stop it."

There's confusion on her face. She looks down at Joey in surprise. When she looks up and sees the knife in her own hand, she lets go of him.

She shakes her head and sucks in air, like a swimmer just coming up from a deep dive.

I feel a scream pushing up from my chest. I can't hold this power much longer. "Bree! Destroy the book. Do it, now!"

She blinks once, then steps around Joey, strides forward and plunges the knife into the book.

The shades and shapes that were groping for the door yowl in frustration. But over that roar is a terrifying scream of pain and hatred as the book begins to smolder, the pages curling up and turning to ash, then blowing away on the remnants of the storm.

Both doors slam shut with a sound like cannon fire. Then nothing.

The knife hilt extends up from the ground where the blade is embedded in the dirt. A wisp of smoke wafts away as the last traces of the book sift down into the grass. Joey is lying face down on the ground, unmoving. I rush over, put two fingers against his neck and feel a pulse.

Bree looks stunned. Her hands go to her face, then she reaches out to me, flinching when I rise and point an accusing finger at her. "What the hell were you thinking?"

"I . . . don't know."

"You don't know? You don't know? You were going to kill him!" I point at Joey. "And open us up to that, that . . . whatever the hell that was!" I lunge for her, but Jeryd steps between us.

"It wasn't her, Merissa," he tells me.

"The hell it wasn't!" I shout.

Bree is crying, folding in on herself like a crumpled paper doll. "It was the book," she whimpers. "All of it."

"Bullshit!" I tell her. "The book chose you, but you didn't have to accept it. You made a choice, too."

Her eyes flash anger and hurt, but there's something else there, too. Something that looks like guilt. Maybe even remorse.

"Merissa." Jeryd's face is flushed and his hands are bleeding, but there is triumph in his eyes, as he places the fingertips of one hand on Bree's shoulder, then reaches toward me with the other. "We need to be united, now."

"United? I'd laugh, but that's not my idea of a joke." I shrug him away.

"I'm serious." He holds out his hand to me again. "We are Triad," he says, a hint of arrogance in his voice.

"Triad? What the hell does that mean?" I ask.

Bree stares at him in confusion, her face mirroring my roiling emotions.

"That we have created a connection unlike any that has been seen in the past century," he says it smugly, like it's something to be proud of. "That together we are stronger than we were as individuals." He looks away for a moment, like he's considering his next words very carefully. When he turns back, he looks me directly in the eye as he says, "That we have formed a magical link. We three are inextricably bound to one another."

Bound? What!?! Is he crazy?

Bree stands there. Apparently, like me, she is stunned into silence.

I shake my head. It can't be true. I'm attracted to both of them and I can't stand either one of them. Could my life be any more screwed up? No way I'm getting sucked into some magical triangle thingy on top of all that. I refuse to be tied to two people I don't even like by some kind of age-old magical power. Not to mention that my parents would kill me and Papaw would have a heart attack if they ever found out I was even hanging around either one of them. "You're kidding me, right?"

I so did not sign up for this.

I look down at the snake tattoo on my wrist, which has miraculously healed. The golden snake, gems and all, shines as if painted in Day-Glo colors. It still tingles, but there's something different about it, now.

"Count me out!" I shout. I leap for the forest,

warm fur enveloping me as I fly through the air. I'm all wolf as soon as my forepaws hit the ground and I run like hell away from them as fast as my four legs can carry me.

CHAPTER FORTY-ONE

Things return more or less to normal, at least for the rest of the town. People don't talk much about the weird things that happened and when they do, it's with uncertainty, like they're not sure if it was real or some half-remembered dream.

No more rampant flu bug. Kids are all back in school. Mr. Rajanni is back to teaching biology. Only he's not teaching at Francis Loring High anymore. Instead, he transferred over to Murdock. There's a star-shaped scar on his forehead now and he's changed the way he runs his classes, but I hear he's still tough and makes kids learn stuff and not just pass tests.

Bree and I have reached a kind of truce for the moment. She seems genuinely confused and remorseful about her behavior—though her apology was less sincere than I'd expected—and I'm not willing to forget it was her arrogant attitude that got us into this mess in the first place. The book may have chosen her, but I know she wanted what the entity offered. Whatever that was. She hasn't been forthcoming on that account, either. And I still haven't figured out how to tell my parents the whole truth about her. I guess it can wait, since it isn't like she and I are hanging out together. Magical triad or not, I still prefer to choose my own friends.

Of course, I still don't actually have any.

Kat's little brother, Devon, is fine. He was already talking and trying to sit up by the time they got him to the hospital. Still, Kat doesn't want anything to do with me. Although, I can't tell if it's because she thinks I tried to hurt her brother, or if she's mortified about having attacked me that day.

As for my parents, they know something happened, but they seem as reluctant to talk about it as I am. The time is coming, though, and I have as many questions for them as they probably have for me.

One good thing that came out of everything I've been through is that I can shift at will and I seem to be better equipped to ignore the pull of the moon, except of course at its fullest. That remains a struggle. And oddly enough, the magic that worked in Other, that allowed me to shift back to human form with my clothes intact, seems to have followed me back, along with my permanent keepsake. Like the bracelet is some sort of magical clothes closet.

Hah! Something else I haven't bothered to mention to my parents.

I also picked out a new leather band to replace the one I tore off my arm that day. This one has a strip of snakeskin right down the middle of it. My mother thinks it's a horrible fashion statement, but other than commenting on my "questionable taste," she's thankfully left me alone about it. I think it's perfectly apropos.

Even with the benefits I've gotten from my tattoo charm, I don't know if I would have kept it, if I'd been given a choice—unlike Bree, who kept the knife, which is some kind of witch-blade, I guess—but I've decided I'd rather not know any more than I have to about witchcraft for the time being.

I'm not sure what Jeryd got out of all of it. I've pretty much made it my life's work to avoid both of them as much as possible. And I do my best to ignore the odd looks I get from Joey, too. Not that he's bothered to try to talk to me. I guess finding yourself passed out in the middle of the woods with grass stains on your hands and knees and no memory of how you got there would be pretty discomforting. Especially for such a supposed bad boy.

On the other hand, since I've clearly got more control over the change, my mom has started to let me go out on my full moon runs without the buzz collar. Of course, she still brings the whistle and waits for me at the car. I thought I'd love the freedom, but for some reason, the responsibility weighs on me more than I expected it to. Seems like

I'm always on guard, now, afraid I might lose control. Odd how something as controlling as a shock collar can also give you a sense of freedom.

I'm still trying to understand that one.

It's awkward to be part of some mystical trio thing, to be bound together as some sort of special magical force, and not even like each other. Bree and Jeryd don't get along any better with one another than I do with them.

Some nights I dream about them. Sometimes I'm kissing Bree and other times, Jeryd, but every dream ends the same, with me confused and alone, unsure of who I am and what I want, whether I like girls or boys. Whether I'm mostly human or shifter. Most days, I wake up with just as many questions and just as few answers as when I went to sleep, and wonder what is wrong with me that I don't know how to answer the most basic ones.

It's not like there's anyone in town I can talk to about it. Speaking of which, I still think there have to be a lot better places to live, but I also know that if anything bad happened to this town—Podunk or not—and the people in it, especially my parents, it would be the worst thing that could ever happen to me. On the other hand, if I could, I would happily give up High School and all the requisite quizzes and tests, like the one I'm supposed to be studying for right now.

Instead, I'm out.

Running.

Without my mom or her stupid whistle.

The moonlight spills down over the path. The

scent of ripe berries fills the air with a sweetness that matches the feel of bounding free. My muscles stretch and contract, blood pumping, heart pounding in exhilaration. Something moves on the path ahead and I slow to a lope. I can smell him before I see him, his earth and fire scent wafting on the air. I pad forward and come to a stop. Jeryd kneels before me, the way he kneeled to his mother that day in Other. My stomach still tightens when I see him, my pulse still races, but I bare my teeth. I'm still pissed about what he did, even if he was trying to trick Andarra. I can't help thinking that he was playing both sides against the middle, waiting to see who would win.

He extends his arms out, palms up. "I would like us to be friends," he says. "Though, truly, I wish it could be more." He turns his piercing eyes on me, a look of flirtation in them.

I sit back and laugh. Of course, it comes out more like a bark.

He shrugs and sits on his heels. "Bound, as we are. We should at least not be enemies," he says.

I glance down at the ring of white fur on my foreleg, then rise and shift in the same moment. I'm becoming more and more adept at this and it feels good to have such control. Papaw would be proud. Although, he wouldn't be too happy about the enabling magical trinket I'm sporting on my wrist.

Jeryd stares up at me, but he doesn't rise. As much as I hate to admit it, I have a momentary urge to kiss him and my face turns warm as my lips tingle. I've sworn off kissing—*anyone*—I remind myself. Instead, I rub at the leather band on my wrist and consider him. "We no longer have an enemy to be joined against, so what would you recommend for motivation?"

"There are always enemies. Dark forces to be fought. Light to be preserved." There is real sadness in his voice. "We are chosen for the roles we play, not always by our own volition, but because the need is so great."

"What? No famous proverbs about enemies?"

"Would you prefer I tell you that war makes strange bedfellows?" he says, standing and brushing the dirt from his knees, mouth curling up into a sly smile.

The gesture makes him seem more human, but I find his suggestive quote and attitude offensive, and I make a disgusted sound.

"I didn't think so. Then how about 'Do I not destroy my enemies when I make them my friends?'"

"We're not friends," I tell him. "You betrayed me."

"I also arranged for your escape," he murmurs. "Twice."

"Give me a break! Do you have any idea what I went through?"

"Yes," he says. "I do. I had to know where you were in order to steer the Hunt away from you." He shoves his hands into his pockets, and for a moment, he looks like a regular teen-aged boy. "And I know I hurt you in the grove. I am sorry for that."

I hear what sounds like real remorse in his voice.

I drop my eyes from his face, wondering what I should believe. Finally, I raise my gaze to his. His silver-gray eyes twinkle in the starlight, reminding me who—and what—he is.

I change, swift and smooth.

He lets out a small whistle, like he's impressed.

I laugh at him, which comes out once more like barking, but I'm pretty sure he gets the point. In an instant, I'm loping back down the path. He bows his head and doesn't try to follow me.

Seeing him took the joy out of running for the night. Besides, it's time for me to go home. Mom will be making her usual bed check soon and it won't do to have her know I'm breaking my grounding by sneaking out.

That I'm running in the forest. Alone.

That while my life may not be what others might think of as normal—and I still don't have all the answers—for now, I'm okay with who, and what, I am.

That I've changed more than they know.

Acknowledgements

A huge round of applause and much gratitude to my beta readers for their honesty and encouragement. You have no idea how much your support and thoughtful feedback mean to me.

As always, a gigantic thank you to my fabulous editor, Anne Lind. You make me a better writer with every single project.

To the amazing staff at Brick Cave Books: Thank you for making my work shine.

Last, but not least, a plethora of appreciation for my incredible fans. I willingly admit that I write because of the voices in my head, but you are why I work so hard to do their stories justice.